.6

"We were discussing _____ the
plant. Do you know _____?"

"According to Monroe's expert, the sap is extracted
by using a cold press, which works just as the name
implies. No heat is used in the process. Our perp
simply ground away at the raw plant fibers and
strained the sap. We're assuming the toxin was added
to the bottle of bubble bath. It's a nasty concoction
when you add the fact that the recipient was highly
susceptible."

Sid's radio squawked to life. He stepped away from
us and carried on a short conversation. When he came
back to the table, his face was grim. "Forget what
I said about that bottle being a nasty concoction. It
was a deadly mix. Eight minutes ago, Leona Harper
died."

★

BINDWEED

Janis Harrison

TORONTO • NEW YORK • LONDON
AMSTERDAM • PARIS • SYDNEY • HAMBURG
STOCKHOLM • ATHENS • TOKYO • MILAN
MADRID • WARSAW • BUDAPEST • AUCKLAND

BINDWEED

A Worldwide Mystery/December 2006

First published by St. Martin's Press LLC.

ISBN-13: 978-0-373-26586-2
ISBN-10:   0-373-26586-7

Printed in U.S.A.

This book is dedicated to my granddaughter,
Jocelyn Nicole Harrison.

You are loved.

ONE

"DEATH HOUSE IS SCARY," said Toby. "People go in on a little bed and come out in a locked box." He eyed the sympathy bouquet on my worktable before turning his anxious gaze on me. "Bretta, are you taking those flowers over there?"

I shook my head. "Not this time. Lew will make the delivery to the funeral home."

Toby heaved a sign of relief. "I wouldn't want nothing to happen to you. You're my bud." His cheeks reddened as he touched the velvety petals of a yellow rose. "Get it, Bretta?" he said, casting me a shy look. "Bud. Buddy. Flower lady."

"Very clever. You're my bud, too." I gave Toby a wink, but kept poking flower stems into the bouquet I was working on. This was the last sympathy order. Once it was finished, I could turn my attention to the final details of a local banker's sixtieth birthday celebration. The man, a bass and crappie pro, fished in tournaments all over the Lake of the Ozarks.

I'd suggested to his wife a party theme that featured brightly colored lures, rods and reels, nets, and inexpensive tackle boxes used as fresh-flower containers. For a dramatic touch, and one that would boost the honoree's ego, we would artistically place his trophies among arrangements of cattails, driftwood, sunflowers, and native foliage. She had loved my ideas as long as I incorporated her collection of lighthouses in the decorations.

I glanced around the room and grimaced. Lighthouses in

every color and size dominated the flower bouquets. The wife had turned a deaf ear when I'd pointed out that the structures might not strike an identifying chord with her River City, Missouri, guests.

River City is located about twenty miles from the interstate that links St. Louis to Springfield. The Osage River flows below the rugged limestone bluffs where our fair city was settled. We have our share of lakes and streams, but mostly we're a farming community with barns and silos dotting our landscape—not lighthouses.

Since the wife had a generous check in hand, I'd bowed to her wishes, but I wasn't happy. The subject of lighthouses had been exhausted. My staff was sick and tired of hearing me vent. So even on this hectic day, Toby was a welcome diversion.

He nodded to Lois, who was arranging bronze and yellow mums in an antique wicker creel, then to Lew, who was making a list of the afternoon deliveries. "You guys treat me good. I'd wash your windows for free, but I like money."

This honest comment made us laugh. Toby's childlike innocence was in sharp contrast to his appearance. He was six feet tall with curly brown hair and hazel eyes. He looked like any other robust, twenty-eight-year-old young man, but oxygen deprivation at birth had damaged a portion of his brain.

Lois walked around Toby to pick up a container of bear grass. She had joined a gym a few weeks ago and looked better than ever. Lois never divulged her age. I wasn't sure how old she was, but from different things she'd said, I had her pegged at fifty-nine. Now that she was exercising, she'd tossed away her cache of chocolates and replaced it with a bowl of grapes, apples, and oranges. She'd also taken to reading books on cholesterol, fiber, elimination, and other titillating, healthful subjects.

"You're looking mighty fine today," she said to Toby, eyeing his tanned, muscular legs. "Have you been working out?"

"Nah. Just pedaling my bike." Toby stuck out a leg. "It's as strong as a spider's web."

Lois grinned. "It would sound more impressive if you said you had muscles of steel."

Toby shook his head. "You're talking about Superman, but I like Spiderman best."

Lew cleared his throat, which was his way of letting us know he had something profound to add to the conversation. I didn't bother to look up. I knew what I'd see. In his late thirties, Lew was losing his hair. The bright ceiling lights would make his chrome-dome shine. His tie would be straight, his shirt collar still starched and fresh even though it was midafternoon.

He was a pompous man, but I could trust him to deliver my flowers with care. Plus, he had personal contact with some of River City's more affluent families. When it came right down to it, Lew was good for my business, if not for my nerves.

Lew said, "Actually, Lois, Toby's comparison is quite correct. A spider's web is Mother Nature's marvel. Engineers have calculated that a web woven of spider silk the thickness of a pencil could stop a jumbo jet in midair."

Lois asked a question, and Lew had the answer. He gave an impromptu lecture on the wonders of the strength, toughness, and elasticity of a spider's web. How it could stop a bee in flight. How legend had it that Genghis Khan conquered Asia because his soldiers were protected from enemy arrows by wearing clothing that had been interwoven with spider silk.

Lois listened to Lew, then said, "I'm hungry. That salad

for lunch didn't stick with me. While you're out making deliveries, pick me up an order of onion rings. That should hold me until I get home."

I was used to this hop-skipping from one topic to another, and picked up on it without missing a beat. "What about your vow to eat healthy?" I asked, wondering if I should get something, too.

"I'll have a salad for dinner," Lois said, digging in her purse for money.

Lew shook his head. "I'm not stopping. The invention of 'takeout,' 'the drive-through window,' and the concept of 'supersized' has put a curse on the human race. Back in my grandmother's day, families worked hard. They ate nutritious meals. They met their obligations without government handouts. It was a matter of pride that kept their noses to the grindstone."

Lew continued in this vein, but I shut him out. I had other, more exciting things on my mind. I smiled to myself. I'd been doing a lot of smiling lately—when I wasn't obsessing about lighthouses. I was in love with a man who loved me, too.

I glanced at the clock. Three hours until I could lock the flower shop door and head for home. Bailey Monroe was coming for dinner, but before he arrived, I wanted to freshen up.

At forty-six, it took more than a dusting of face powder to make me feel desirable. My hair was more gray than brown. My blue eyes had circles under them. Physically, I was showing my age. Mentally, I was twenty again—at least where Bailey was concerned.

I came out of my daydreams when Toby jiggled my arm. Leaning close, he whispered, "Bretta, I don't want to listen to Lew." He pointed to a lighthouse that had been painted to resemble red brick. "I don't like that either."

I agreed with Toby in both instances. Hearing Lew's views on any subject was always irritating. As for the lighthouse, that particular one was especially offensive to me. It towered over my arrangement, reducing the flowers to insignificant spots of color. My artistic sensibilities were insulted by my own work, but I'd had no choice if I wanted to please my customer. However, Toby wasn't under my same restrictions. I wondered why he disliked the arrangement.

When I asked him, he pressed his lips tightly together and shook his head. Thinking he didn't want to criticize the bouquet, I said, "You won't hurt my feelings, Toby, if you don't like that arrangement of flowers."

His eyes opened wide with surprise. "All flowers are beautiful." He turned his back to the lighthouse and sighed. "Mostly, I'd like to get paid."

I chuckled. "That can be arranged."

Toby pulled a sales book from his shirt pocket. Directing a quick glance at Lew, he said, "I need quiet so I don't make a mistake on this bill."

There wasn't much chance of that. The amount never varied. I paid Toby eight dollars to wash my flower shop windows, adding a two-buck tip. I went to the cash register and waited for Toby to finish writing up the bill. After he'd handed me the receipt, I counted ten singles into his hand because he only accepted ones as payment.

After he'd carefully tucked the money into his billfold, he said, "Mr. Barker has a new lady at the bakery. I don't like her. She says funny things."

"Funny how?" I asked.

Toby's face scrunched into a frown as he thought hard. "Like I couldn't track an elephant in four feet of snow." He shrugged. "It's September, Bretta. There ain't no snow, and we ain't got no elephants here in River City, so why would I try to track one?"

Lois scowled. "Well, it's clear we've got a baboon."

Toby turned to Lois. "You mean like the three monkeys. 'Hear no evil. See no evil. Speak no evil.'"

"Words to live by," said Lew piously.

"But what is evil?" asked Toby, staring at me with trusting eyes. "Tell me how I'd know evil."

Lois ran a hand down the slender curve of her hip. "If it looks good, feels good, and tastes good, then it's probably—"

Not to confuse the issue, or Toby, I spoke quickly, "Evil is anything that causes others pain or harm."

"Oh," said Toby with obvious relief. "Then I'm okay. I wouldn't hurt nobody."

I touched his arm. "We know that. Ignore this new woman when she makes her comments."

"Hear no evil, right?" asked Toby.

"Exactly."

"But it's evil to steal, ain't it?"

"Of course."

"Then there's an evil person coming onto my land. I told Sheriff Sid about this stealing, and he said I needed to hire you." Toby frowned. "Is it because my mother's flowers are being cut down?"

I went back to my workstation and picked up another yellow rose. It was easy to visualize Sid's mocking expression when he'd steered Toby in my direction. Before my husband, Carl, passed away, he'd been one of Sid's deputies. Sid had never liked the idea that Carl shared the facts of his cases with me, but then, Sid had never been married. He didn't understand the bond between a husband and wife. Carl and I had discussed everything—my work at the flower shop, his work with the Spencer County Sheriff's Department.

I have to admit that Carl's topics were more interesting than whether I should change plush-animal suppliers or add a line of designer chocolates to my flower shop inventory. But Carl had listened, just as I had when he talked about the crimes around Spencer County. I'd given him my opinion, which had some satisfying results.

Since Carl's death I'd done more than hypothesize. I'd taken an active part in solving several crimes, much to Sid's irritation. Sid could be a crotchety, belligerent man. He was also possessive of any notoriety connected with his cases, especially now that he was running a tight race for reelection. When I receive credit, I'm as welcome to him as a ragweed bouquet to an allergy sufferer.

So I ignored Toby's reference to Sid, and zeroed in on the other part of his statement. "Someone is stealing your mother's flowers?"

"That's right. Sheriff Sid said maybe the deer or the rabbits are having supper. But these aren't munchy plants, Bretta. Just big old woody stalks chopped off at the ground. They've got pretty flowers." Toby measured a six-inch diameter with his hands, which I took to be an exaggeration on his part.

"What kind of plants are they?"

"I don't know." Toby's voice quivered as he added, "Before my mama died, she showed me how to pick the seeds and make them grow in a pan by the kitchen window. She told me to plant six new rows every year." He smiled sadly. "I've done just like she said. They look pretty when they bloom."

"Why six rows?" asked Lew.

Toby's chin came up. "Because Mama said to plant six rows. She said some might go away."

Gently, I said, "What did she mean by 'go away'?"

Toby shrugged. "I guess die. Everything dies." He blinked a couple of times, then whispered, "Even Mama."

Agnes had beat cancer twice in her life, but when it reoccurred a third time, she'd put aside her pain long enough to make sure her son's future was secure. My flower shop is located on Hawthorn Street. Agnes had worked at the pharmacy just a few doors down. She'd been friendly in a general way, helping me as a customer, but I hadn't known her well. Fact was, I hadn't known she had a son until a month or so before she passed away. She'd brought Toby around to different shops along Hawthorn, introducing him to owners, explaining that he would be on his own soon and would need work. She'd said Toby couldn't handle being cooped up in a center or a factory, but he could wash windows, sweep sidewalks, and carry out trash.

I'd been deeply touched by the sad situation and had assured her that Toby could come to me if he needed help. I'd also suggested that she talk to Avery Wheeler, a lawyer and a dear friend of mine. He could assist her by tying up any legal ends regarding Toby's future.

Toby took a shaky breath. His voice was stronger as he said, "But these plants didn't die. They were chopped down." Toby stared at me. "You'll come to my house, won't you? Sheriff Sid said you would be there with bells on. I don't think we'll need the bells, unless you think they'll scare off the bad guy."

Lois and Lew snickered. I ignored them and said, "Of course I'll come by. Tomorrow is Saturday, and my day off. I have an appointment at ten, but I can be at your house about one o'clock. Will that be all right?"

Toby's happy smile chased away his gloom. "That'll be good. I gotta go, but I'll see you tomorrow." He walked to the front door and lifted the latch. Before he stepped outside, he looked back at me. "We'll be buds for years and years, won't we?"

I nodded. "Years and years."

As Toby closed the door, he gave me a fond look. His expression brought a lump to my throat. He was such a sweet young man, but he was so alone. After Agnes died, I'd asked around and discovered that he lived on Hawthorn, at the edge of town. He had no other family. The individual store owners his mother had introduced him to were his only friends. So sad.

Behind me, Lois called, "Hey, Bretta. I thought this big lighthouse was supposed to shoot out a beam of light. I get nothing when I plug it in."

Before I could reply, Lew said, "Let me handle it, Lois. I watched your husband last week when he rewired Mother's favorite floor lamp. I know exactly how to proceed."

I rolled my eyes and sighed. Yeah, right. This ought to be good.

SIX HOURS LATER, I was in the company of the man I loved. We were stretched out in a hammock, in my garden, staring up at the sky. The September evening was cool, but I was warm, wrapped in Bailey's protective arms. I lay with my back against his broad chest. My head was cradled under his chin. I'd been telling him about my day, ending the tale with a "shocking" conclusion. Lew had tried to fix the lighthouse's electrical connection, but had gotten zapped in the process.

Bailey's laughter rumbled in his chest. "What does a proper man like Lew say when he comes close to getting electrocuted?"

"He couldn't speak at first, but when he recovered, he blurted out, 'I'm tingling like I just got laid.'" I grinned. "I still can't believe Lew said that. And you should have heard Lois. She wouldn't let up on him. Kept asking him what kind of wattage he was used to. What was her name? Why didn't he bring his *hot mama* around so we could meet her? Lew said his hand was burned. He left work early to have it treated, but I think he left because he was tired of Lois's teasing."

Bailey nuzzled my ear. "Speaking of *hot mama,* why don't we take a walk over to my house? Maybe I could interest you in a little *tingling?*"

I grew still. Over the last few months, we'd done our share of fooling around, but we hadn't done the deed—yet. Bailey's invitation couldn't be plainer. He wanted me in his bed. I wanted to be there, but I hesitated. I had issues. They weren't of a sexual nature, or at least I didn't think so.

I was fully conscious of how our bodies melted together. How his legs twined with mine. How his arms tightened around me. I closed my eyes and tuned into my body's rhythms. My heart thudded. My pulse raced. A flash of heat warmed my face and spread down my neck at the thought of being intimate with Bailey.

Nope. My problems didn't stem from a lack of carnal urges. I had plenty of those. It was other areas in my life that needed tending.

He cleared his throat. "Since you haven't leaped up to lead the way to my house, I'm taking that as a no."

I twisted around so I could see his face. I'd met Bailey when I was in Branson at a floral convention. He'd been a working undercover DEA—Drug Enforcement Administration—special agent. I'd been exposed to the lying, scheming, suspicious persona that made up his disguise, but some part of me had seen the true Bailey Monroe. My attraction to him had held through the long weeks after I'd left Branson, thinking I'd never see him again. Then out of the blue, he'd popped up on my doorstep, the proud owner of the cottage located next to my property. We'd shared some rough times, but our love had grown. He was retired now and was writing a book about his career as a federal officer.

There was just enough light left from the sunset to shine on his coppery eyes. His full lips were turned down in an exaggerated frown. I stroked his cheek. "Buck up, sweetheart. Tingling *is* on my mind, just not tonight."

"What's bothering you? More important, do you want to talk about it?"

I settled back against his chest. "Not particularly, but it doesn't have to be a long conversation. I can sum it up in two words—my father."

Bailey chuckled. "Two words, but they encompass a passel of emotions."

"Isn't that the truth? I've forgiven him for running out on me when I was eight years old. I'm trying to accept him as the meddlesome busybody he is. He's likable. He's kind-hearted. He has good intentions, but they always seem to backfire on me."

"I sensed a coolness between the two of you at dinner. What's going on?"

"Without asking me, Dad hired an interior decorator to do

the upstairs bedrooms. He and this DuPree woman have been plotting and planning for the last two weeks, but he only deemed it necessary to tell me this morning before I left for work."

"DuPree? Does she have a business here in River City?"

"Yes. Ms. Abigail DuPree is the owner of Par Excellence Interiors. When Dad told me he'd set up an appointment so I could meet her tomorrow at ten, I decided that forewarned was forearmed. I drove by her store. I planned to go in and scope it out, but I was overwhelmed when I saw the display in her front window."

Bailey rubbed my shoulder. "That bad, huh?"

I wanted to wail my frustration but settled for a pitiful moan. "It was ghastly. Bolts of zebra-striped material formed the backdrop that showcased some crudely carved furniture. Accents of leopard skin, vases of peacock feathers, and, would you believe, there was a stuffed armadillo perched on a red leather ottoman."

"It sounds…uh…unique."

I snorted. "That's one way of putting it." I swung my feet over the edge of the hammock and, after a couple of tries, I managed to stand up.

Bailey sighed. "I guess our moment of togetherness has passed." When I didn't comment, he got up, too. Once he was at my side, he said, "Don't take offense at what your father has done. Redecorating seven bedrooms is a big project. In the long run, you might welcome Ms. DuPree's assistance."

I didn't answer because Bailey had stated the obvious. It was a big project, but it was my decision on how the renovated rooms were to be finished. Granted, I had turned the supervision of the remodeling over to my father, but I'd never dreamed he'd take on the decorating, especially without consulting me before he called in what he termed a "professional."

As a florist, I knew color, contrast, and design. But most of all, I knew that my Greek Revival home did not warrant zebra print or leopard skin accents.

I tried to ignore the voice inside my head that told me I wasn't being fair to Abigail DuPree. The whole point of a window display was to grab the attention of potential customers. I used that ploy at the flower shop, but I'd learned to soft-pedal the outrageous. Abigail's mistake had been combining too many flamboyant components in one exhibit. If I'd been doing it, I would have—

I shrugged. Why go there? It was obvious that my approach to design differed from hers. There was no getting around it. I'd been put off by her window display, so I didn't have confidence in her ability to decorate my beloved home.

The trunk of a gigantic maple tree blocked my view. I moved around it so I could see the house. I sighed with satisfaction. There it stood in all its historic glory—gleaming white paint; tall, stately columns; wide, elegant veranda.

My home. My pride and joy. My sanctuary. Or it had been until my father moved in and took over. I frowned as I pondered those last two words. Maybe I was being too harsh on Dad, too.

"Bailey," I said softly, "am I wrong to feel betrayed by my father? It's as if he doesn't trust me to make the right decisions for my own house."

"I don't think he had that in mind. He knows you're busy. He's trying to help."

My shoulders slumped. "I've heard that before. Remember

when he poked his walking stick at that crack in the plaster and the entire ceiling came down?"

"I remember."

"And what about the time my car was vandalized? My father arranged for salesmen to bring all those new vehicles out here just so I could choose one."

Bailey nodded. "I still think you should have picked the Viper. That's one hell of a car."

I raised an eyebrow. "Are you missing my point?"

Before he could answer, DeeDee came out the terrace doors. She had the cordless phone in her hand and a concerned expression on her face. "What's wrong?" I asked, hurrying to meet her.

She thrust the phone at me. "It's the sh-sheriff. H-He wants to s-speak to you."

DeeDee is my twenty-three-year-old housekeeper. When she came into my employment, she was a shy waif of a girl. Because she stutters, her overprotective parents had nearly ruined her prospects for a happy, productive life. Giving her the responsibility of running my household had bolstered her confidence. Now, I'm proud to say, she's full of vim and vigor and even has the courage to speak her mind, especially where my welfare is concerned.

I took the phone, placing my hand over the mouthpiece. "Did he say what he wanted?"

"No, but if h-he's calling you, it can't be good n-news."

That was true, but I put a positive note in my voice. "Hi, Sid. What can I do for you?" I was prepared for his usual caustic tone, which was always present when he spoke with me.

"Bretta," he said quietly. "I thought you'd want to know. We just put Toby Sutton in an ambulance. He's in bad shape. The outcome doesn't look good."

TWO

THE NEWS ABOUT Toby blew me away. My jaws worked, but I couldn't form any words. I swallowed hard, and finally managed, "He was fine this afternoon. I'm supposed to go by his house tomorrow at one."

Sid's voice was gruff. "You can scratch that date off your calendar. The house is a crime scene now."

I gasped. "Crime scene? Oh no. What happened?" When Sid didn't answer, I said, "Please, I don't need the details. Just the general picture, okay?"

"Hornets."

I waited, but Sid didn't elaborate. "That's it?" I said. "That's all you're going to tell me?"

"You figure it out. You're the supersleuth."

I cringed, expecting him to slam down the receiver, but Sid didn't hang up. I was in no mood for his game, but I knew that if I was going to learn anything, I had to do this his way. I mused aloud. "If hornets are involved, and Toby's on the way to the hospital, I'm assuming he's been stung. But what's the connection between the hornets and his house as a crime scene?"

Sid's sigh whistled in my ear. "They were in his bedroom. We're dealing with a hornet's nest that's more than a foot across. The nest was rigged with a length of string tied to the bedroom doorknob. When Toby opened the door, the nest fell off the wardrobe and broke open."

"Why did he have the nest tied to the doorknob?"

"*He* didn't. A window was jimmied open."

The implication of that statement hit me almost as hard as the news about Toby's condition. "Someone deliberately did this to Toby? Why? Who?" I stopped, took a breath, and let it out slowly. "Is Toby conscious?"

"He made the 911 call, and was able to tell the dispatcher what had happened before he collapsed. The dispatcher could hear the little bastards buzzing over the telephone. Toby was unconscious in the kitchen when the EMTs arrived. They couldn't get into the house until the hornets were gassed. It's been a bitch. Keep what I've told you under your cap, Bretta. That's it."

This time I didn't stall Sid. I'd heard enough for now. I pushed the disconnect button and handed the phone to DeeDee. "Run get my purse," I said. "I'm going to the hospital. I'll meet you around in front."

DeeDee hurried away. Bailey kept pace at my side as I loped along the brick path to my SUV. "Toby doesn't have any family," I said. "I have to be there for him. I need to call Avery Wheeler, but I can do that from the hospital."

"I got the gist of the story from your end of the conversation, but let me get something straight. Sid thinks this hornet's nest was intentionally placed in Toby's house?"

I nodded. "He said a window was jimmied open for access into the house. A string was tied from the nest to the doorknob of Toby's bedroom. When Toby opened the door, the nest fell off the wardrobe and broke open. Sid said the nest is more than a foot across."

Bailey muttered an obscenity.

DeeDee came down the veranda steps with my purse. The

keys jiggled in her hand. She held them out to me, but Bailey intercepted. "I'll drive," he said to me. "You're too upset."

I didn't argue. I went around and climbed into the passenger seat. Bailey got behind the wheel, and we took off. We didn't talk on the way into River City. Toby was in my thoughts, but I couldn't express my feelings without tearing up. I huddled on my side of the SUV, worrying about Toby's condition, wondering why anyone would want to harm such a kind, sweet man.

Over and over I asked myself the same question. What was the motivation? Why would anyone put a hornet's nest in Toby's bedroom? But I couldn't get beyond the fact that it *had* happened. Why? Anger slowly replaced the numbness that had taken over my body since Sid had phoned.

Bailey turned into the hospital parking lot. He had to circle a few times but finally he found a slot. As soon as he'd shut off the engine, I had my door open. Before I could get out, Bailey touched my arm. I stopped and looked at him. The interior lights showed his concern for me.

He nodded as he gazed into my eyes. "I knew it," he said. "You were too quiet on the ride here. You're already thinking about suspects, motive, and opportunity."

I shrugged. "Mostly motive. I hadn't gotten around to the other two—yet."

"Just be careful, Bretta. I know you're upset about Toby, but we don't know what we're dealing with, or who. A good investigator doesn't piss off possible suspects until he's gathered as much information as he can."

I stared at him. "What suspects? I'm going into the hospital to be with a good friend."

Bailey swept a hand toward the lighted parking lot. "Look

around us, sweetheart. You're not Toby's only friend. I've spotted three Hawthorn Street business owners since we arrived. Isn't that Abner Garrett, of Garrett's Grocery Store, crossing the lot? Harmon Purvis from Purvis Pharmacy is walking through the hospital's front door. In front of him was Diana Shott. I'm not saying any of these people are suspects, but I'm sure Toby visited with them, just like he visited with you. They may have information, but it'll take skill and finesse on your part to retrieve it."

He leaned over and kissed my cheek. "Be cool. Listen to what's said. Don't be too quick to voice your theories."

I nodded solemnly before I got out of the SUV. Bailey's advice was sound. I hoped I could follow it.

We entered the hospital, stopping at the front desk to ask for Toby. We were told he was still in the emergency room, but the lady directed us to an area at the end of the corridor.

I knew the place all too well. I'd waited there for news of Bailey's condition when he'd been involved in a car crash. That event had happened several months ago, but I'll never forget my feelings of desolation when I thought I might lose him. He'd made a miraculous recovery. I prayed that Toby's fate would be the same.

Bailey opened the door and I stepped into the room. When Bailey had been hurt, I'd waited here alone. Tonight all the chairs were occupied. I took a quick head count. Including myself, there were seven Hawthorn Street shop owners present. Several acknowledged me with a brief nod. Others offered a sad smile.

"Bretta," said Melba Cameron, coming wearily to her feet. She owned a candle and gift shop called Scent-Sational. A dainty, middle-aged woman, she always smelled of vanilla and cinnamon. "I'm so glad you're here. I phoned your house and a young woman said you were on your way."

I looked from one familiar face to another. "How did all of you know to come to the hospital? Who notified you?"

"I started the ball rolling," said Yvonne Pritchard. She owned The Treasure Trove, an antiques shop that was located a couple of blocks from Toby's house. Nodding to her brother, Phillip, she explained, "We heard the ambulance race past the store." She picked up a magazine and fanned her plump face. "When it pulled into Toby's driveway, you could have knocked me over with a feather."

It would've taken a substantial feather to accomplish that feat. Yvonne weighed close to three hundred pounds. She was a talented seamstress and made all her clothes, favoring smocks and polyester slacks with elastic waists. She'd had knee-replacement surgery on both legs and walked with a cane.

I said to her, "And you called everyone to come to the hospital?"

"I called Melba. We put together a list of Toby's customers. She took half and I took half. It was quicker that way even though there are only eight of us. We didn't talk directly with Mr. Barker from Merry's Delights, but we told his wife, Martha."

I asked the room in general if there had been any news concerning Toby's condition.

Melba shook her head. "Not one word. But Avery Wheeler knows we're here. He said someone would update us as soon as possible."

It eased my mind that Avery was with Toby. There was nothing to do but wait. Since no extra chairs were available, Bailey and I leaned against the wall near the door. I forced myself to keep my lips shut and listen to the conversation. The topic was speculation on what might have happened to Toby.

Leona Harper of Leona's Boutique spoke up. "What a sad situation. Toby is such a precious young man. Before Agnes died, I told her Toby needed more in his life than a bunch of busy shop owners. He needed a caretaker, but she wouldn't even discuss the subject."

Leona was in her midfifties, with blond hair and big blue eyes. While the rest of us were dressed in jeans and sneakers, she wore a buff-colored suit, plum silk blouse, and heels. She'd told me once that in her line of work, she had to be meticulously groomed at all times. She believed in facials, wrinkle creams, and using layers of cosmetics to achieve that "natural" look.

She shook her head. "I know Toby loves critters, as he calls them, but why would he bring a hornet's nest into his house?"

I could have set everyone straight, but I bit my lip and kept listening.

Melba said, "Surely Toby would have known better. Besides, where in the world would he have found one?"

Diana Shott, who owned Buck-A-Roo, a discount store, said, "I had a nest under the eave of my house." With everyone's attention on her, she squared her shoulders and took a deep breath. The swell of her breasts pushed against the thin material of her shirt. She wasn't wearing a bra, but just in case none of us had noticed, she drew all eyes to her cleavage by toying with a delicate gold necklace.

Harmon Purvis, the pharmacist, seemed unaffected by her display. He smirked. "What you had was a paper-wasp's nest. They're cousins to the hornet, but not nearly as aggressive." Lean and fit, Harmon stood over six feet tall and looked like

Mel Gibson fifteen years in the future. "I've seen some large hornets' nests hanging from tree limbs in the timber. They're shaped like inverted teardrops and would measure about eighteen inches in length. They look like they're wrapped in gray tissue paper. At the base is a funnel-like opening where the hornets can come and go."

I wanted to know why Harmon was so knowledgeable about hornets, but before I could ask, Melba beat me to it. "You're a regular walking encyclopedia of information, Harmon. How come?"

He shrugged. "I've seen some severe cases of hornet stings. I know the damage a swarm can do when they feel threatened." He lowered his voice. "Look, I shouldn't be telling you this, but you all need to be prepared. Toby was on medication for his heart. This trauma to his body is extremely critical. We're dealing with a life-or-death situation."

I hadn't known about Toby's heart problem and, apparently, neither had any of the others. Conversation ceased. The room grew quiet except for Yvonne, who sniffled into a handkerchief.

My throat was tight with unshed tears. Bailey took my hand and gave it a gentle squeeze. After a few minutes, Diana said, "I was too busy to visit with Toby today when he came by, but I got the impression he was upset about something." She crossed her long legs and asked, "Do any of you know what was wrong?"

Yvonne sighed. "That's partly my fault and mostly Phillip's." She gave him a hard look.

Phillip was a tall, handsome man in his sixties. He had a broad face, dark eyes, and a ready smile. Tonight his lips were twisted into a grimace. "I said I was sorry, Yvonne. I don't know what more I can do."

Yvonne spoke to the rest of us. "Toby came by our house early this morning. If he knocked at the door, we didn't hear him. Phillip was in the shower, and I was getting dressed. When Toby didn't rouse anyone, he went down to Phillip's workshop, which Phillip usually keeps locked. I was in the kitchen cooking breakfast when I noticed that the barn door was open. I told Phillip, but by the time he got dressed and went to investigate, Toby had touched a chest of drawers Phillip had just stained and varnished."

Phillip took up the story. "He didn't just touch it, Yvonne. He left handprints all over it. Said it felt funny. Of course it did. It was still tacky. I'll have to wait for it to dry, then sand off the ruined finish and start over."

Yvonne stared at her brother. "But you could have been kinder. You yelled at him."

Phillip ducked his head. "I know, and I'm sorry. I should have handled Toby differently, but I lost my temper. I'll try to make it up to him."

Abner Garrett, the grocer, turned to me. "Toby was real excited about you coming to his house tomorrow. I asked him why you were coming over, but he wouldn't say." His tone was light, but underlying it was a sharp edge. "What's that young man been telling you?"

Abner was the third generation to run Garrett's Grocery. I didn't shop there. He and I had an ongoing feud over the semi-trucks that unloaded his merchandise in the alley. Because the trucks had to angle their way to the back of his store, they penned in my delivery vehicle. It often took some major fi-nagling on Lew's part to free the van.

I'd asked Abner for some cooperation. If he'd let me know when a truck was on the way, Lew could park in front of the flower shop. Abner had tactlessly informed me that he had more important things to do than alert me to an impending delivery.

Giving Abner a wide-eyed, innocent look, I said, "What do you think we talk about?" Turning his question into a question irritated him.

He glared at me. "If Melba or Yvonne didn't get in touch with you, Bretta, how did you know that Toby had been brought to the hospital?"

Bailey gave my hand a warning squeeze, but I ignored him. "The sheriff called me."

Heads jerked up. All eyes were on me. Melba asked, "Why did Sheriff Hancock call you?"

When I didn't answer right away, Abner snorted his contempt and walked across the room. I watched him, wondering if something was bothering him—other than me. He stared out the window, seemingly unconcerned with this new topic of conversation, but his head was cocked, as if he was straining so he wouldn't miss a word.

Bailey whispered in my ear, "Not cool, sweets. How are you going to get out of this?"

I was wondering the same thing when that decision was taken out of my hands. Attention shifted from me when the door opened. Avery Wheeler shuffled into the room. He looked like a sad old walrus, baggy body, short neck. His prominent salt-and-pepper mustache drooped. His bulbous nose was red, his eyes weepy. The hand on the crook of his cane trembled. His gaze swept one and all until his eyes met mine.

For a moment his somber expression lightened, and he almost smiled. But his burden was too great. Wearily, Avery shook his head. "It's over. Toby is gone. He never regained consciousness."

Silence greeted his announcement. Then I heard the tiniest of sighs. Was relief behind that gentle gasp of expelled breath? Was Toby's killer in this room? Did he or she feel safe now that Toby was dead?

Overwhelmed by my thoughts, I turned and buried my face in Bailey's broad chest.

THREE

I MANAGED TO WAIT until Bailey and I were in the SUV before I demanded, "Did you hear that sigh when Avery said that Toby never regained consciousness?"

Bailey shook his head. "I can't say that I did."

"Damn. I was hoping you could help me pinpoint where it came from. Then I'd have a clue as to who I should question first."

"Whoa. What's incriminating about a sigh? We'd just been told that Toby had passed away. I felt like sighing, too."

"It sounds weird, Bailey, but the more I think about it, the more convinced I am that I heard a sigh of relief, not sorrow. It makes me think the killer was in the waiting room with us. He or she was relieved that Toby didn't have the chance to—"

"Bretta, Bretta, what am I going to do with you?"

My chin shot up. "Don't patronize me. Someone maliciously tied a hornet's nest to Toby's bedroom doorknob. Harmon knew Toby had a heart problem. I don't like Abner Garrett. He's irritating. I don't know if there was something going on that would make him target Toby, but I can find out. In fact, I need to research all the Hawthorn Street business owners. Did I tell you that Toby never strayed from our street?"

"No, you hadn't mentioned that."

I grabbed my purse off the seat and rifled through the

contents. Unsuccessful, I said, "Could you switch on the dome light, please?"

Bailey hit the switch and the interior blossomed with illumination. "What are you looking for?" he asked.

"Found it." I held up a notebook. "I want to make a list of suspects while they're fresh in my mind. And I can't forget Mr. Barker." In case Bailey wasn't familiar with the name, I added, "He owns Merry's Delights, the bakery. I don't suspect him, but did I tell you the new woman he has working behind the counter made a derogatory comment to Toby?"

Bailey shook his head. "Bretta, are you hearing yourself? You're rambling on and on, snatching and grabbing any theory that pops into your head. Slow down, honey. You're on an adrenaline rush. When you crash, it's going to hurt." His tone softened. "Nothing you do tonight or tomorrow or even next week is going to change the fact. Toby is dead, sweetheart. Catching his killer won't bring him back. Take time to mourn his passing, or at least acknowledge that he's gone."

"What good will that do?" I fought back tears. "If I keep busy, it won't be nearly as painful."

We rode in silence for a while, then Bailey said, "If you truly believe that, then ask your questions. You won't win any popularity contests, but if it helps keep you sane, then go for it. I'll cover your back."

I froze. No "Mind your own business." No "Keep out of this." No "Let the authorities handle it." *I'll cover your back.*

Bailey's caring offer opened the floodgates. Tears filled my eyes and brimmed over. I slumped against the seat. "It's not fair, Bailey. Why Toby? He was so uncomplicated, so unassuming."

Bailey pulled into my garage and shut off the SUV's engine. Before he hit the button to lower the garage door, he gathered me tenderly in his arms. "Bretta, Toby had ties to the people on Hawthorn Street, but what about the rest of his life? Just because you briefly visit with him a few times a week doesn't mean you really *know* him. There are too many unanswered questions. A good investigation is conducted in layers."

I sniffed a couple of times. "Carl taught me that. To make his point clear, he used a zinnia as an analogy."

"Why a zinnia?"

I wiped my eyes on my sleeve. "Obvious reason. I'm a florist. I can relate best to a flower."

Bailey shook his head. "I get that, but why a zinnia specifically?"

"Oh. It's because the zinnia belongs to the composite family of plants. The flower heads have tight layers of petals. Carl said the stem of the zinnia is the foundation, which is what a case is built on. Next is the outer row of petals. Most of the time he believed this was relevant but fundamental information. Each consecutive row of petals overlays the preceding row. Just like fact upon fact has juxtaposition."

Bailey leaned back. "I get it. The progression of petals grows smaller and smaller as they near the center of the flower."

"Just as a case advances toward the ultimate goal—capturing the villain."

Bailey's eyes twinkled with humor. "I think I would have liked your husband. Carl sounds as if he was a fine man."

I reached up and put my hand against Bailey's cheek. "He was, but so are you."

He turned his head and kissed the sensitive area near my

thumb, kissed my wrist, but eventually he found my lips. I wound my arms around his neck. I put my thoughts aside and lost myself in this man who understood me so well.

I'M NOT A LIGHT SLEEPER, but the noise that woke me the next morning could have roused the dead. I winced as my thoughts touched on Toby. Last night's events were surreal. Who was responsible for the hornet's nest in Toby's house? Why? Why? Why?

Thump. Thump. *Thump!*

I listened to the sound of a heavy object bumping down the attic stairs. I glanced at the clock on my side table. Quarter after eight. What was going on? Swinging my legs over the side of the bed, I grabbed my robe and went to investigate. I stepped out into the hall and saw my father wrestling with a trunk that was wedged in the doorway that led to the attic.

Albert McGinness was in his seventies. I'd inherited his blue eyes, and was working up to a full head of gray hair just like his. He was a handsome, distinguished man with a pile of money in his bank account. He'd invented some branding gizmo in Texas that had netted him a small fortune. He's artistic and creative, and we're just enough alike to cause friction.

I'd been unusually busy at the flower shop lately, so I hadn't paid much attention to my father. I saw that he'd dropped a few pounds. His paunchy stomach was flatter, his skin a deep golden tan. I glanced down at my arm and saw the pasty white of a woman who spent too much time indoors. But my stomach was in better shape than it used to be.

I'd lost one hundred pounds after Carl died, but food was my nemesis. I tried to remember that I ate to live, not lived to eat. In the past, any emotional upheaval in my life had been

remedied by devouring whatever was close at hand. Chocolate, potato chips, ice cream, and cashews were all comfort
foods, but they defeated my attempt to keep the lost weight
from reappearing. Why is it that when I'm upset, I never
crave radishes or carrots?

Just watching my father made me wonder if I could talk
DeeDee into fixing French toast topped with blueberry syrup
for breakfast. I pushed that thought away, and said, "What are
you doing, Dad?"

He whirled around. "Bretta. You're awake." He waved a
hand airily. "That's just as well. You need to get dressed and
eat breakfast. You'll be more receptive to Abby's ideas if you
have a full stomach."

"Abby?" I murmured. Then remembered. Abigail must
equal Abby, which in turn equaled the interior decorator. I
shook my head. "The meeting has to be canceled. A friend of
mine passed away last night. Lois can't handle the flower shop
alone."

"But this is your day off, and I have the library almost
ready for our presentation."

"*You* have it ready? Isn't it up to that DuPree woman to
see to whatever needs to be done?"

"She's doing more than her share, Bretta. And please don't
refer to her as 'that Dupree woman.' She has excellent ideas.
We're lucky to have her helping us."

It was showdown time. I wasn't in the mood for any of this,
but I had to get a couple of things straight. In a reasonably
kind tone, I said, "Dad, I haven't hired her yet. I haven't
given my okay to anything. The last time I looked, *my name*
was on the deed to this house."

I knew I'd gone one step too far when my father's eager

expression changed to one of dejection. "I know this is your home, daughter. Nothing concerning the furnishings has been ordered or decided. All I ask is that you give Abby and me an hour. I think you'll be pleased with what we have in mind." His tone turned wheedling. "Can't you call Lois and tell her you'll be late? I told Abby you'd be a hard sell, but I think we've hit on the right theme for the rooms up here. We've put in a lot of time on this presentation. Can't you give us one hour?"

I thought about the schedule involved in Toby's funeral. Avery had told us last night that he would plan Toby's funeral service for Tuesday. If that was the case, we wouldn't do any designing until Monday, when Toby would lie in state. Lois could probably handle the calls that would come in this morning. If Lew was in an agreeable mood, he might lend a hand. He would be at the flower shop getting the banker's birthday bouquets loaded in the van for delivery to the country club.

My father saw I was considering his plea. As an added incentive, he said, "It might not take an hour. Once you get the general drift of what we have in mind, you can look over our ideas at your leisure."

I nodded. "All right. I'll stay, but I have to call Lois again. I told her last night that Toby had passed away and to be ready for a hectic morning. Once the word gets out, we'll be inundated with orders."

My father shuffled uncomfortably. "I guess you should know, the word is already out. The newspaper has the story on the front page. It says the sheriff's department is investigating your friend's death because of 'suspicious circumstances.'"

I waited for his inevitable questions about what these

suspicious circumstances might be, but Dad fooled me. He went back to the attic doorway and attacked the trunk with renewed energy. He got it free of the door frame and hefted it onto a two-wheeled dolly that leaned against the wall.

As he rolled the trunk past me, he said, "Don't come into the library until we call you. I want to see the surprise on your face when you get your first glimpse of our proposal."

If he'd taken the time to look at me, he would've had a preview of that anticipated look of surprise. I couldn't believe my father had passed up the opportunity to probe the meaning of the "suspicious circumstances" surrounding Toby's death.

When my father lived in Texas, he'd subscribed to the *River City Daily* newspaper, where he'd read of my success in solving a couple of cases. He'd come to Missouri with the wild notion of forming a partnership—McGinness and Solomon Detective Agency. I'd put a stop to that. It was one thing to dabble in sleuthing, but a totally different realm of existence to do it for pay. When I'm involved in an investigation, it's because I'm personally motivated. I either knew the deceased or someone I care about is under suspicion and I want to prove his innocence.

My father's lack of interest in Toby's death was puzzling. I followed Dad to the elevator that saved steps from the first and second floors. "So?" I said. "Did you draw any conclusions from the newspaper article?"

Dad pushed the button, and the elevator door creaked open. "Not really. Just skimmed the piece. I had other things on my mind."

I moved so I could see his face. Not one iota of curiosity, just a few beads of sweat trickling from his hairline down to his temple. I helped him roll the dolly into the elevator, then stepped back into the hallway. Before he pushed the button, I offered him a juicy tidbit. "I have inside information that came directly from Sid."

Dad's lips twisted into a grimace at the mention of the sheriff's name. Sid and Dad didn't get along. There's an antagonism between them that just won't go away. They'd almost come to blows the first time they met, when my father had boasted to Sid about the detective agency. Sid was proprietorial about his law-enforcement position in Spencer County and took my father's idea as a personal affront.

My father's lips smoothed into an ingratiating smile. "It's about time the sheriff recognized the fact that my daughter has brains as well as beauty." He beamed at me like a proud papa.

It was too much sweetness before breakfast. I didn't understand my father. Just when I thought I had him pegged, he did an about-face. Where was his curiosity regarding Toby's death? Since my father had moved into this house, he'd poked his nose into anything that had a surreptitious feel to it. Toby's untimely demise certainly qualified. What was the deal?

The elevator door started to close. I took a step toward my room but stopped. Abigail. Abby. My father was quite the charmer, quite the lady's man. Maybe he was infatuated with Ms. Dupree.

I frowned. Something about him had struck me as different. I'd noticed his weight loss and his tan, but I suddenly realized it was his clothes. Whether my father was puttering around the house or going out on the town, he favored dress slacks, polished leather shoes, and conservative shirts. This morning he was dressed in faded blue jeans, sneakers, and an ordinary white T-shirt. His arms looked muscular for a man in his seventies. Was he going for the youthful look? Why?

I spun back to the elevator and pressed my lips to the crack around the door facing. "Dad, how old is Abigail Dupree?"

His huffy answer echoed up the elevator shaft.

"That's hardly relevant, daughter."

I walked to the horseshoe-shaped staircase that curved gracefully to the bottom floor. Leaning over the railing, I looked down into the entry hall. After a few minutes, my father came into view. "Dad, Ms. Dupree's age might not be relevant, but I'd like to know."

He glanced up at me but continued on to the library with his burden. "She's thirty-two years old," he said. Then he added testily, "Your mother raised you to be a courteous, thoughtful woman. I expect to see that person present in the library when Abby and I are ready for you."

Uh-oh. I rarely heard *that* tone from my father. I saluted his back, spun on my heel, and walked back to my bedroom.

FOUR

I GOT DRESSED BEFORE I called Lois about my change of plans. I assured her I'd be at the flower shop no later than eleven o'clock. It wasn't even nine, but she said the phones had been ringing when she'd come in the back door. I told her to put a couple of lines on hold and do the best she could.

It's faster going downstairs by the back staircase, but this morning I took the main steps to the entry hall. I loved the view from this lofty perch. With time on my hands, I paused on the polished oak riser to appreciate the beauty. The morning sun shone through the windows that flanked the front door. The light caught the cut-glass prisms on the chandelier that was suspended from the second-story ceiling, and created a mosaic pattern on the parquet floor.

I'd painted the walls a soft butternut, a warm, neutral shade that showcased the house's antique furnishings. The horse-shoe-shaped staircase blocked the view from the front entrance down the long central hall, but I knew each room intimately. I'd personally gotten down on my knees and brought the gloss back to the wooden floors. I'd refinished woodwork until my hands were so sore I could barely grip my florist knife, but the labor had paid off. The rooms were just as I'd envisioned.

The ground floor contained the library, formal dining room, ballroom, and kitchen. Connected off the kitchen were my father and DeeDee's living quarters. When my father first arrived, I'd offered him his choice of rooms upstairs, but he'd declined, saying he liked the proximity to the kitchen.

At the end of the hall, a pair of French doors led to a terrace that looked out on a garden in the process of being rejuvenated. The work had come to a halt while Missouri experienced one of its hottest, driest summers on record. Now that it was September, the weather was cooler, and we'd had some much-needed rain. Eddie, my landscaper, was going full steam. He knew exactly what I wanted in the garden, so I wasn't concerned with his progress. The same couldn't be said for my next project. Turning this mansion into a boardinghouse had been an idea born out of loneliness.

Carl and I had lived in a modern ranch house in River City. Our lives had been full of love, work, and laughter. We'd gone out to eat, had friends in, but mostly, we had each other. Once Carl was gone, my social life shrank. I received invitations, but rarely accepted. Our friends were couples, and I was the odd woman out. My flower shop business saved my sanity through those first months, but coming home to an empty house had been difficult.

The solitude had forced me to make a drastic decision. I'd taken Carl's life-insurance money and made the down payment on this house with the idea of surrounding myself with people, even if they were renters.

I walked down the rest of the staircase and turned so my gaze could follow the graceful curve of the stairs. The balustrade drew the eye to a balcony that circled the upper floor. The doors to all seven bedrooms were closed, but the smell of new wood and fresh plaster had seeped into the main house.

It was a comforting aroma, one I needed this morning. Toby's death weighed heavy on my heart.

My father came out the library door, saw me, and pointed to the kitchen. "Please, go eat your breakfast. Abby just called. She's about a mile down the road. If you cooperate, daughter, we'll get this show on the road before schedule."

I liked the sound of that, so I hurried across the hall and entered DeeDee's domain. The room was state of the art for creating exquisite cuisine. White walls, white floors, stainless-steel appliances, copper-bottomed pots and pans hanging from hooks over a preparation island, and every electric convenience known to woman. Bright red, blue, and yellow calico-print curtains and chair cushions softened the sterile environment, giving the room a bright, homey feeling. The television was tuned to the food channel. Wolfgang Puck was removing the bones from a chicken.

DeeDee didn't take her eyes off the TV screen. "Albert told me to f-fix you a s-substantial breakfast. I heard you coming down the s-stairs, though you t-took longer than usual. I hope your f-food isn't cold."

I sat down and unfolded my napkin. Glancing up at the television, I saw raw pink flesh and blood-tipped bones. When Wolfgang picked up a cleaver, I grimaced. "Can we dispense with the chicken surgery until after I've eaten?" DeeDee hit the remote button and the screen faded to black. I smiled my appreciation. "Thanks. Maybe you can catch a replay another time."

"He'll be on later t-today." She poured coffee for both of us and sat down. "Are you ready for the m-meeting with the decorator?"

"As ready as I'm going to be." I lifted the warming lid that covered the plate and sighed happily. Coddled eggs were nestled in a blue dish that was surrounded by slices of oranges, strawberries, and kiwi fruit. Crisp curls of turkey bacon begged me to take a bite. Calorie wise, this was a dieter's dream. That it was attractively presented was an added bonus.

Since DeeDee had discovered that she loved to cook, I'd reaped the benefits. She revised high-fat recipes to suit my dietary needs. The results were always scrumptious. With her expertise, I figured she could take an old piece of shoe leather, arrange it on a plate, and the sight would make my mouth water. But I didn't have to contend with shoe leather. Everything she made was luscious, and my weight remained stable.

The front doorbell rang. Our heads swiveled in that direction. My father bellowed from the hall, "I've got it. Don't come out. Stay right where you are."

I rolled my eyes and picked up my fork. The bite of egg was as tasty as usual, but annoyance with my father made the yolk stick in my throat. I took a swallow of hot coffee, and then popped a piece of kiwi into my mouth to cool off my scalded tongue. The tartness of the fruit made my lips pucker.

DeeDee caught my sour expression and said, "Give them a ch-chance, Bretta. I think Abigail's ideas are v-very good."

I didn't bother to explain why I was making a face. "You've seen these ideas?"

"I haven't s-seen anything, but Albert needed s-someone to talk to, so he used me as a s-sounding board."

"You never said anything to me."

She shrugged. "I was s-sworn to s-secrecy."

"I can appreciate that, but I want to know more about these ideas." Seeing her mulish expression, I lowered my voice.

"Look at it this way. If I'm prepared, I won't blurt out some awful remark that will cause trouble."

DeeDee nodded. "You do have a knack for s-speaking your mind."

"So?" I said, whirling my hand in a get-with-it motion.

DeeDee stared at me with troubled brown eyes. She glanced over her shoulder at the kitchen door before whispering, "Attic."

I pushed my plate aside and leaned my elbows on the table. "What is it with the one-word clues? First Sid, and now you. Attic, huh? Well, I'm not in the mood to play Sherlock, or Nancy Drew, or Miss Marple." I scooted back my chair. "I'm going to the library and get this over with. I have other fish to fry. Other papers to peddle. I'm out of here."

I got up and started for the kitchen door. As I passed DeeDee, she put a hand on my arm. "You're at the sh-shop all day, so you haven't s-seen how hard Albert has worked. He l-loves you and wants to please you. Give him a ch-chance."

I didn't say anything, but my exasperation fizzled. Knowing my father, I was sure he had worked diligently. Look at how he'd wrestled that trunk from the attic. I frowned as I left the kitchen. And why was he doing all the heavy work? Why wasn't Abigail helping? I caught sight of my grumpy reflection in a mirror that hung by the dining-room door.

I stopped and gave myself a pep talk. "Be nice. Be polite," I murmured. "Be open-minded. Look for something that can be complimented." I tried a smile but it was too forced. "Relax," I said under my breath. "Be charming." I eased my lips into a slow, gentle curve. "That's much better." Chuckling, I gave myself a congratulatory cheek-splitting grin that exposed all my pearly whites.

The library door opened. In the mirror my gaze connected with my father's. My affected smile dissolved into slack-jawed embarrassment.

He shook his head and motioned for me to go in ahead of him. "We're ready for you."

In a hearty tone, I said, "And I'm ready, too."

My father wasn't fooled. In a soft voice, he said, "Abby and I have taken this decorating very seriously. I had hoped that you would, too." He put a hand on my back and gently propelled me forward.

Contrite, I shuffled into the library. With the walls paneled in dark walnut, the room would have felt oppressive if I hadn't lightened the mood by having the furniture reupholstered in moss green, cream, and gold. The Oriental rug picked up those colors and added a bold splash of peacock blue.

Posters and swatch books covered the sofa. A portable movie screen had been set up in front of the bookshelves. In my swift appraisal of the room, I also saw an overhead projector, but then my father directed my attention to the woman standing by the fireplace.

"Abby, this is my daughter, Bretta. Bretta, this is Abigail Dupree."

She looked younger than thirty-two. She had a round, cherub face sprinkled with freckles. Her auburn hair was twisted into a braid that reached below her narrow waist. She wore a pair of khaki slacks, topped with a white knit shirt. Her smile was shy, but her blue eyes twinkled with excitement.

She made the first gesture, holding out her hand. "Bretta,

I've looked forward to meeting you. I have everything lined up, ready to go. Albert told me you were crunched for time. We can get started right away."

I gave her hand a light clasp. "Nice to meet you," I murmured. My first thought, that Dad was infatuated with this woman, bit the dust. She wasn't his type. But something was going on between them. It was as if they were on the same brain wave. She had only to glance across the room and my father adjusted the blinds. He lifted one shoulder, and she gave him a tight smile and nodded.

My father was an active man—an active, wealthy man. I'd kept him busy with the remodeling upstairs, but that job was completed. Was he looking for a new vocation with Abigail? Was she looking for an investor in a fledgling business?

Dad urged me toward a chair that had been placed facing the screen. "Sit here," he said, "and we'll begin."

Abigail picked up a notebook from a table next to me. Her hands trembled. My father had said he'd told Abigail that I would be a hard sell, which couldn't have eased her mind about making this presentation.

My attitude softened toward her. "Relax," I said, and flashed a genuine smile. "I'll try not to interrupt your delivery, and I'll try to be open-minded."

She drew a hand across her brow and heaved a deep sigh. "Whew, that takes the pressure off." She giggled as she took a firmer grip on the notebook. "I've felt like an invader, coming around while you've been at work, but Albert thought that was the best way to gather our data. Your home is lovely. The woodwork with its scrolls and carvings are superb. I liked that you stayed with the period of the house for the decor downstairs, but for a boardinghouse, where each room is the living quarters for an individual, I felt that the decorating theme needed to be modernized."

Modernized how? With zebra and leopard print? I gnawed my bottom lip to remind me that I'd said I'd keep quiet.

Abigail smiled. "I can see you don't agree, but have you thought about the type of person who might want to rent a room? Wouldn't they bring their own memorabilia? Decorating a boardinghouse is different from a bed and breakfast. With the latter, your guests arrive with luggage, to spend a few days before leaving. You provide a lovely, comfortable room with chairs, bed, tables, and such. But what about renters who want to move in with their own bed or Grandma's favorite rocking chair? What if those items don't fit into the room's color scheme or decor?"

Abigail held out her hands. "I've tried to work around your idea of a boardinghouse, but I'm stymied. How much furniture do we incorporate into the theme? Do we simply paint the rooms and furnish window treatments? Or do we go all the way and add accessories such as prints, vases, and figurines? These are questions you need to consider, but because you're pressed for time, we'll skip that discussion and move on.

"Albert liked the idea of naming each room for identification, rather than tacking a number on a door. The blue room, the pink room sounded too mundane for such a classy old house. Since flowers are an integral part of your life, we researched that category. I have to say we've considered everything from amaryllis to zinnia."

Zinnia reminded me of my conversation with Bailey concerning the stages of an investigation. My mind flitted away from Abigail's words. What had Sid found out? Would he tell me if I called him? Had he questioned the proprietors on Hawthorn Street? What would he ask each one? Did he have a suspect yet?

"—that's why we settled on it," finished Abigail. "There are so many different varieties with such visual names, though I wouldn't be so presumptuous as to tag your private quarters. We've chosen only six names for the seven bedrooms."

She consulted her notebook. "Golden Dawn. Crimson Charm. Vanilla Blush. Lavender Lace. Cocoa Magic. Coral Duet." When she raised her gaze to meet mine, her eyes were shining. "Doesn't each name evoke its own portrait? Once we'd settled on the names, the rooms seemed to take on lives of their own.

"Golden Dawn calls for buttery yellow accents against fern green walls, with contrasts of deep indigo blue. Crimson Charm begs for brass and glass with touches of elegant damask in shades of rich, vibrant burgundy. Vanilla Blush is a perpetual bloomer with red hips among luscious ivory flowers that are tinged with shell pink."

Abigail waved her hand. "I could go on and on, but a picture is worth a thousand words. Albert, if you'll dim the lights, it's time to show Bretta our incentive for making the bedrooms fabulous."

I'd lost the thread of Abigail's speech while I was day-dreaming, but picked it up again when she mentioned "red hips." I assumed she was talking about roses. She switched on the overhead projector and slid a transparency into place. An exquisite picture of a rose came into focus on the screen. Under the photo, in elegant script, were the words "Lavender Lace."

Abigail's voice was soft. "See how the petals are infused with splashes of deep purple edged with white fringes? I visualize pale gray walls, a deeper gray carpet with an undertone of lavender. Accents would be with pewter and touches of dainty lace trim. It would be a feminine room, but I think any woman would love to call it home."

As Abigail talked she put another image under the projector. This time I saw the words "Cocoa Magic." A russet rose with a chocolate glaze was the only way to describe the sensational reddish-brown color combination.

"This would be a man's room," continued Abigail. "The wood floor would be left exposed, but area rugs in cream or ecru would add contrast. There's a sleigh bed in the attic that would set the room off to perfection."

She turned to me, and I saw her teeth gleam in the dusky light. "And speaking of the attic. There's a gold mine of antiques upstairs. Most are in excellent condition. Some need a few minor repairs, but I know a man who does wonderful restoration. But getting back to the roses. Your father painted all the transparencies. Once the walls are finished, we'll use this overhead projector to cast the image of the rose on the wall of the corresponding room that bears its name. Your father will then paint that image directly on the plaster, giving the room its monogram."

Abigail switched off the projector, and my father turned on the lights. She locked eyes with me. "I know this is too much to take in all at once. I have more elaborate sketches of each room, with placement of the furniture and the fabrics I'd like to see used. I can leave everything for you to look over, or you can ask me questions, if you have time?"

My mind was in a whirl, but in a good way. I was truly impressed. I loved the use of the roses. I loved the names attached to the rooms. In fact, I didn't see anything that hit a jarring note.

Abigail and my father stood side by side watching me, waiting for my reaction. I had plenty of questions, but asked only one. "Dad, what was in the trunk you brought down from the attic this morning?"

Before he could speak, Abigail said in a dramatic whisper, "A corpse in need of a final resting place."

I supposed she was trying for humor, but I wasn't amused. I cocked an eyebrow, but kept quiet.

Abigail's lightheartedness vanished. She glanced at Albert as if for help, then back at me. "I—uh—you—uh—your father has told me about your extracurricular activities." Her voice grew cool. "Since my spiel only prompted a question concerning the trunk, I thought I needed to grab your attention another way."

"I'm listening," I said.

Her eyes narrowed. "But are you seriously interested?"

Keeping my voice even, I replied, "I'm still here, aren't I?"

My father stepped forward. "Now, girls," he began, but choked off in midsentence.

I glanced at him and caught a pained expression. Concerned, I touched his arm. "Dad? What's wrong? Are you ill?"

He shook his head. "No. No. Disappointed is more like it. I'd hoped this first meeting would be productive as well as amicable. Bretta," he said, "I know you're upset about your friend's death, but try to be patient." Looking at Abigail, he added, "Let's keep to the business at hand. Show her the contents of the trunk."

Abigail pressed her lips tightly together and led the way around the sofa. The piece of furniture had blocked my view, so I was surprised to see the carpet spread with bright pieces of material. The fabrics had been carefully fanned out in color-coordinated stacks.

"These vintage textiles are fabulous," said Abigail. She picked up a shimmering piece of vermilion-colored cloth, unfurling it like a flower opening its petals. "I've done a fabric identification using the burn test. This is pure silk."

My gaze swept the fabric, but I saw nothing that marred the sheen. "Burn test?"

Still miffed, Abigail replied in a monotone. "I snipped a piece from the selvage, touched a match to it to determine if the fabric is natural, man-made, or a blend of natural and man-made fibers. Silk is a protein fiber and usually burns readily. The odor reminds me of singed hair. The ash crumbles easily, but the fire can't be extinguished as quickly as it can with linen or cotton."

I picked up the edge of the fabric and let the sensuous material slip though my fingers. "So this is real silk? It feels wonderful, but I'd be afraid to use it. With my luck, I'd spill something on it and it would be ruined."

Abigail's lips twitched. "I can be a klutz, too, but silk is wearable, durable, and is a classic. It never goes out of style. No other fabric generates the same reaction as silk. It's one of the oldest textile fibers know to man and it's the strongest. A filament of steel the same diameter as silk will break before a filament of silk."

"Stronger than steel?" I stared down at the fabric in my hands. "If it does all you say, then why isn't it used more often in clothes and such?"

"Cost. Pure silk like this is taken from the cocoon of the silkworm."

I nodded. Anything that took time to produce raised the price. I looked down at the other fabrics displayed on the sheet-covered floor. "Are these silk, too?"

"Some are." Abigail gently folded the length of silk and placed it back with the others. Pointing to a fuchsia piece that was almost transparent, she said, "That's chiffon. Over there is a georgette sheer crepe. It's heavier than chiffon and has a crinkle surface. Organza is similar to cotton organdy except it's made with silk."

"And those heavier-looking materials?" I pointed to a lovely plaid of scarlet, green, and navy.

"That particular piece is tartan. It's made from wool and is a twilled plaid design that originated in Scotland."

"Since you had Dad bring these fabrics down from the attic, I'm assuming you have plans to use them in the decorating upstairs?"

"With your permission, of course. Some of the pieces are too small to do much with except make accent pillows. But there's enough of this vermilion silk to cover the Queen Anne chair I found in the attic."

"I understand that silk is durable, but do you think covering a chair is making the best use of this material?"

Abigail shrugged. "At least it's being utilized. Stuffed in a trunk, it's doing no one any good."

"That's true." I studied the range of fabrics. They were lovely to look at and a pleasure to touch. The filmy texture of the chiffon was sensual in my fingers. The woolen tartan made me think of wintry nights, curled up with a good book and a cup of hot chocolate. "These fabrics set a mood, don't they?"

My casual comment caused Abigail's eyes to light up. "You get it, don't you? The principles that apply to arranging flowers are color, texture, and placement. The same is true of fabrics. Whether plaids, gingham, or pinstripes are used, layering vintage fabrics is a wonderful strategy. Brocade has a raised pattern that resembles embroidery. Damask is a mix of plain and lustrous weaves and has a formal air for draperies and slipcovers. Taffeta is crisp and plain, but pair it with velvet and the room comes alive. Whether it's curtains or draperies, or dust ruffles around a four-poster bed, or chiffon draped in a canopy, I think using these fabrics will make each room unique."

I was listening to Abigail, but I sneaked a quick peek at the clock on the mantel. Apparently, I wasn't as furtive as I thought. Abigail saw the direction of my gaze and stiffened again. "Here's my phone number," she said, taking a business card from her pocket. "If you decide to hire me, I'll clear my schedule and begin immediately."

I needed time to think things through, and promised Abigail I'd be in touch by the first of the week. Both she and my father looked crestfallen at the delay, but I stuck by my decision. Her comment about a boardinghouse versus a bed and breakfast had opened up several new thoughts, but I had to get to the flower shop. I said my good-byes, picked up my purse, and headed for work.

FIVE

AS I DROVE INTO River City, I decided that I liked Abigail Dupree. She was a little too prickly, and my father was taking this redecorating much too seriously. It was as if he had a personal stake in whether I decided to hire Abigail. Again I wondered if he'd put some of his own money into her venture. But I couldn't see why he'd do that unless he was bored and looking for a new outlet for his creativity. Painting the roses on the bedroom walls might satisfy the artist in him, but he could do that without Abigail's influence.

Abigail's presentation had appealed to me. She'd been straightforward. Her ideas were pleasing, and her use of colors that coordinated with the roses had stimulated my creative imagination. I could understand her wanting to do this job. Browsing the attic for furniture, pairing the pieces with vintage fabric and accessories that didn't figure into a budget would be exhilarating. Now that she'd reminded me of the possibilities lurking in the attic, I was tempted to nose around on my own. But first things first. I had a flower shop to operate.

I entered River City on Chestnut, traveled about eight blocks, and then made a right on Millstone Road. Normally, I stay on this lesser-traveled course until I'm in the same block as my shop, and then I cross over to Hawthorn. I had other plans today. I cut to Hawthorn immediately so I could see the route Toby took each day when he left his house.

I was at the south end of the street, where country gave way to city. Missouri State Highway 12 divided fields and pastures before becoming Hawthorn. If I wanted a look at Toby's house, I would have to turn away from town and go outside the city limits. There wasn't time, so I had to fight that urge. I stepped on the gas and eased into the flow of traffic that would take me to the flower shop.

I knew this area well, but I tried to see it through Toby's eyes. What would it be like to frequent only one street when hundreds crisscrossed our city? Hawthorn was high traffic, with every kind of business imaginable. Fast food, cafes, ethnic fare, insurance offices, bars, dress shops, liquor stores, discount stores, a grocery store, a pharmacy, a hardware store, a tire-repair shop, and so many more.

Everything a person needed to sustain life was on this one street. There wasn't any reason to go farther afield, which must have been in Agnes's mind when she planned her son's future. Had she picked each of us because Toby might require our services? Abner's grocery store, Harmon's pharmacy, and Diana's discount store were places Toby would need to frequent, but Leona's dress shop or Melba's candle shop didn't sell anything necessary for Toby's well-being. As for my business, I'm sure there are people who live a lifetime without entering a flower shop. So why was I chosen? Why Leona, Melba, and Yvonne? And I couldn't forget Mr. Barker and his bakery. Mr. Barker was a kind gentleman. As were Leona, Melba, and Yvonne. I liked to think I'd fit into that same category. So had we been chosen because we'd take an interest in Toby?

We'd cooperated with Agnes's wishes, but what was in

Toby's mind? I knew he had trouble comprehending some things, but for the most part he functioned on his own. Avery took care of the financial aspects of his life. How did Toby spend his days? Did he always work? He came around my business frequently, but I'd never stopped to wonder what he did the rest of the time.

I parked in front of the flower shop, gathered up my purse, and stepped out of my SUV. I glanced next door to the Happy Hour Video store and caught a glimpse of the store's owner, Josh Wainwright, peeking out at me. I raised my hand to wave to him, but he quickly ducked out of sight. That roused my curiosity.

Last night at the hospital, no one had mentioned contacting Josh about Toby's condition. And yet, I'd seen Toby sweeping Josh's sidewalk and washing his windows. Why hadn't Melba or Yvonne called Josh? Did that mean that Josh wasn't on Agnes's list of store owners?

I changed direction. No harm in asking a few questions. I pushed open the door of the video store and stepped inside. Josh was behind the counter. He was in his thirties. His taste in clothes ran to baggy pants, tight T-shirts, and loafers without socks. He always looked as if he needed a shave, but the scruffy hairs on his jaw never materialized into a full beard.

He glanced up when the door opened and flashed me a quick grin. "Bretta," he said, "I figured I'd be seeing you today. Our friendly neighborhood sleuth is hot on the trail."

"What do you mean?"

"That hornet's nest was *intentionally* put in Toby's house." Josh's eyes narrowed. "Get the bastard, Bretta. Whoever pulled such a nasty trick deserves to be charged with murder."

"I agree, but how did you find out about the nest?"

Josh shrugged. "Sheriff Hancock isn't as devious with his questioning as he thinks. I drew my own conclusions."

"How well did you know Toby?"

Josh hesitated. "So-so," he finally said.

"Have you ever see anyone hassle Toby? Push him around? Tease him?"

Josh stared at me. "Do you think someone has been picking on him?"

"I'm not sure, but I'm not ruling it out completely. I can't understand the motive. Why Toby? Did someone carry a grudge against him? Was Toby a threat in some way?"

Josh's eyes opened wide. "Toby, a threat? You've got to be kidding."

"I'm serious. Why put the hornet's nest in his house if not to cause serious injury? Maybe the perpetrator didn't plan on Toby's dying, but that's what happened."

Josh nodded. "I see what you mean. I'll give it some thought, but nothing comes to mind at the moment."

"You weren't at the hospital last night."

Josh raised an eyebrow. "Was I supposed to be there?"

"I thought maybe Yvonne or Melba might have called you."

"Why would they call me?"

"Toby swept your sidewalks and washed your windows. I assumed you were one of the people Agnes asked to employ her son."

Josh shifted uneasily from one foot to the other. "Never met the woman."

"So Toby took you on as a client after his mother died?"

"That's right."

"Do you know if he stopped at any other stores along Hawthorn besides the ones his mother had chosen for him to do business with?"

Josh raised his chin. "I don't know what Toby did after he left my shop."

I had one more thing I wanted to ask. This was always the difficult part of my amateur sleuthing. I had no right, or the badge, to back up my impertinent question, but I asked it anyway. "Where were you yesterday?"

For a second, anger flashed in Josh's eyes. A tight smile twisted his lips, but he answered my question. "Right here. Two of my employees didn't show up for work. I was here from nine o'clock in the morning until I closed at ten." He touched the keyboard of the computer next to him. "I have a list of customers from yesterday. With the touch of a finger, I can print you out a copy, complete with addresses and phone numbers. I've already given one to the sheriff, but it's no problem to make a copy for you."

My cheeks felt hot. "That isn't necessary, Josh, but surely you understand why I asked?"

His voice was cold. "I understood when the sheriff asked me, but not you." He picked up a stack of video cases and turned his back to me.

I sighed softly and walked out the door. Pausing on the sidewalk in front of the flower shop, I glanced across the street to Kelsay's Bar and Grill. I could use a snack. My conversation with Josh had left a bad taste in my mouth. Maybe I could entice Lois away from her diet with some of Kelsay's curly fries. We could split an order.

Sounded good to me. I took a step in that direction. The door behind me opened, and Lois stuck her head out.

"Don't even think about going over to Kelsay's, Bretta. I need you inside right away. I can't take another minute of this lunacy."

Thinking she was talking about orders for Toby's funeral service, I said, "It's been hectic, huh? Didn't you put two of the phone lines on hold?"

Lois rolled her eyes. "Flower business I can handle. Being interrogated about a murder investigation has gotten to me." She held the door open wider. "You deal with them. I've had it."

"Them?" I said as I entered the shop. "I thought you were talking about Sid." I looked over the front counter to the workroom. Melba, Yvonne, and Leona had made themselves at home. I walked slowly past the display of green plants, my gaze fastened on the trio. They were seated on stools around what is usually my workstation. Cans of soda and sheets of paper were spread over the tabletop.

"Well," said Melba. "It's about time. While you've been at home, we've been busy gathering information." She pushed several sheets of paper toward me. "Here, take a look. We've made a list of possible suspects and motives. We've done all that Yvonne's brother will allow. He says we're inviting trouble, but we had to do this for Toby."

I sensed a movement to my right and turned to see Phillip Pritchard sitting in a chair by the ribbon rack. He came slowly to his feet. "Sorry for the invasion, Bretta. I've tried to keep a tight rein on these ladies. Since I'm their designated driver for the morning, I've curtailed their movements, but I can't stop them from theorizing."

He held out his hands in a helpless gesture. "Back when I was working, I could keep twenty employees toeing the line. These women don't recognize that *there is a line*. Maybe you can talk some sense into them. Yvonne has been on the phone since we got home last night from the hospital. I finally went on to my room, but at some point she and these two," he said, waving a hand at Melba and Leona, "decided to write up every detail they could remember about Toby's life. I went along with that, but when I heard them mapping out a strategy for interviewing people along Hawthorn, I took a stand."

Yvonne shifted her weight on the three-legged stool, making the wood creak. I was worried that the stool was about to give way, but Yvonne had other things on her mind. Her eyes blazed. "Stand? Ha! You invited yourself along and have been treating us like underlings."

Leona's lips tilted up in a smile. Her heavily applied makeup creased, forming tiny lines around her mouth. "I think it's cute that he's worried about us. I haven't had such consideration in ages." She stood up. Today she had on a calf-length belted dress in shades of peach and toast, with swirls of burgundy. "I have to get to my shop."

She stacked the papers that were in front of her into a neat pile. "Bretta, these are for you," she said, handing the sheaf to me. "We've dredged up all the information we have about Toby, his mother, Agnes, and anything else we could think of that might be relevant. We've signed our names to our own work, so if you have any questions, you'll know who to contact."

Melba stood, too, but she was such a little lady, I had to dip my head to meet her direct gaze. As she came closer, I caught a whiff of what smelled like blueberries. I sniffed a couple of times and my stomach rumbled in response to the wonderful aroma.

Melba laughed. "Hungry, Bretta? I was unpacking a new shipment of blueberry-muffin-scented candles when Phillip arrived. That particular fragrance must have been a good choice on my part judging by your reaction."

"You're right about that." I glanced at the papers in my hand. "I appreciate the trouble you've gone to, but why don't you give this info to the sheriff?"

Leona spoke up. "We did. We made copies, but he didn't seem impressed. That's why we're giving you a set, too. Sheriff Hancock was more concerned with where we were yesterday. That's why the three of us got our heads together. We have airtight alibis for the entire day. We have witnesses who are willing to swear that we never left our businesses, but the same can't be said for some of the other owners."

Melba tapped the papers in my hand. "We've put it all in here, Bretta. My mind is already made up as to who is guilty. You can bet your last dollar that I won't be buying groceries at Garrett's anytime soon."

Phillip snapped to attention. "That's enough," he said. "Melba, you cannot make comments of that nature." He shook his head wearily at me. "These women don't understand the seriousness of such rash statements. I can try to watch over Yvonne, but Leona and Melba are alone." He held out his hands. "What can I do to protect them? Right now, they're their own worst enemies. Melba's remark said to the wrong person could result in uh—well—uh—" He faltered to a stop.

I nodded. "Phillip is absolutely right. You can't discuss your thoughts or your theories with anyone. You'll only endanger yourselves. I appreciate this information. I'll read it carefully, and if I see anything pertinent, I'll call it to the sheriff's attention. My best advice to each of you is to go back to your businesses and carry on with your normal activities."

There was grumbling, but Phillip herded his group out the

door. Once they were gone, I heaved a sigh. "Whew," I said, sitting down. "I didn't need that."

Lois fanned a bunch of orders at me. "And I did? In between taking phone calls, I had to listen to them. They've been here for over an hour, flinging out names of possible suspects, asking me what Hawthorn store owner I liked as a possible killer. They wanted to know if I'd seen anything suspicious. Had I noticed any covert meetings taking place in the alley behind the flower shop? Did Abner have any nefarious visitors coming in the back of his grocery store? And it went on and on." Lois shook her head. "I feel sorry for Phillip. I only had sixty long minutes of that kind of garbage. The one good thing is their age. Their energy levels peter out fast. By the time you arrived, they'd begun to run down."

The phone rang. Lois was standing by it, but she didn't make a move. When it rang a second time, and she still didn't reach for it, I heaved myself up and said, "Stay where you are. I'll get it."

"Seems only fair," she muttered.

I picked up the receiver and said, "The Flower Shop."

Sid's voice filled my ear. "Bretta, who have you questioned? What have you found out?"

No pleasantries here. "I assume you're referring to Toby's murder investigation?"

"I don't have time for chitchat. Why beat around the bush? You know and I know that you can't control your snooping. So what have you found out?"

"You're not being very nice, Sid. I've been at home all morning." Reluctantly, I added, "Before I came into the shop, I spoke with Josh, next door."

"And?"

"He figured out from your questions that the hornet's nest was intentionally put in Toby's bedroom."

Sid's tone sharpened. "He says my questions tipped him off? That's interesting."

"Why is that?"

"Because I purposefully confined my inquiry to his relationship with Toby. Not once did I mention the cause of death. Josh Wainwright didn't get anything from my questions, but that's not to say he couldn't already have firsthand knowledge about the nest." Sid chuckled nastily. "I love these unexpected slipups from suspects. Keeps me on my toes. What else do you have?"

"Yvonne, Melba, and Leona were here at the flower shop when I arrived. They gave me some compiled information on Toby. They told me they gave you copies, too. Have you read what they've written?"

"Skimmed the malarkey. Nothing jumped out at me." He was silent a moment, then said, "Three hundred feet doesn't sound like much, but it's the difference between active or peripheral involvement."

I frowned. "I don't know what you mean."

"Toby's house sits three hundred feet outside the River City limits. That makes this case a Spencer County inquiry. Police chief Kelley is assisting, but jurisdiction belongs to me. Success or failure, good media coverage or bad, it all falls on my office."

He heaved a sigh that whistled in my ear. "My luck sucks. This case is high profile. Every step I take, every move I make will be under scrutiny. I'm already getting calls from around the county. Citizens are demanding that I step up patrols in outlying areas. People are appalled that someone like Toby was targeted by a person or persons as yet unknown."

"I'm surprised that Toby's name is recognized by so many people. I thought he only traveled down Hawthorn."

"It isn't. He did."

My mind scrambled to piece that together. By the time I had it figured out, Sid was saying, "—is being memorialized because he was mentally challenged. The media is feeding the frenzy, playing up Toby's death for all it's worth. I haven't seen the news reports, but a couple of my deputies say there have been interviews with mental-illness experts, family services, and any other government agency that has an ax to grind."

"Why are they involved?"

"Because Toby didn't depend on the government for assistance. He didn't have a social worker. He didn't fall through any cracks in the system. His death wasn't the result of a bureaucratic slipup. In short—no one screwed up. In most cases a man of Toby's—uh—type would have received some kind of government aid. Since he didn't collect a monthly check, his death is being blamed on society as a whole, with all the social services adding their spin on the circumstances."

"The only person to blame is the one who put the hornet's nest in Toby's room."

"Yeah, well, that brings me back to my questions. What have you heard or observed?" He stopped and reluctantly added, "What conclusions have you drawn?"

In the past Sid had repeated time and time again that if I didn't know something to be a fact that could be substantiated, then I was to keep it to myself. My success had changed his tune, but his tone made it clear he didn't like requesting this song.

I sank onto a stool and massaged my forehead. "Observations? Drawn conclusions? You don't ask for much, do you?"

"If I don't ask, I get nothing. Let's hear it. Begin where you want, but don't go off on a tangent. My time is limited. I'm meeting a bug specialist at Toby's house in about an hour."

"What do you hope an entomologist will tell you?"

"I don't know anything about hornets except that when riled, in close quarters, they can be lethal. Go on, Bretta, start talking."

I took a few minutes to get events set in my mind. I had several things I could tell Sid, but I needed to do them in chronological order so he could see how each piece fit in with the next.

I began with Toby's visit yesterday. I related the conversation as best I could, but I put emphasis on the bakery employee's belittling comment to Toby. I told Sid about Toby's invitation to me, concerning the flowers that were being stolen from his garden. I continued with the names of the people in the waiting room at the hospital, the conversation that took place there, and how Harmon Purvis seemed well informed on the subject of hornets. Sid listened without comment until I came to the part about the sigh I'd heard when Avery told us Toby had passed away.

Sid grunted. "A sigh. Big deal. What's with a sigh? I do it all the time. I'm doing it now." He huffed out a breath of air. "See? What's that prove? It's hot air. I need something tangible. I'll talk to the bakery employee, but it sounds like nothing."

"I want to see Toby's garden."

Silence. Finally Sid said, "Why? Because Toby said the flowers were being stolen?"

"Yes. Do you know what kind they were?"

"Does it matter?"

"It might make a difference, and then again, it might not."

Sid chuckled. "Playing it safe, huh? Okay. Come by the house. I'll be there for the next hour or so." He didn't say thanks. He didn't say good-bye. He simply hung up.

I returned my receiver to the cradle and it immediately rang again. This time I didn't wait to see what Lois would do. I picked it up, saying, "The Flower Shop."

On the other end of the line, a soft, feminine voice said, "Avery Wheeler calling Bretta Solomon."

"This is Bretta."

"Just a minute, please."

I heard a click, and Avery's modulated tone filled my ear. "Bretta? I wasn't sure if my secretary would find you at the flower shop. It's getting on toward noon and I know you close early on Saturday."

"That's right. How are you doing?"

"Okay. I'm getting Toby's affairs in order, which is why I called. I'll need a nice spray of flowers for the top of his casket, and a bouquet from me personally. Send both bills to my office."

I pulled an order form in front of me. "I have standard questions I ask when I take an order for flowers for the casket."

"Proceed with your questions."

"Will the casket be open or closed?"

"As you know, the body is at Delaney Funeral Home. Bernard has assured me that the sting marks on Toby's face will be covered by makeup. I'm to do a viewing tomorrow afternoon. At that time, I'll make the final decision. Knowing Bernard's fine work, I'm going to say the casket will be open."

"What color will it be?"

Avery cleared his throat. "Mahogany, with a copper bead around the beveled edge of the lid."

I hesitated before I made that notation. A mahogany casket seemed rather extravagant, but I didn't comment. "And Toby will be wearing what color suit?"

"No suit. He didn't own one, didn't feel comfortable in a tie, either. I've had my secretary buy a pair of navy dress slacks and a blue shirt."

"Toby loved all flowers. Do you think I should use red roses or red carnations?"

"He thought highly of you, Bretta. Whatever you choose would please him and will please me as well."

My eyes burned with unshed tears. "Thank you, Avery. That means a lot to me. Toby was very special."

Avery cleared his throat. "Since I have you on the phone, I'm going to take this opportunity to request that you attend the reading of Toby's will. I'll also be contacting Lois Duncan and Lew Moffitt as well."

I turned so I could see Lois as I repeated, "You want Lois, Lew, and me to be at the reading of Toby's will?" Lois's eyes widened with surprise.

"That's correct," said Avery. "I've scheduled the meeting for seven-thirty Tuesday evening. That should make it easier for all the beneficiaries to attend."

"Beneficiaries?" I repeated. Now I couldn't contain my

questions. "How many are you talking about? You did say a mahogany casket? Isn't that top of the line? What kind of legacy did Toby leave?"

Avery's voice was cautious. "I'm not giving out any more information, Bretta." He murmured a soft good-bye, and hung up.

SIX

WHILE LOIS AND I closed the flower shop, we hashed over the few facts Avery had divulged. It didn't surprise me that Toby had a will. Since Toby had a heart condition, I would have expected Avery to advise Agnes to make some sort of provision in the case of his unexpected death. It didn't even surprise me that I was a beneficiary. He had no family. Just friends like me, and Lois, and Lew. It was a pretty good assumption that all of Toby's Hawthorn clients would be in Avery's office on Tuesday evening.

Would his killer be there, too?

I didn't voice that question to Lois. She was excited that Toby had thought enough of her to include her in his will. I didn't bother trying to explain that Toby probably had nothing to do with the bequests. Those issues were surely settled before Agnes passed away.

Lois and I said our good-byes. Since I was parked out front, I locked that door, leaving Lois to take care of the back. Traffic was light for a Saturday. The day was gorgeous. Bright sunshine, a gentle breeze, and the sky so blue it hurt my eyes.

I'd always felt blessed that my flower shop was located on Hawthorn, a direct route to the Spencer County Courthouse and other municipal offices. Business at my store was often brisk and had netted me a good living over the past years. Other parts of River City hadn't been as fortunate. In the last decade, since the interstate had looped our metropolis, little mom-and-pop operations had vanished. Because most major growth tends to sprawl near the congestion of heavy traffic, the outer-loop highway had become the place to open a new venture. Westgate Mall featured forty-five shops, advertising "all your needs under one roof."

While I welcomed sightseers into my shop, I knew without a doubt that my economic success depended on River City's thirty thousand residents, along with the people living in the outlying areas of our county. I had to please them, not the owners of the vehicles, racing down the interstate, looking for a fast potty break or a place to buy a quick snack. To the people in and around River City, the shops on Hawthorn offered more than service. We were familiar with their wants and needs, and we tried very hard to please.

Traffic thinned even more as I arrived at the end of Hawthorn. Highway 12 was well paved, with shoulders wide enough that Toby could pedal his bike safely. I hadn't traveled far when I saw the city limits sign. I applied my brakes. Just as Sid had said, three hundred feet later I made the turn into Toby's driveway.

I parked behind Sid's patrol car, leaving another car room to back out onto the main road. I took my time getting out of my SUV. Sid and a man, who I took to be the entomologist, were conversing in the front yard. The man said something to Sid. Sid nodded and the man went to his car and got in. I waited until he'd backed out before joining Sid.

The sheriff of Spencer County was a few inches taller than my height of five feet seven. He had a round face, light red hair, and a multitude of freckles on his pale skin. He rarely smiled. This moment was no exception. My arrival hadn't put the bright light of welcome in his sober eyes. "Was that the entomologist?" I said.

"Yes. He spouted information until my head feels like it's full of cotton batting, and I've got a pain in my gut." He rubbed his stomach and winced.

"Did you hear anything that might help your investigation?"

Reluctantly, Sid pulled out a notebook. "The word *wasp* is derived from the Anglo-Saxon words *waefs, waeps, waesp,* which when loosely translated means to weave, which refers to the way they build their nests. Hornets have a scientific classification as being members of the *Vespidae* family. These vespoid wasps are also called yellow jackets as well as hornets."

He looked at me, then back at his notes. "According to the bug guy, hornets' nests aren't prevalent. They're social insects because they live in colonies that number upward into the thousands. Easily provoked, these insects will attack and drive their stinger into flesh while injecting venom into the wound. Hornets make large paper nests by masticating wood and plant fiber. With dedication, they apply layer upon layer until they have a hive that might measure about half the size of a bushel basket."

I raised an eyebrow. "Those are fantastic notes. You must have copied everything he said word for word."

Sid flipped his notebook shut and tucked it in his shirt pocket. "When he started talking, I wasn't sure what was important and what wasn't. So I used my own cryptic brand of shorthand to get it all down. Now I see it as a waste of paper."

"I heard you say that hornets' nests aren't prevalent. I take that to mean they aren't hanging from every tree branch. Whoever decided to use the nest had to know where it was and have access to it."

"The bug specialist says he's located ten nests in the county. He figures there could be more, but he's been alerted about these because people don't like them on their property. He keeps tabs on the nests, knows when the hornets are about to swarm. He's going to check to see if any are missing. If we can pinpoint where the nest came from, we might get a handle on who grabbed it."

I was skeptical. "That sounds like a very long shot."

Sid glared at me. "You got any better ideas?"

"No. I'm just saying—"

"I know what you're saying. I'm not putting much stock in it either, but the bug guy volunteered. And just to let you know, I went by Merry's Delights and questioned that employee who made the comment to Toby. That was a long shot, too."

"But why did she say what she did to—"

"Forget it. I talked to her and crossed her off my list." Changing subjects, he asked, "Have you been in Toby's house?"

Sid might have crossed the employee off his list, but I hadn't. However, he didn't need to know that. "I've never had any contact with Toby outside of the flower shop."

"I didn't figure you had or you'd have said something. We'll see the garden, but first we're going inside."

I frowned. "Is that necessary?"

Sid rubbed his stomach as he stared off into space. "Yeah," he said. "It's necessary. I want your take on what's inside."

"My take?"

Impatiently, Sid said, "Your impression, Bretta. I want to know what you think."

I turned toward the house. It was white, square, and unpretentious. At a guess I'd say there were two bedrooms, a living room, a kitchen, and a bathroom. There was a cement front stoop covered by an A-shaped overhang. Blinds hung smooth and straight behind the windows.

I glanced at Sid. "What kind of impression do you expect me to have?"

Sid didn't answer. He strode off, leaving me to follow, which I did. I was more than curious, and not just about the interior of Toby's home. I wanted to know why Sid was so intent on my going inside.

Sid led the way down a sidewalk that ran alongside the house. We turned the corner and stepped on the porch. I glanced at the backyard but my view was blocked by a row of thick hedges. For the time being, I put the garden out of my mind and moved to the door that had been propped open. The blades of a box fan whirled, blowing the smell of chemicals past me. I wrinkled my nose at the odor.

Sid explained, "You're smelling the vapor the exterminator used to kill the hornets. If you think it's bad now, you should have been here last night. The house reeked of it, but I've been assured that the lingering odor isn't toxic."

He stood aside and motioned for me to go in. "The house has been processed, with most of the attention centered on Toby's bedroom. As I told you, the window was jimmied open, but we didn't find any prints except Toby's."

I nodded and stepped into the kitchen, wincing as my feet crunched on the dead hornets. They lay in droves on the floor, speckling the white linoleum like giant commas punctuating a blank page. Conscious of the insects under my feet, it was hard to take in everything at once.

The walls were painted yellow, with green-checked curtains at the windows. The cabinets followed three walls, interspersed with a stove, a refrigerator, and double sinks under the window that faced the drive. That windowsill was wider than most and held an aluminum pan filled with soil. Seedlings had sprouted, but lack of care had sent them to an early grave. The counters were clean, only an electric can opener, a coffeemaker, and a toaster in sight. A table with two chairs was by the back door. The room was tidy except for the dead hornets on the floor.

I glanced at Sid, but he gave no indication of what he expected from me. I walked farther into the room. On my left was an open door. I looked in and saw what must have been Agnes's bedroom. The walls were painted a pale pink, with fussy curtains at the windows and a floral spread on the bed. A collection of mementos was displayed across the top of a chest of drawers and night tables.

I turned my attention back to the kitchen. On the wall next to me was a bulletin board. Tacked to its surface were three large charts. The first one was labeled: "Menu # 1." What followed were thirty squares that contained thirty days of planned meals. I read the first day:

Breakfast: Scrambled eggs, bacon, toast, and orange juice
Lunch: Tuna sandwich, lettuce and tomato, and a glass of milk
Supper: Taco salad and a glass of milk
Snacks: An apple, a banana, and grapes

I looked at the second and third charts and saw that the meals were well-balanced and nutritiously complete.

Sid said, "I spoke with Abner Garrett at the grocery store. He says that before Agnes died, she made up the menus, compiled the grocery list, and gave it to him. Each month he delivers the necessary items that will coincide with Toby's planned menu, and sends the bill to Avery Wheeler."

Sid opened a cabinet door. Inside were a few cans of vegetables, soups, and fruits. "We found an empty peach can filled with dollar bills. It looked like quite a wad, but there was only forty dollars. According to Avery Wheeler, Agnes didn't want Toby to have an allowance. Any pocket money Toby had was to be earned from the jobs she'd gotten for him before she died. All bills were paid by Avery." He lowered his chin and stared at me. "Keep that bit of info in mind as we proceed through the house."

I nodded and walked across the room to the refrigerator. I didn't open the door. I was interested in the instructions pasted on the surface. Each note had been cut from what originally had been brightly colored construction paper. Time had faded the green, red, and yellow squares, but the writing was bold and clear.

Winners never cheat, and cheaters never win.
Always wear clean underwear.
Idle hands are the devil's workshop.
Waste not, want not.
Always be polite.

As Lew would say, "Words to live by."

Frowning in concentration, I moved on to the front of the house. The living room contained a sofa and two hard-looking chairs that were covered with clear plastic to protect the upholstery. None of it looked as if it had ever been sat on. Lacy doilies covered tabletops. Everything was spotless. There were no newspapers, but six stacks of gardening magazines sat on the coffee table. All were still in their mailing covers. There wasn't any radio or television, but an old phonograph sat in the corner. Next to it was a stand that held record albums. I glanced at the names of some of the artists— Lawrence Welk, Glenn Miller, Tommy Dorsey, and Ray Conniff.

I said, "The whole house looks as if time has stood still since Agnes died. Six piles of gardening magazines for the six years she's been gone. She must have liked music, but I don't see a radio. And these albums are outdated." I pulled out a couple. "They're instrumental. No lyrics." I looked around the cold, stark room. "No newspaper. No radio. Music but no lyrics. Nothing to evoke any kind of emotion, whether it be anger at a story or lyrics from a love song." I sighed. "Toby must have missed his mother very much. She was gone, and yet she influenced his life right down to the food he ate each day."

Sid chuckled. "Do you think so?"

I shot him a hard look. "I'm assuming that since you've asked, you know differently."

He nodded to the closed door off the living room. "His room is in there."

My heart picked up its rhythm as I turned the doorknob. This was the same action Toby had taken that had unleashed the hornets. When the wooden panel swung open, I slowly crossed the threshold into Toby's domain.

The single bedstead had been crammed against the wall to make space for two televisions. Stepping farther into the room, I saw one hooked to a VCR, the other to a DVD player. An oversize recliner faced the electronic setup, four remote controls within easy reach on a side table. A kitchen utility cart held a microwave. Next to it was a TV tray with a stack of paper plates and a roll of paper towels. The door of a cabinet was open wide enough that I could see boxes of microwave popcorn and bags of candy on the shelves inside. An apartment-size refrigerator hummed quietly. Near it were two overflowing wastebaskets. One contained empty Coke cans. The other looked like a Dumpster for every fast-food restaurant on Hawthorn. Pizza Hut, Taco Bell, Wendy's, and McDonald's were all represented, along with empty, oily popcorn bags and the wrappers from many, many candy bars.

I shook my head. "I would never have guessed that Toby was into junk food. I wonder if this is why he didn't want to listen to Lew talk about the curse of the fast-food restaurant."

"I had my men show Toby's picture around these restaurants, but no one recognized him."

"How did he get the food?"

"Beats the hell out of me. I'm not even sure that it matters."

"It seems important to me. It's an unanswered question."

"I have plenty of those." Sid looked at the empty containers and shook his head. "All I can say is that it's a damned good thing Toby rode his bike every day, so he got some exercise, or it would've taken a crane to hoist him out of here."

Sid pointed to the recliner. "By the way, I mentioned the contents of this room to Avery Wheeler. He said he hadn't authorized the purchase of the chair, televisions, VCR, or DVD player."

I frowned. "Those were a rather large purchase for someone picking up pocket money washing windows." I continued to stare at the trash. "I don't know how long that garbage has accumulated, but if he ate this kind of thing all month long, there must be an excess of groceries in the kitchen."

Sid didn't look happy. "You figured that out, huh? As it happens, the contents of Toby's cabinets are sparse. So why isn't there more food in the kitchen, if he was eating takeout? He surely wasn't gorging on both—the required meals, as well as all this, too."

I heard Sid, but I didn't comment. I was still taking in Toby's room. Stuffed animals in all shapes and sizes were stacked on his chest of drawers, on the bed, and from shelves that had been hung from the walls. There were pictures of deer and skunks and birds and rabbits. A few were framed but most were taped directly onto the wallpaper.

Toby had kept the rest of the house spotless, which led me to believe that he rarely used the other rooms. But here, he'd indulged in his own personal vices. He'd literally turned his room into his own personal comfort zone.

Looking at the overflowing trash can, I wasn't sure if the fast food versus Agnes's menus was important, but the motivation behind Toby making that choice could be. Agnes had tried to watch over her son from the grave, steering him on a righteous path with proverbs stuck to the refrigerator, planning nutritious menus, arranging for the appropriate food to be delivered directly to his door. She had tried to keep him healthy in body as well as mind, but once she wasn't around, he'd picked up some new habits.

I frowned. Was it important that Toby had disobeyed his mother's wishes that he eat healthily? If he was compelled to deviate from one of Agnes's rules, wasn't it possible that he turned aside from others?

I went slowly back through the house, looking at everything more closely. I peeked in the bathroom, but it was immaculate. No dirty clothes on the floor. No bathtub ring. The cap was on the toothpaste. The lid was down on the toilet.

I went into the kitchen and opened the door to an almost-empty refrigerator. There was milk, some condiments, and a couple of shriveled carrots in the vegetable bin. The freezer compartment held a small carton of sugar-free, fat-free frozen yogurt. It had never been opened.

As I closed the door, I stared at Agnes's grouping of proverbs. Given my present thoughts, two stood out. *Waste not, want not.* What was Toby doing with the food he didn't eat? *Idle hands are the devil's workshop.* Had Toby's hands been idle? Was there someone lurking in the shadows luring him down a path his mother would have considered unacceptable?

Toby had asked me about evil. When I'd told him that evil was "anything that causes others pain or harm," he'd seemed relieved, assuring me that he "wouldn't hurt nobody." But what if he knew something, or heard something, or saw something?

See no evil. Hear no evil. Speak no evil.

Why had he recited those words? I searched my memory for the context of our conversation. Lois had made a comment about baboons. Toby had picked up on it, bringing up the subject of his mother's flowers. Was that relevant?

My thoughts were getting me nowhere, and Sid was obviously impatient. He paced about the kitchen, rubbing his stomach, making faces. I gave him a quick nod. "I'm ready to see the garden."

He snorted. "That's just fine and dandy, but what about your impression of the house? Have you got any thoughts?"

I annoyed Sid to no end when I said, "Several."

He waited. When I didn't elaborate, his face turned red. "What the hell is that supposed to mean?"

"It means that I'm still mulling over all I've seen. I'm not ready to express an opinion."

Sid glared at me. I kept quiet even though his ferocious stare was intimidating. He stomped to the back door muttering under his breath. The only words I caught were "—holes and opinions. Everybody's got one, but they're useless if you don't put them to work."

SEVEN

I STEPPED OFF THE porch and onto a grassy patch. Huge bushes towered over me, blocking my view. Wondering what variety the shrubs were, I plucked a leaf and identified them as crepe myrtle. I filed that information away. If I needed a thick screen in my garden, these plants might fill the bill.

While Sid turned off the fan and shut up the house, I made my way through the break in the shrubs. I was eager to see a fabulous array of plants. Once again I was in for a surprise. There were plenty of specimens, but the quality was lacking. All the shrubs were overgrown and undernourished. They'd been planted too close together, so that each overlaid its neighbor, creating a woven mat of foliage. There were bird-houses and squirrel feeders everywhere I looked. Little dishes filled with cracked corn and seed were sitting under the shel-tering limbs of the raggedy shrubs. I counted three black trash cans with lids firmly clamped to the rims.

"What's in the trash cans?" I asked Sid as he hurried past me.

"Grain and rabbit pellets."

I gestured to the full dishes. "The animals aren't eating much."

Sid mumbled something. When I asked what he'd said, he replied, "The animals in this garden are eating their fool heads off. I just filled the dishes myself. No sense letting the grain in the big cans go to waste." He glared at me. "Do you want to see the chopped-off plants or are you more interested in the diet of—"

I quickly said, "The plants, please."

Sid grumped as he walked on ahead. I followed, trying not to trip on the tangle of weeds. I craned my neck, wanting to see everything. There were so many different varieties of a species. Tenacious day lilies had poked straggly blooms through a thatch of crabgrass. Morning-glory vines slithered over an old wheelbarrow that had been abandoned. As we went deeper into the garden, the plants grew wilder and taller.

Abruptly Sid stopped. Looking around him I saw a wall of burgundy-colored leaves. The shrubs formed an interwoven line that ran approximately forty feet on the longest side, which was closest to us, and about thirty feet the other way. The branches stretched twelve feet into the air.

"Here we are," said Sid. "I don't know what this stuff is, but it has thorns."

"Red barberry," I said. "It makes a great deterrent if you want privacy."

"Down here is a break. We can go through it."

After about twenty feet, we came to the gap. Sid stepped aside. I entered a well-maintained garden, trading one wall of vegetation for another. The plants in front of us were six to eight feet tall, with thick, robust stalks. Each leaf was the size of my hand and had points like a maple leaf. Stroking the felted surface of one, I looked around and spotted a few pink and white blooms. Toby hadn't exaggerated the size of the blossoms. They were a good six inches in diameter. I recognized the plants as hibiscus, though I was used to selling the tropical variety in my flower shop.

Sid said, "There's a narrow path that laps this entire enclosure. Over there, to your left, are the plants that have been chopped off." His radio squawked. He unclipped the walkie-talkie from his belt and turned away to carry on a private conversation.

I used the time to examine the stumps. It looked as if the stalks had been about the size of a half-dollar. This particular grouping was several years old, judging by the number of stalks each rootstock had produced.

After Sid had clipped his radio back on his belt, I said, "I'm assuming you know these are hibiscus plants?"

"That's the information I got. Actually, I was told they are hardy hibiscus—perennial in our area." He jerked his head at me. "Let's go. I'm needed back at headquarters."

"I'd like to stay—"

"Nope. You're leaving, too."

"But, Sid, I haven't seen enough. I want to—" I stopped. His sour expression told me I was wasting my breath.

As we left the area, Sid said, "Hibiscus flowers come in shades of burgundy, pink, pale pink, and white. According to what I've learned, these are much taller than the new hybrids that are available now. My source says that before breeders decided to shrink the plant, it wasn't uncommon to see hibiscus as tall as a fence post."

"Who supplied your information?"

"Eddie Terrell."

"Eddie is landscaping my garden. I'm surprised you called him. I got the impression from Toby that you didn't think the chopped-off plants were important."

Sid's voice was grim. "That was before Toby died. When his heart stopped beating, everything connected with his life became significant." He looked over his shoulder at the plot we'd left and scowled. "Though I can't for the life of me understand the reasoning behind taking the stalks."

"Toby told me his mother showed him how to start new plants on the windowsill. I saw some in the kitchen, but they were all dead. Agnes also told Toby that some of the plants might 'go away.' He assumed she meant that they would die, but what if she knew someone would be cutting them down?"

"For what reason?"

"I don't know. Did Eddie have a theory?"

"I didn't ask him." Sid stopped next to his patrol car. "Do I dare ask if you have an opinion on the plants? Or are you keeping *that* to yourself, too?"

In a calm tone I said, "I'm not being difficult, Sid. I need to think through what I've seen in the house and this garden. You'll be the first to know when I have something worthwhile to tell you."

Sid snorted. "You're being as cagey as a lawyer."

"What's that supposed to mean?"

"I talked to Avery Wheeler about the details of Toby's estate. At first Avery wasn't going to cooperate, but after I pointed out that capturing Toby's killer should be the top priority, the old walrus stopped hemming and hawing. He said that Agnes made provisions if Toby should die young. Money that is left after burial expenses is to be equally divided among the eight shop owners who took an interest in Toby's well-being. I've seen the projected numbers, and you'll all get a nice chunk of change, but it doesn't feel like the motive for this murder. This feels spontaneous, spur of the moment."

I didn't agree and said so. "It would seem premeditated to me. Someone had to go out into the woods and find a hornets' nest. The task of getting it safely out of the tree and back to Toby's would take time and, I would think, expertise. Even rigging it to the doorknob of Toby's bedroom would take a certain kind of finesse. I wouldn't have a clue how to go about it."

Sid flashed me an annoyed glare. "I don't mean that. I'm talking about the emotion behind the killing. It doesn't feel like a smoldering rage. The kind of hate that builds and builds until murder seems to be the only option. Every action the killer took was smooth and calculated. Maybe I'm letting the suspects color my judgment, but this was the act of someone used to making quick decisions."

At first I didn't get what he meant, but as understanding dawned, my tone showed my outrage. "You mean because we're owners of our own businesses, and have the ability to resolve problems, any one of us is capable of murder?"

Sid nodded slowly. "That's right. Our killer is cool and detached. But leave yourself out of this equation, Bretta. Those aren't words I'd use to describe you."

Before I could think of something profound to say, Sid got into his patrol car and drove away.

IN THE LAST FEW WEEKS, my Saturdays have fallen into a pattern. I come home from the flower shop at noon, if work allows. Spend time in my garden, using muscles that don't get used the rest of the week. Hot and grimy, I shower, dress, and go over to Bailey's where we watch TV, fool around on the couch, and then he walks me back to the house.

Ho-hum. Bailey and I had fallen into a rut. The same old same old. We needed something fun and exciting to do. Something to raise my spirits and get my mind off how unfair life can be.

I parked my SUV on the concrete apron in front of my garage, but instead of going inside, I took the path to Bailey's house, which sat at the farthermost edge of my property. At one time the cottage had been part of this estate, but when I'd bought the mansion and the land, that piece of real estate had been excluded from the sale. I'd tried to buy the cottage, but before I could wear down the owner's resistance, Bailey had stepped in with an offer that had been snapped up.

I'd been upset when I first learned he was the new owner. I'd had plans to make that cottage into a wedding chapel. Once my garden was restored, I hoped brides would flock to me with orders for their nuptial flowers. I still thought it was a good idea, but not at this time. Having Bailey in my life was more important than a wedding chapel, and strangers parading around my garden.

I paused on the path and stared at the cottage. It sat east of the mansion and was a charming structure with a steep-pitched roof and dormers. Its exterior was white and it used to have robin's-egg-blue shutters. Bailey had painted black over the blue, and he'd removed the window boxes because he said the plants needed too much care. His idea of decorating had been to nail a rack of deer antlers above the front door.

Without any color, the cottage looked drab. My designer's eye saw a grapevine wreath hanging between the wooden interior door and the glass storm door. Bright fall leaves with German statice, and maybe some pheasant feathers to pick up the hunting theme. It would add a welcoming touch and wouldn't need watering.

Would Bailey agree? It couldn't hurt to ask. I took a couple of steps toward the house, but stopped when Bailey skulked around the corner of the cottage. His back was to me, his chest plastered against the clapboards. The object of his attention seemed to be the window next to the front door. I would have called to him, but the gun clutched in his hand scared me speechless. He had on a bulletproof vest—another fact that frightened me. I was out in the open, an easy target if there was gunfire.

I had to let him know I was close by. I opened my mouth, but before I could get a word past the lump of fear in my throat, Bailey bellowed, "This is Special Agent Bailey Monroe. I have a warrant for your arrest. Come out with your hands up! Do it *now!*"

His harsh, authoritative tone made goose bumps ripple down my spine. My wide-eyed stare swung to the door, but nothing happened. I looked back at Bailey. He advanced another cautious step. Ragged breath squeezed out of my lungs.

He shouted, "Come out now! The house is surrounded."

Surrounded? My head swiveled. I hadn't seen anyone. I blinked in confusion. Was he bluffing? Had he cornered someone in his house? Before I could complete another thought, Bailey took another step toward the door. He cocked the gun. The ominous sound was my undoing. I squeaked, "Ohh."

Bailey spun on his heel. Gripping the gun with both hands, he aimed the barrel at me.

EIGHT

THE EXPRESSION IN Bailey's eyes was ruthless. The copper color had hardened to a flat, lackluster metallic. Unable to move, I barely breathed. He glared at me, then blinked as recognition dawned. The muscles in his arms relaxed and he lowered the gun.

"Bretta? Good Lord, what are you doing sneaking up on me?"

I gulped. "I wasn't sneaking. I—uh—came over to—uh—" I stopped and shook my head. "I can't even remember why I'm here." I glanced at the house, then back at him. He wasn't paying any attention to the cottage. Totally confused, I asked, "Is someone inside?"

"No."

I stared at his hand. "If you don't need that gun, can you put it away? It makes me nervous."

"It isn't loaded," he said, but he slipped the weapon behind his back and into the waistband of his jeans. "Is that better?"

"I'm not sure." I'd been paralyzed with fear, but now that my preconceived notion of danger was gone, my knees buckled. Bailey was at my side in an instant and helped me over to the porch steps. He sat next to me and took my icy hand in his.

I asked, "What were you doing?"

He gave me an embarrassed grin before he explained, "I'm working on a scene in my book. It's been a while since I've been decked out in a vest and held a gun in my hand. I was hoping that if I reenacted a search-and-seizure scenario, I could describe it more accurately."

"If you can capture on paper the tension I just witnessed, you'll have one helluva book. I was terrified."

"I'm sorry. If I'd known you were anywhere around, I'd have clued you in."

I thought about that for a moment, then said, "No. That wouldn't have worked. You'd have been self-conscious. This way you were right there in the role. When you identified yourself as 'Special Agent Bailey Monroe' in that stern, no-nonsense tone, I got goose bumps. If I were a criminal, I'd have been out that door in a flash. I'd have surrendered in a heart-beat."

Bailey arched an eyebrow at me. "Really?" He ran a finger along my jaw. "So, if I want you to surrender to my wishes, all I have to do is talk in a stern, no-nonsense tone and identify myself as—" His voice deepened. "I'm Special Agent Bailey Monroe. Drop your defenses and come into my arms."

I complied with a giggle, pressing my cheek into his shoulder. The vest was stiff and hard against my skin. I wiggled about but couldn't find the familiar hollow where I liked to rest my head.

With a sigh of regret, I leaned away from him. "That vest stops more than bullets, Special Agent. It puts the kibosh on intimacy. I feel as if I'm trying to cuddle a hunk of wood."

"I can take it off. Come inside, and we'll get comfort-able." He waggled his eyebrows at me.

I jerked upright. "That's why I came over here." Bailey's eyes widened. I hurried to say, "No. No, not that. Let's go on

a real date tonight. We can get dressed up. Go to a nice restaurant. Maybe even find some music where we can dance."

Bailey thought about it. "We can do that. Why the
change of plans?"

I touched his cheek before standing. "I want to forget
work, death, and murder for an evening. I want to be happy
and carefree and spend time with a handsome man."

Bailey stood and put his arms around me. Once again the
vest kept me from getting as close to him as I wanted. Miffed,
I said, "I'm glad you don't wear this thing often. Carl had
one, too, and he wore it whenever he was on duty. I'm sorry
to say it's still as unromantic as ever. I could have sworn Carl
told me years ago that some new product was being researched to make these vests lighter, less stiff, and more
user-friendly."

"Really? That's interesting. I need to do some checking in
that area. I've decided to include a chapter about the equipment we use to make an arrest. Technology advances at such
a fast rate that, once I write this particular segment, it will
probably be outdated, but I'm going to give it a go."

I ran my hands over his padded chest. "The vest may be
stiff and unromantic, but I'm glad it's kept you safe." I looked
up at him and gave him my rendition of the eyebrow waggle.
In a sultry voice, I said, "But you won't need this extra protection tonight."

Bailey chuckled. "Since you brought up the subject of
protection—" He left his sentence hanging suggestively.

My cheeks warmed to a fiery red. I gulped. "I—uh—we—
uh—" I floundered to an embarrassed halt.

Bailey shook his head. "You're a tease, Bretta Solomon,
but I can play that same game. The *protection* I'm referring

to has to do with your feet. You might want to wear steel-toed shoes tonight. I'm not much of a dancer."

A SHORT TIME LATER I walked into my home with a bounce in my step and a smile on my face. As I approached the kitchen, the bounce turned to a shuffle, and the smile shriveled like a tender flower that had been nipped by frost. My father's voice was expected, but the trill of female laughter that followed his comment wasn't. I stepped to the doorway and looked in.

My father was squeezing the juice of a lime into a shallow bowl. Next to him on the counter were a blender, an ice tray, a box of powdered sugar, a bottle of gin, and a bunch of green leaves. Abigail DuPree was at his side, soaking up every word, grinning up at him with unabashed adoration.

He was saying, "The trick to a good mint julep is the powdered sugar. It dissolves quickly and doesn't leave granules to spoil the silky smoothness of the drink."

"And we have fresh mint from the garden, too," said Abigail. "That has to improve the flavor."

"Most assuredly," said my father. "As will the paper-thin goblets I found in the china cabinet. Bretta is fond of saying, 'Presentation is everything.' "

I spoke up. "Really? I say that?"

My father turned a beaming smile on me. "Yes, you do, and I'm glad you're home. I should have the drinks ready in a jiffy. We're having ours out on the veranda. Would you care to join us?"

I shook my head. "You two go ahead. I have to get ready. Bailey is picking me up later. We're going out tonight."

My father put down the lime and faced me. "But you can't. I have this evening all planned. Abigail is joining us for dinner. DeeDee has fixed a true Texan feast. We're going to eat, drink, and play Scrabble. It'll be a good chance for you to get to know Abby, and it'll be something different to do."

My eyes narrowed, but I kept my tone even. "I want something different tonight, too, but my plans involve relaxing with Bailey."

"But—"

Abigail touched my father lightly on the shoulder. The gesture was fluid and easy, as if she'd done it a hundred times. "It's fine, Albert," she said. "Bretta can sample the beefsteak chili tomorrow. As for Scrabble, it might be best if it's just the two of us. Spelling is not my strong point. I'd hate to embarrass myself in front of a prospective client."

Her easy way of accepting the situation and soothing my father was appreciated, but I still didn't trust her. What was her game? I nodded politely and turned to go upstairs, but stopped when Abigail said, "I have a suggestion you might want to consider."

I waited to see where this was going, though I had a pretty good idea. Neither Abigail nor my father understood that decorating the bedrooms *was not* my primary concern. They didn't know that thoughts of Toby intruded on my peace of mind time after time.

I didn't want to argue. I wanted to go gently into this date with Bailey. I needed time with him. I needed that more than I needed rooms painted and papered and prepared for strangers who might not appreciate the final outcome.

I was primed to utter those very words when Abigail said, "If you have a teal blue dress, I suggest you wear it tonight. That color with your eyes will knock Bailey's socks off." She smiled at my surprise and said quietly, "A woman has to maintain her sanity any way she can. Dressing up and going out with a handsome man often helps."

I smiled uncertainly and took myself off to my room. As I climbed the stairs, I thought about the stressful week coming up. On Monday we'd fill the sympathy orders for Toby's funeral. That evening I planned to attend his visitation. The funeral was on Tuesday, with the reading of the will later that day. So much sadness lay ahead, but this was only Saturday. I had tonight.

When I closed my bedroom door, I left my sorrow in the hall. I lounged in a bath of bubbles, played soft music on the radio, and dressed in the teal blue sheath dress I hadn't worn in ages. To my amazement, the dress fit even better than before I'd pushed it to the back of my closet. I strapped on sandals with heels that showed off the delicate curve of my legs. I fussed over my hair, my makeup, and my choice of perfume. When six o'clock rolled around, I was ready and waiting.

Right on time, Bailey parked in the driveway. I was watching for him, but when he didn't immediately get out of the truck, I waited to see what he would do. He sat there behind the steering wheel, staring at the house, expecting me to materialize. Stubbornly, I waited him out. I wanted to be collected at the door. When I didn't show, he grinned, got out, and headed up the front walk.

I stepped away from the window and waited for the doorbell to ring. The melodious chimes made my heartbeat quicken. Taking my time, I crossed the foyer and opened the door. Bailey was dressed in cocoa brown dress slacks with a cream shirt and plaid sports jacket. He wasn't wearing a tie, but he didn't need one to impress me. The open neck of his shirt was enough. The evening was already off to a wonderful start. Then he held out a single red rose.

When I didn't make a move to accept his gift, a frown creased his face. "Is it wrong to give flowers to a florist?"

Finding my voice, I whispered, "Nothing could be more right." I took the rose, slipped my hand through the crook of his arm, and we went out to his truck. He opened the passenger door for me and stole a kiss once I was seated.

On the ride into River City, I encouraged Bailey to talk. Since he'd just gotten off the phone with his agent before picking me up, the progress of his book was uppermost in his mind.

"I told Elaine about my plans to include a chapter on the equipment we use in the line of duty. She agreed it would make for interesting reading, but I'd have to preface the chapter with something like 'as of this writing' because innovative marvels are being created almost every day.

"This afternoon, after you'd gone, I did some preliminary research on Kevlar. It's a petroleum-based material. Since it's manufactured from toxic chemicals, other options are being explored. Apparently, back in the midsixties, during the Vietnam War, military scientists began searching for an alternative to Kevlar for protecting soldiers on the battlefield. I've come across a program that's being funded by an army research grant. The man in charge is a molecular biologist in Wyoming. Genetic engineering is involved and it sounds bizarre."

As we crossed the city, we discussed books we'd read and movies we liked. We touched on several subjects, but not in any great depth. It was an evening made for light, easy conversation.

The restaurant Bailey had chosen was an old favorite of mine. The food was excellent, the company superb. During dinner I listened to stories about his career, about his plans for the book he was writing. And all the time I drifted in a rosy glow.

Once dinner was over, Bailey took me to a lounge that featured music from the sixties. We found a dark corner and settled in, holding hands and gazing into each other's eyes. When the band played an old Ray Charles tune, "I Can't Stop Loving You," Bailey led me onto the dance floor. It was romance at its finest. Our bodies blended to the rhythm. His arm around my waist kept me snug against him while we circled the room.

We danced to several more songs, but by eleven o'clock the floor was crowded. Serious partygoers had arrived, and the noise level had escalated. I suggested it was time to go. Bailey agreed, and we headed for his truck.

The night had turned cold. Streetlights wore halos of wispy fog. A gentle breeze swirled the mist in an eerie pattern, blowing leaves across the windshield of Bailey's truck. We were only a few blocks from Hawthorn. I had the urge to see the street one more time before I went home.

Unsure how Bailey would react, I kept my voice casual. "Do you mind driving by the flower shop? I don't want to go inside, but I'd like to give it a—uh—visual check." I glanced at Bailey's profile to see how he took my request.

"If I turn here," he said, easing the wheel to the right, "we can travel the entire length of Hawthorn. Would that suit you?"

I met his knowing gaze and shook my head. "Am I that transparent? I should keep you guessing, but that takes too much effort."

"Has Toby's death been on your mind all evening?"

"No. Thanks to you, I've managed to push it away." I patted his thigh. "You were the perfect date. This evening was wonderful. It was just what I needed. But I can't squash my thoughts forever."

"Bretta, with me you don't have to try. I've been there. I know how a case can eat away at you. It's the controlling part of your personality. You have to have all the questions answered."

I made a face. "I'm not sure I like that description. *Controlling* sounds overbearing and not very charming."

"You've already charmed me. I wouldn't have you any other way."

We drove in silence for a time, then I asked, "Did I tell you that Sid took me into Toby's house this afternoon?"

"No. Was the experience enlightening?"

"It was, up to a point." I proceeded to tell him what I'd seen. When I finished, Bailey commented, "Sounds to me like Toby was programmed."

"Programmed?"

"Yes. Agnes tried to anticipate every eventuality in her son's life—a home, a job, his meals, his recreation, his friends. Over and over, like a recording, she drilled into him how he should spend his time."

"Do you think she threatened him with dire consequences?"

"I doubt it. She probably felt it wasn't necessary. Toby was impressionable. Agnes had years of directing Toby—what he should do, where he should go, and to whom he should speak. He wasn't ever going to be what society terms 'normal,' but Agnes knew Toby couldn't be without human contact. A recluse is an oddity and vulnerable to outside forces. By introducing him to people of her choosing, she could give him a controlled environment, hoping to bind him to a life she thought would keep him safe."

"Before she died, do you think there was already someone in his life she feared might influence Toby in a bad way?"

"That's highly possible. It would go a long way toward explaining why Agnes went to such lengths to make provisions for Toby."

Seeing that we were on Hawthorn, I wiped a spot of moisture off my side window. "Drive slow, if you can."

"It's late enough that there isn't much traffic."

Bailey let the truck's engine idle us along. One by one I gazed at the stores that represented Toby's clients. Mr. Barker's bakery, Merry's Delights. Leona's Boutique. My flower shop. Agnes hadn't chosen Josh from the video store as one of Toby's stops. After seeing the electronic setup in Toby's bedroom, I decided I needed another chat with that young man. Abner Garrett of Garrett's Grocery Store was next. Followed by Harmon Purvis's pharmacy, Melba's candle store, and Diana's discount shop.

Musing aloud, I said, "It must have worried Agnes no end that Toby might meet someone she thought would be unacceptable. Those last few months before she died must have been heart wrenching as she planned Toby's life."

"That's where the protectiveness comes in. From what you've told me, she did everything she could to make his future secure."

"But it didn't work, did it?"

"That's a given, since Toby is dead."

"But why is he dead? Was he mixed up in some devious plot? Was someone exploiting his naiveté? I feel sure that Agnes taught him right from wrong. Are we dealing with some slick-tongued shyster who preyed on Toby's gullibility? Did this person see an opportunity to use Toby? And to what purpose?"

"Again, those are excellent questions, but you'll have to ask someone who's more attuned to the facts. I've picked up bits and pieces from what you've—"

"Look, Bailey. Flashing red lights." I leaned forward, peering through the windshield. "I can't tell, but they look like they're at Yvonne's house." I quickly amended that statement. "No. No. They're at Toby's."

Bailey eased down on the accelerator. We could have closed the distance quickly, but Bailey had to brake when an officer waved us to a stop. Bailey rolled down his window. "What's going on?" he asked.

"Police business. You'll have to take another route."

From my perch on the edge of my seat, I scanned the uniformed figures. Sid had to be here. Finally I spotted him, leaning against the rear fender of one of the patrol cars. I opened my door and started toward him. Hearing rapid footsteps behind me, I glanced over my shoulder, expecting to see Bailey. The officer was bearing down on me. I didn't want trouble, so I stopped, but I called out to Sid. "Sheriff? Can I speak to you?"

Sid looked up and grimaced. But after a moment, he said, "Let her through."

I didn't need any more encouragement.

NINE

SID GAVE ME THE once-over, taking in my stylish dress and high-heeled sandals. He looked past me to Bailey's truck and said, "Out and about on a Saturday night? Must be nice."

"What's going on, Sid?"

"Did you have a pleasant evening?"

Patiently, I said, "Yes, Sid. We had a lovely time. Why all the patrol cars?"

Wearily, he rubbed a hand across his face. "I've wrapped up this case. We have a suspect in custody."

Craning my neck, I could see a silhouette in the backseat of Sid's car, but I couldn't make out who it was. I turned to Sid for answers but bit back the words when he winced as if in pain. Taking a closer look, I saw he was paler than usual and his eyes were bloodshot. I asked, "Are you okay?"

"Been better. I suppose you had a tasty meal in some fancy restaurant." In a wistful tone, he said, "I remember a time when I ate at a leisurely pace from an honest-to-goodness plate." He tried to take a deep breath but flinched. "Haven't felt good all day. Earlier I had a chili dog served on a flimsy piece of cardboard, followed by a nasty case of indigestion."

"I have some Rolaids in my purse. Do you want me to get them?"

"Nah. I have my own stash. We've about got things wound

up here. Once I do a couple hours of paperwork, I can go home."

"Who are you—uh—processing?"

Sid mumbled, "All that trash from the fast food in the bedroom and almost nothing to eat in the kitchen. If Abner Garrett delivered the groceries, and if Avery Wheeler paid for them—then where's the food?" His lips turned up in a sly smile. "I let it be known to a couple of blabby Hawthorn Street store owners that I was reprocessing the house tomorrow, concentrating on the inside of the kitchen cabinets, where I hoped I'd find new evidence." Sid swayed on his feet, then jerked upright. "Feel kind of woozy."

I touched his arm and felt the radiating heat. "You're sick, Sid. I think you're running a fever."

He dashed a hand across his forehead. "I'm sweating like a porcupine in a balloon factory, but it's cold out here." He tried to stand up straight but couldn't quite make it. "Don't have time to be sick. Pain in my gut, but I've been able to ignore it. Garrett used Toby to make money. Scammed him out of the groceries. Damnedest motive for murder I've ever seen."

"Scammed him out of the groceries?" I looked back at the car. "Is that *Abner?*"

"That's right. What a jerk. He crept back to the house tonight to have a look around, and we nabbed him. When we read him his rights and snapped the handcuffs on him, he broke down." Sid licked his lips and closed his eyes. "Admitted that he'd taken advantage of Toby. Abner had followed Agnes's instructions. He received full payment from Avery Wheeler for the food, but then he bought back the groceries from Toby at a ridiculously low price." He opened his eyes and blinked at me. "Don't give me that look, Bretta. I don't like it."

I wasn't surprised that my dubious expression didn't please him. "Sid, has Abner confessed to putting the hornets in Toby's bedroom?"

"Not yet, but he will."

"Sid, you're too sick to see—"

"I don't want to hear it. Get her out of here," he said in a hoarse tone. Two officers stepped forward. One was reaching for my arm when Sid doubled over in pain. Through clenched teeth, he muttered, "Fire in my gut."

"Call an ambulance," I said. "The sheriff is sick." When neither man moved, I took Sid's arm. "You need to go to the hospital, Sid. Let a doctor check you out. You might have food poisoning from that chili dog."

He gasped. "Hurt before I ate that piece of—oh God." He rode out the pain with his arms folded across his belly. After a few minutes, he looked around. "Deputy Hawkins, you're in charge of getting the prisoner to the jail and processed. Sam, take me to the emergency room." Another pain bent him almost double.

Sam grabbed one arm. I took the other, and we helped Sid into a patrol car. They took off with the siren blaring and the lights flashing. I watched the car disappear down Hawthorn before I turned to the car that Deputy Hawkins was entering.

I crossed to the driver's window and leaned down. "Get back, ma'am," said Hawkins. "*I* won't put up with your meddling." He jerked the gearshift into drive and pressed on the gas. In the backseat, I had a glimpse of Abner Garrett. Tears streaked his face, but his eyes met mine. Sadly, he shook his head.

I FOUND OUT THE NEXT MORNING that Sid had undergone an emergency appendectomy. The surgery had gone well, but as a precautionary measure, he'd been placed in intensive care for observation. Deputy Hawkins was running the sheriff's office—which meant I couldn't get an ounce of information about Abner Garrett's arrest.

It was Sunday afternoon. I was out in my garden, taking a stroll, enjoying the peace and quiet. The garden's progress was coming along nicely under the guidance of Eddie's capable hands. A stretch of soil appeared devoid of life, but labels stated that spring bulbs nestled beneath the surface. I tipped my head to look above me. The hard maple trees were just starting their fall parade of colors. In sharp contrast, the green of the cedars, pines, and junipers made a crisp backdrop to the perennial plantings.

I hadn't been sure how Eddie was going to blend one plant group into another. He'd suggested that we let nature be our guide. He had pointed to the sky, using the shape of the clouds as inspiration, arranging the first group of plants in a pear shape, then reversing the next bed so that it ran along behind the other. The results were flowing and not too fussy. From the bottom bed he'd used a "drift" of flowers. This was a thin, longish line of plants that carried the eye to one of the focal points of the garden. In this instance it was a swing.

I'd had an old tire swing hung from a stout tree branch, but then I'd complained to Eddie that the rubber stained my clothes. His alternative was an elegant glider set under an arbor. Given time, the wood would be covered by a clematis vine. The variety Henryi had been settled on.

Earlier this summer I'd enjoyed the star-shaped white blossoms. I love white flowers in the garden. At night they have an unearthly quality in the moonlight. But I also want to be surrounded by lots of color. Purple makes peace, while red shrinks the beds and blue makes them appear larger. Yellow borrows a ray of sunlight from the skies, while green adds tranquility to the soul. I'd learned all of this by listening to Eddie, who in turn had inherited his wisdom from his father.

I went to the glider and sat down. As I leaned back I saw a huge garden spider hanging from a web that was anchored to the wooden crosspieces that formed the swing's frame. Spiders don't bother me, and this one was a beautiful specimen with an oval abdomen patterned in yellow and black. She was sitting head down at the web's hub. I assumed she was waiting for her next meal, though she looked as if she'd been eating regularly. She was a portly creature, but when I set the glider in motion, she moved with grace along the gossamer strands of her home.

The spider reminded me of the main character in the book, *Charlotte's Web*. That indomitable creature had immortalized her friend, a pig named Wilbur, by weaving words of praise into her web.

"Well, Charlotte," I said aloud. "I could use some insight. I don't suppose you could draw on your shrewd lineage and weave the name of Toby's murderer into your web?" I peered at the spider and saw a leg quiver. "Go ahead," I encouraged. "Don't be shy. I won't tell a soul."

I chuckled softly and reached into my pocket for the papers Melba, Yvonne, and Leona had given me. While I'd waited for lunch to finish cooking, I'd read over their notes but hadn't found anything that was helpful. I'd hoped that in a different setting, I'd find some informative nugget that would push me in the direction of a solution.

I started with Melba's notes first, but I was shaking my

head by the time I'd finished reading. She made it abundantly clear that she didn't like Abner Garrett. I wasn't crazy about him either, but in a murder investigation it paid to be open-minded and without prejudice. Melba hadn't been able to do that. Everything she'd written directed suspicion to the grocer. In view of his arrest, Melba might be right. I didn't have any trouble believing Abner capable of scamming Toby with the groceries, but I just couldn't see him prying open a window and rigging the hornet's nest.

I laid Melba's notes on the seat next to me and picked up Leona's. The tone of this writing made me uneasy. From the first line, she hinted that Toby's death had sexual undertones. For some reason she knew the length of time Toby spent in several of the shops. She equated that time with fooling around. She stated three different instances when she'd witnessed Diana touching Toby's arm, patting his shoulder, or smoothing his shirt collar even though no adjusting was necessary.

Leona went on to say that Diana wasn't happy in her marriage and had used Toby to pass away the time until she'd reached a decision on whether to stay with her husband or move on. Down at the bottom of the page, Leona had written, "I called a neighbor of Diana's and asked how 'things' were progressing in that part of River City. My friend knew exactly what I meant. It seems that Diana and her husband have reconciled, and they're acting like newlyweds. I think this only proves my point further. Diana led Toby on. When she reconciled with her husband, she became concerned that Toby might have taken her attention seriously. Afraid that Toby might tell someone, Diana decided Toby needed to be stopped, so she found a hornet's nest and—"

I rolled my eyes. "What a crock," I muttered aloud. It

sounded to me as if Leona was a sexually frustrated woman with a galloping imagination. Folding the papers together, I laid them on top of Melba's and picked up Yvonne's. I'd saved hers for last because her notes were more interesting and had more details that involved Toby.

She had lived closer to him than the rest of us on Hawthorn Street, and she felt she knew him very well. To reinforce that statement, she'd included several anecdotes. A couple had caught my eye. The first had to do with Toby going duck hunting with Phillip and Harmon. Phillip had been against the idea, but Harmon had argued that Toby needed a man's influence in his life. The outing had been disastrous.

Yvonne wrote, "Toby left the house in high spirits. I wasn't sure if he understood what was going to happen, but the guns intrigued him. Once the hunters were situated behind the duck blind, Phillip said it was difficult to keep Toby quiet. All was fine until the first flock of ducks appeared. Harmon took aim and fired. Toby was horrified when one of the ducks nose-dived into the water. When the men brought Toby home, he was an emotional mess. I couldn't leave him alone at his house, so he stayed with me that night. Toby was too tenderhearted to take hunting, and I'd told the men that would be the case."

I stared somberly into the distance. It wasn't Toby's reaction to the death of a duck that interested me. It was the fact that it had been Harmon's idea to take Toby hunting. He had to know that Toby would be upset by the killing of an animal. Why allow him to come along? Was Harmon being malicious? Or was he merely thoughtless?

Glancing up at Charlotte, I saw she'd crept closer to the edge of the web. It seemed as if she was peering directly at me. "See what you think," I said to her. "I'll read this last bit aloud."

I scanned the sheet until I found the right passage. "Agnes and I were good friends," wrote Yvonne. "After my divorce, I often got lonely. Agnes was a widow. Her husband had worked for the railroad and was killed while switching cars on the railway. The accident happened only a month before Toby was born. I was the one who took Agnes to the hospital and stayed with her through the delivery. I watched Toby grow in stature and mourned with Agnes when he didn't develop mentally.

"Harmon was wrong to assume none of us knew Toby had a heart problem. I knew. Agnes tried to protect Toby from everything. He wanted a pet desperately—a cat, a dog, a rabbit, a bird—but Agnes said they carried germs and disease. Agnes didn't have to work when Toby was young. The railroad paid her a substantial sum of money, but even scrimping as she did, the money ran out about the time Toby turned eighteen. That's when Agnes went to work for Harmon.

"Agnes had a host of regulations that she expected Toby to abide by. In my opinion, he went astray from Hawthorn Street. Someone influenced him in a bad way, and our beloved Toby has paid the price."

I stared down at the paper. Perhaps the reason I liked Yvonne's writing best was because she didn't point fingers. She simply laid out the facts as she knew them, and all could easily be verified by asking around. I didn't think that would be necessary because I couldn't see any reason for Yvonne to lie. I also found it interesting that she thought someone outside of Hawthorn Street had influenced him.

"Bretta? Am I interrupting you?"

Since I thought Charlotte and I were the only ones in the garden, I jumped at the sound of the voice. I looked around and saw Abigail standing off to my left.

She said, "I heard you speaking and followed the sound. I hope you don't think I was eavesdropping."

I picked up the notes and folded them together before I stuffed them back into my pocket. I didn't feel particularly welcoming, but I wasn't going to be out-and-out rude. However, I wanted to make a point. Raising an eyebrow in feigned bewilderment, I said, "I'm amazed. I could have sworn this was Sunday, but here you are. It must be the first of the week."

My sarcasm would have made a weaker woman cower. Abigail only shrugged. "It's still Sunday," she said, "and I'm not here for your decision about hiring me. As it happens, I love gardens, and I hate my apartment. I thought about going to the park, but didn't want to be surrounded by people chasing balls or Frisbees. I decided to take a drive, and my car brought me here. I didn't even ring the front doorbell. I slipped around the house, like the trespasser I am, hoping to find a bench where I could soak up a few rays."

I moved over. "It's not very sunny under this arbor, but the view is restful."

Abigail sat down next to me. We didn't talk, but stared at the garden. After a while, she put out a foot and pushed against the ground. The glider moved gently. Glancing at me, she pushed again and again. The peaceful rocking accelerated to a faster pace. I grabbed the armrest and added my own foot action. Soon we were swinging so high the chains that attached the glider to the crosspiece overhead squeaked in protest.

Whoosh. Whoosh. *Whoosh!*

I laughed out loud, delighted by the wild rush of air in my face. We kept up this madcap pace until we were both breath-less. We stopped pushing and gradually the swing slowed to a more gentle rhythm. Abigail leaned back and caught sight of the spider.

"Wow!" she said. "That's one beautiful orb weaver."

I followed her gaze and smiled. "That's Charlotte. She and I met for the first time this afternoon. What did you call her?"

"She's an orb weaver. Better known as a common yellow garden spider. They like to build their webs in grassy areas near houses. She's harmless except for the insects that get too close to her web. When that happens, she shrouds them in a silk-wrapped cocoon."

"What else do you know about her?"

Abigail's smooth brow wrinkled. "Gosh, Bretta, you're asking me about things I learned back in high school."

"You're closer in age to that source of information than me. It's been way too long since I studied anything in school."

Abigail pursed her lips thoughtfully. "If I remember right, she has eight legs, two body parts, an outside skeleton, and eight eyes. She's very patient. She will wait all day for her next meal."

"That's when it becomes tangled in her web?"

"Not so much tangled as stuck." She turned sidewise so she could stare at me. "Are you really interested in this stuff? Or are you trying to keep me from discussing my decorating ideas?"

I smiled. "Probably a little of both, but Charlotte does intrigue me. What do you mean 'stuck'? Like glue?"

"I don't remember all the technical terms, but normally a spider has three pairs of spinners. The small tubes inside the spinnerets, as they're called, are connected to glands that are located at the back end of their abdomens. From these tubes the spider spins a watery fluid into a thread that we can't see unless sunlight is reflected on it."

I looked up at Charlotte. "She's even more impressive than I thought." I turned and contemplated Abigail. "So are you," I said, paying the compliment easily.

She seemed pleased. Today she'd twisted her long hair into a bun at the nape of her neck. It was a sedate style, but with her adolescent features, she looked like a teenager playing at being an adult. While this fountain-of-youth attribute would serve her well when she hit fifty, I wondered if she had a hard time convincing clients that she was capable of the job. She had mature ideas regarding the redecorating of my home. My father had recommended her, but what did I really know about Ms. Abigail Dupree?

I didn't realize I'd been staring until Abigail asked, "Is something wrong?"

I shook my head, then started my interrogation into her personal life with what I considered to be the gentle approach. I'd learned that if I wanted information, I had to give before I received. So I said, "I don't know how much my father has told you about our history. I've had a difficult time accepting him back into my life. I understand why he left all those years ago, but those same years have changed him. He's more aggressive, more outspoken, and more opinionated. He's different from what I remember."

Abigail clasped her hands tightly in her lap. "But your memories are those of a child."

"That's true. But the father I knew led, he never pushed. He patiently taught me to swim, to ride a bike, to make a whistle from the hollow stem of a squash plant." I smiled up at Charlotte. "He even taught me the itsy, bitsy spider song." I turned to Abigail. "What are your parents like?"

Abigail tried to pass off my question with an indifferent

shrug, but I kept quiet, waiting for an answer. Finally, she said rather lamely, "Average, I guess."

After my personal disclosure, her reply was sadly lacking. I persisted, "Are they both still alive?"

"Yes, but they're divorced."

Common ground. I jumped on it, putting a sympathetic note in my voice. "Were you very old when they split up?"

"I was twenty."

I waited for her to elaborate, but she pressed her lips together. It was obvious that she was perturbed. She sat woodenly at my side, staring down at her hands. Seeing no need to upset her further by pursuing the issue, I switched topics, talking instead about the work Eddie had done on the garden.

A few minutes later my father appeared on the path. When Abigail saw him she leaped up from the glider like she'd been waiting for an excuse to get away. I followed more slowly, wondering about this woman I was about to hire.

I'd looked over Abigail's prospectus for the bedrooms. I liked everything she'd outlined concerning the decorating, but the businesswoman in me was uneasy. Abigail hadn't included any professional information. No references or referrals that would confirm the fact that she was capable of completing the job. And yet I was going to give Abigail this chance, if for no other reason than to get to know her better. I was curious—a trait of mine that usually got me into trouble.

TEN

WHEN I JOINED ABIGAIL and my father on the path, my father was saying, "—been calling and calling your cell phone. Don't you have it with you?"

"I left it in my car, Albert."

My father frowned. "You had me worried. I didn't know where you were."

This conversation baffled me. "Dad," I said, "Abigail has a life outside of her job. Besides, it's Sunday. She deserves a day of rest."

My father quickly nodded. "Of course. You're right, Bretta, but there's been a—uh—development."

I asked, "Development concerning what?"

My father shuffled his feet and switched his cane from one hand to the other. He glanced at Abigail, but fastened his uneasy gaze on me. "I don't want to upset you, since nothing has been decided, but I—uh—took a piece of furniture from the attic to have a watermark removed and the finish restored."

"Oh really," I said, raising an eyebrow. "Is this piece of furniture for you personally, or do you have plans to use it somewhere else?"

"It's a writing desk, and we thought it would fit into the Golden Dawn room, especially if the oak finish has been successfully restored. I can pick it up today, and I thought Abigail might like to ride along."

I asked, "Who did the work?"

"Phillip Pritchard. He has a workshop behind his sister's antiques store."

"I know Yvonne," I said, touching my pocket where I'd put the notes. I wanted to talk with her, and today would give me more time than tomorrow when I'd be busy at the flower shop. "If you both don't mind, I'd like to tag along. If Phillip is going to do the furniture restoration for the bedrooms, I'd like to see the first sample of his work."

Abigail's head swiveled toward me. I nodded. "That's right. You have the job."

At the very least, I expected a joyous whoop. Her smile was almost sad, which confused me. "I'll try to live up to your expectations," she said solemnly.

My father was more exuberant. He grabbed me in a bear hug, squeezing the breath out of me. In my ear, he whispered, "I knew you'd make the right decision, daughter. This is wonderful. Just wonderful."

He released me and stood back to smile at us. "We've got plenty of work ahead of us, ladies, but I'm sure this experience will form an enduring friendship."

Abigail answered his presumptuous statement by saying, "I'll meet you at Phillip's."

Determined to have his way, my father overrode Abigail's objection to riding with him. She wanted to drive her own vehicle back to River City. He informed us that we would ride together in his truck so we could get to know each other better. He further stated that once we had picked up the writing desk, we would bring it home so we could see how it fit under the window in the Golden Dawn room.

Under my breath I muttered, "Push, push." I was referring

to my earlier conversation with Abigail about how my father had changed. She was so quiet, so downbeat, I was hoping to reestablish the amicable link we'd shared while making the glider soar through the air. But Abigail ignored me. To my father she said, "Whatever you want, Albert."

My father took her simple words as law. On the ride into town, he outlined plans and made assessments as to the amount of time involved in the redecorating project. I kept waiting for Abigail to add her professional opinion, but she was quiet, letting my father ramble.

I was bewildered. Didn't she want the job? Had she changed her mind? Her entire attitude had undergone a transformation. When she'd arrived in the garden, she'd been open and friendly. Now she seemed standoffish, withdrawn from me. I tried to think of what I might have said that would have brought about this aloofness. Was it the criticism of my father or my questions about her parents? I thought about asking her, but if I broached the subject in front of my father, he would only assure me that everything was "wonderful"—a word I was beginning to despise.

So for reasons of our own, Abigail and I rode in silence, allowing my father control over the conversation. "The Treasure Trove is closed this afternoon," he explained as we arrived at our destination. "But Phillip told me he'd be out in the barn."

The Pritchard property rested within the city limits. Back in the midfifties, the farm had been a thriving dairy operation. The white clapboard farmhouse was Yvonne's antiques showroom. Each room held pieces that pertained to that particular living space. I'd taken DeeDee with me one time when I was looking for a dining-room chair to match the three I'd already found. I hadn't been able to get her away from the kitchen. She'd been fascinated by the utensils used in bygone days.

The porch had red geraniums blooming in old crocks, dented buckets, and other unique containers. A trellis made from an iron bedstead supported a yellow climbing rose. Iron wagon wheels attached to posts formed a boundary that marked the business end of the property.

Yvonne and Phillip lived in a double-wide modular home that had been squeezed in next to the store. Sharing the rest of the land was an old barn with an attached silo, and a chicken house complete with a flock of laying hens. Scratching in the dirt behind a wire fence were some ducks, a couple of geese, a few sheep, and a goat.

Following Phillip's instructions, my father took the driveway that divided the business from the Pritchard's home. I'd never been down this hedge-lined road. Once we passed their residence, a tall woven-wire fence with an iron gate barred our way. A sign directed us to "HONK." My father tapped the truck horn. After a few minutes, the gates opened electronically, and we entered the barnyard.

The barn was a Dutch design with a gambrel roofline. The huge sliding door was open. Yvonne sat in a pool of sunlight working a spinning wheel. The setting was picturesque and tranquil with a herd of sheep grazing in a nearby pasture, and the silo casting its elongated shadow across the grass.

We got out and Abigail turned to me. "Do you like horses?" she asked.

"From a distance. I don't ride, but I think they're beautiful."

Abigail smiled. "Watch this. Yvonne showed me this trick the last time I was here." She whistled a couple of high to low notes. A white horse ambled around the corner of the barn.

Under her breath Abigail said, "This is the neat part." Raising her voice, she called out, "Come, Sugar Cube." She pointed her finger at the horse.

The horse pricked up its ears. Abigail lowered her arm, then raised it again to point at the horse. "Come, Sugar Cube."

"Are you offering it a treat or is that the horse's name?"

"It's his name." A wide smile stretched across her face.

I looked at the horse. With his head held high, he clip-clopped across the barnyard straight to Abigail. She stroked his nose and tugged gently at his ears. "Isn't he a sweetheart? I so miss being around a horse."

"You have horses where you used to live?"

Before she could answer, Phillip came to greet us. The smile he turned on me was welcoming, his handshake firm. "I didn't know you were bringing guests, Albert," he said. "We've just brewed a pot of tea. I'll have Yvonne hunt up more cups."

I demurred, saying we didn't want to cause them any trouble, but Phillip was already striding back to the barn with a purposeful step. He spoke to Yvonne, who got up slowly from her seat at the spinning wheel. She waved to us before disappearing from view.

As we entered the barn, Abigail and my father showed no particular interest in their surroundings. They took off to the back of the building where Phillip was waiting. I lingered, trying to see everything at once. I was standing on smooth concrete. High overhead, oak beams formed the skeletal structure. The floor of the hayloft provided a portion of the ceiling. Milking stanchions ran the length of the building, with wooden troughs facing the main alleyway of the barn.

Dishes clattered off to my right. I called, "Yvonne, I hope it's all right that I came along with my father and Abigail."

She came out of the room pushing a tea cart. "Bretta, you're always welcome." She gestured to the cart. "Here in the barn I don't use my good china, so we'll have to make do with mismatched cups and saucers, but I do have homemade oatmeal cookies."

"You really don't need to do this. We aren't staying long."

She parked the cart and offered me the tin of cookies. I chose one and took a bite. After swallowing, I said, "These are delicious. I like them soft and moist."

Yvonne waved away the compliment. She had more on her mind than cookies. "I heard Abner was arrested for Toby's murder. From what I hear, Abner had a scam going. For a mere pittance, he was buying back the groceries he'd already billed to Agnes's estate."

I nodded. "That's what I heard, too."

She groaned as she sat back down at the spinning wheel. Rubbing her knees, she said, "I suspect we'll soon learn that he was also padding the original grocery bill."

"That's possible," I agreed. "I read the notes you gave me about Toby."

"Were they helpful?"

"You did a very good job. I was particularly interested in the duck-hunting episode."

Yvonne shook her head. "Poor Toby. He was crushed when he came back. He didn't take to the idea of killing any critter. It was a—what do you call it?" She stopped and thought. "Traumatic experience," she said with a nod. "Phillip and I both tried to tell Harmon that Toby wouldn't like hunting, but he had it in his head that Toby needed a man's influence in his life."

"You wrote that in your notes. What exactly was Harmon talking about?"

"Since Agnes worked for Harmon at the drugstore, he had a front-row seat when it came to Toby. Harmon thought that Agnes babied her son. Harmon even tried to get Agnes to send Toby away to a state school, but she wouldn't hear of that."

"What business was it of Harmon's? Just because Agnes was an employee didn't mean he had any say in Toby's welfare."

Yvonne eyed me. "I figured you knew that Harmon loved Agnes, especially with you being right down the street from the pharmacy. It was common knowledge. But Harmon wouldn't take on Toby as part of the marriage package. When he made this clear to Agnes, she turned him down. Before Harmon could get Agnes to change her mind, she found out the cancer was back and that this time it was terminal."

"Did Agnes love Harmon?"

Yvonne held out her plump hands. "I'm just guessing that she did. She never said as much, but she loved someone. There was a man in her life, and if it wasn't Harmon, then I don't know who it was."

I was curious. "Why do you think Agnes had a man in her life?"

"Because she sparkled. There was a light in her eyes that even the cancer couldn't dim."

I ate the last of my cookie as I pondered this information. I wasn't sure how it fit into Toby's death. If Agnes loved this man—whoever he was—she surely would have trusted him to look after Toby once she was gone. But that didn't work with my theory that Agnes feared someone in Toby's life would have a negative influence on him—unless it was Harmon.

I dropped the topic of Agnes's love life, and asked, "Do you think Abner is the one who put the hornet's nest in Toby's bedroom?"

"My instincts tell me no. Melba thinks Abner did it, but she doesn't like him."

"Do you know if there's a specific reason?"

"Abner put in a line of candles and potpourri at his grocery store. Melba was furious. As she said to me, 'I don't plan on selling milk, bread, or cheese. Why should he infringe on my territory?'"

"She has a point. I know that Abner sells blooming plants, which are usually priced lower than what I'm selling. I don't like it, and I don't particularly like Abner, but I can't see him messing with a hornet's nest."

"Then who did it?"

I shrugged. "I don't know."

"Have another cookie?"

Reluctantly, I declined.

Yvonne sighed. "I wish I had your willpower. I'm so big I can't do the things that used to give me pleasure. Sugar Cube is my horse. I loved to ride him, but now I can't get my foot up high enough to put it in the stirrup. And even if I accomplished that feat, I'd be afraid my weight would hurt him." She turned her sharp gaze on me and demanded, "How did you do it? How did you lose so much weight and keep it off?"

I gave her a quick version of how I ate lots of fruits and veggies. I ended by saying, "Quick, convenient food is the most damaging."

"But it's so good. Agnes was always lecturing me on the danger of fast food. She never went out to eat. She didn't buy potato chips or Coke for Toby. She told him restaurants were dirty and that the food could poison his body. According to her, nature's bounty was the only thing he was to put in his mouth. Apples, oranges, bananas, peanuts—unsalted, of course. Popcorn, no butter. Lemonade, with little sugar. Her special treat for Toby was a frosted shredded wheat biscuit."

Yvonne chuckled. "I can't tell you the number of times I watched him lick off the sugar and toss the fiber to the birds or break it up and feed it to Sugar Cube. Toby gave that horse carrots, celery, and other bits of healthful snacks that Agnes thought necessary for a long life." Yvonne sighed. "And then that woman up and died young. What was the point of depriving herself—"

From the other end of the barn, Phillip called, "Yvonne, will you hunt up that chart that shows the different colors of stains? I think it's in on my desk."

"I'll be right back," she said, levering herself up from her seat at the spinning wheel. She stood upright slowly. "My knees are giving me fits. I've had replacement surgery, but my doctor says another won't do any good unless I lose the weight." She waddled across the alleyway and into a room.

I looked at the tin of cookies that was within easy reach. Then I looked at the door where Yvonne had disappeared. It wouldn't be polite to stash the cookies out of sight, but I could take myself away from temptation. I jumped up and meandered over to one of the milking stanchions and ran my hand over the smooth, glossy boards.

Behind me Phillip said, "I can't get that kind of finish with a sander. The cows slicked up that wood with constant contact while poking their heads through the stanchions to eat. When I turned this place into my workshop, I thought about tearing all this out to make more space, but I didn't have the heart. This is a piece of Americana that can't be duplicated."

I agreed. "Destroying it would have been a sin. It's good to see a barn of this type being preserved. So many are left to literally fall down in disrepair." I turned in a complete circle. "I grew up on a farm and we had an old barn, but it was nothing like this. There isn't any hay, or straw, or cobwebs."

Phillip laughed. "Since I use this barn to stain and varnish furniture, the days of storing hay are long gone. But there are cobwebs. They're just up so high you can't see them."

I walked farther into the barn, noticing a faint, unpleasant odor. I'd identified the expected turpentine, varnish, and paint that Phillip used in his work, but this odor was different.

When I commented on it, Phillip said, "After years as a dairy farm, the essence of cow still lingers."

I sniffed again. "This doesn't smell like cow."

Phillip frowned and took a deep breath. His brow cleared. "I know what it is. I'm so used to it that I don't even notice it. Follow me." He led the way to the back of the barn. "I think you're smelling the silo. I haven't done any renovating in this area. Structurally, I think it's sound, but several bricks are missing, and the top is gone."

He took a ring of keys from his pocket. "Keeping doors and gates locked can be a nuisance, but for insurance reasons we were forced to make certain restrictions. I had problems with Yvonne's antiques customers roaming all over our property. The silo is a real draw for kids and adults. The original iron ladder is still attached on the exterior, but the first rung is an unhandy ten feet above the ground. Our insurance agent wanted the silo dismantled, but I balked at the idea. To pacify him, I put locks on every door, and fenced and gated the immediate property near the store."

Phillip opened the door, then stood aside so I could enter. I walked slowly over the threshold into a corridor with a dirt floor. Filthy windows allowed a murky light to penetrate the gloom. The odor was stronger.

Phillip said, "This covered area was used by the farmer to bring the silage to the cows."

I nodded. "Now I recognize the smell. When I was a child, a neighbor chopped corn-and-grain sorghum. He stored the green fodder in a pit. After a few months of hot weather, the wind would pick up the stench and carry it to our place. My mother said the stuff smelled too rancid to feed to an animal."

"Once the plant fibers start to break down, the smell can be offensive, but only if the silage hasn't been properly packed into the silo. If all the air is forced out, then the fodder doesn't spoil because mold can't survive without air."

Phillip flipped through his ring of keys. "This isn't the right set," he grumbled. "I must have left the silo key on my desk." He touched the bricks. "There isn't much to see, but if you want, I'll run get the key. Once I get the door open and you look up, all you see is sky, because the top is gone, but it's an interesting piece of architecture."

Before I could answer, Yvonne hollered that she'd found the chart he wanted.

Phillip sighed. "I guess I'd better get back to work. You come out another time, I'll give you a proper tour. I love this old barn. It was built back in the late twenties, and the beams in the original main alleyway don't have any nails. They were put together with pegs."

As we walked back to the main entryway, Phillip continued my education on the construction of barns. He pointed out the different woods that had been used for siding, and the size of the trees that had been hewn to make the massive support posts.

Up by the front door, my father was sipping tea. Yvonne

and Abigail were looking at a length of cloth that was spread across one of the milk stanchions. At my side, Phillip picked up his pace. When he reached the women, he said, "Sister, sometimes you amaze me. I've told you I'm not ready to—"

"Now, Phillip, don't be upset," Yvonne said in a placating tone. To the rest of us, she explained, "My macho brother doesn't want people to know that he weaves cloth in his spare time. He thinks the task is too sissified."

Phillip rolled his eyes. "That's not it at all. Yvonne, you and your cohorts think that everyone's life should be in the public domain." He picked up the end of the cloth. "I will not begin a new business venture until I'm sure I can provide quality work. Until then I don't want to be hounded with questions and requests. Upholstering is a natural sideline to my refinishing furniture, but I'm not confident in that area of expertise yet."

A spark of anger flushed Yvonne's face. "My 'cohorts,' as you refer to them, are good friends. We respect privacy, but Toby's death changed the rules."

Phillip sighed. "I suppose you're right—on that issue." Taking a couple of steps back, Phillip started to wind the material into an untidy ball, but a corner was caught on the head of a nail that protruded about a quarter of an inch from the wooden stanchion.

I was closest. Before I could free the fabric, Phillip gave it a tug. I expected the cloth to rip, but the nail bent double, allowing the fabric to slide free. Tucking the wad of material under his arm, Phillip said, "I have the bill for the desk in my office, Albert, if you'd like to follow me." He shot his sister a sharp glance before disappearing through the doorway to his office.

Yvonne shook her head. "I know better than to talk about

Phillip's hobby. But when Abigail mentioned the wonderful fabrics she found in your attic, Bretta, I wanted to show off my brother's creation. He's very talented and has shown a real aptitude for blending natural fibers."

Before I could speak, Abigail took up the conversation. She went into great detail, describing one particular piece of brocade she'd come across. Annoyed, I kept waiting for a break so I could ask what Yvonne and her "cohorts" had been doing that involved Toby's murder. Before I could get a word in, my father returned alone from settling up the bill.

With the business dealings done, my father wasn't in the mood to hang around. In a flurry of good-byes, we thanked Yvonne for her hospitality and went out to the truck.

While my father checked the ropes that anchored the desk to the truck bed, Abigail said, "I wish I could buy some of that cloth from Phillip to use in the Cocoa Magic room. The neutral color would go well with what I have in mind for the area rugs. They would need a stout backing, but that wouldn't be a problem."

"What was the fabric like?" I asked absently. Had Phillip only been referring to the notes the three women had given me? I thought back over my conversation with Yvonne. Nothing raised a red flag that she and the other women might be involved in pursuing another line of inquiry into Toby's murder.

"Jute comes to mind," said Abigail, "but this had a softer feel and a fabulous shimmer. It was the weight of the weave that intrigued me. When I get back to my apartment, I'm going to look through some of my catalogs. I don't dare ask Phillip what blends he used, and I'm not sure it would be a good idea to bring up the subject with Yvonne. She might mention to Phillip that I was interested, and that might upset him so much that he wouldn't do our refinishing. His work is excellent, and I wouldn't want to hunt up another restorer."

My father heard her as he climbed into the truck. "That's exactly right, Abby. We *need* Phillip for this project. We don't need his weaving talents."

As we drove out the gateway, I glanced back at the brick silo. The afternoon sun touched on a metal rung near the rim. In the strong shaft of light, the weathered metal glinted like a beacon.

My mind leaped to the lighthouses I'd incorporated in the banker's birthday bouquets. I shook my head at my analogy. The silo and a lighthouse had nothing in common except their cylindrical framework. And yet, something niggled at me.

ELEVEN

BEFORE I WENT TO THE flower shop on Monday morning, I detoured by Merry's Delights to have a word with the employee who had made the belittling comment to Toby. Sid had said his interview with the woman had gone nowhere, and he'd crossed her off his list. I wanted to meet her for myself and draw my own conclusions. I knew I might be wasting my time hoping to have a private conversation. Mornings were chaotic at the bakery. Impatient customers wanted fast service so they could get to their jobs. I had the same pressures facing me, but I made the time.

I walked into Merry's Delights and got in line. There were three people behind the glass-fronted counter where the goodies were kept. The smell of freshly baked yeast bread, cinnamon, and vanilla edged past my resolve to talk, not buy.

I was trying to make up my mind which pastry to choose when someone tapped me on the shoulder. I turned to find the owner, Mr. Barker, at my side. He was as round as a bagel and covered from neck to knees with a green apron that was powdered with flour. He was bald and wore gold wire-rimmed glasses, which he had the habit of peering over.

"Hi," I said, smiling. "Looks like business is good."

"Pays the bills," he said, tilting his head so he could study me over the rims of his glasses. "You don't come in as much as you used to."

Since I lost weight, I'd taken my daily stop at Merry's Delights off my schedule. "That's right," I said. "I miss your apple fritters, but if I indulge too often, I can't snap my jeans."

"So you're here for the apple fritters?"

Something in his voice told me I'd better be honest. "They aren't my primary reason this morning."

"I figured as much." He turned and nodded to a window that looked into his kitchen. "I was standing there kneading dough when you walked in. As soon as I saw you, I knew you'd want to have a word with Elsie."

"If she's the one who upset Toby with a rude comment."

He took my arm and led me across the room to a private area. "It ain't going to happen, Bretta," he said in a low voice. "You can't talk to her. She's high-strung. When the sheriff questioned her, she was so upset she had to take the afternoon off."

"I won't upset her."

"Yes you will. If you say anything to her other than to give her a pastry order, she'll be worthless for the rest of the morning, and I don't have time for that."

I looked at the three helpers. "Which one is she?"

Mr. Barker hesitated, then said, "The young woman dressed in pink."

Elsie's dark hair was tucked under a net. Her eyes were wide spaced, her mouth drawn down in a frown. She didn't look particularly cheery, but she was fast. As I watched, she took care of more customers than her two fellow employees put together.

I turned back to Mr. Barker. "She gets the job done. Does she ever smile?"

"Rarely, but at this time of day, my customers don't care.

They want to be efficiently served. She's not rude. She just doesn't make small talk."

"But she did with Toby. Do you know the context of the conversation they had?"

Mr. Barker pursed his lips in disapproval. "Since you're going to pursue this, it's better that you talk to me instead of Elsie." He folded his arms over his pudgy tummy. "I witnessed the entire episode. It started before Toby came in. Elsie was cleaning off tables and tipped over a glass. The liquid soaked the front of her slacks. Toby came in, saw the damp spot, and asked her if she'd peed her pants."

I grinned. "I see."

Mr. Barker shook his head. "Anyone else would have laughed it off, but Elsie was mortified. She told Toby that he was dumb. That he 'couldn't track an elephant in four feet of snow.' "

He held out his hands. "It was a rude remark, but Toby's observation was, too. Those of us who knew Toby forgave his odd ways. He wasn't the brightest bulb in the chandelier, but he *brightened* our life—my life. For Toby to die under such circumstances is ironic."

"Ironic, how?"

"Toby loved animals. Even the ones that could do him harm. I know it's an overworked cliché, but Toby truly wouldn't hurt a fly. About a month ago, he found an opossum lying by the side of the road. A car had hit the animal, but it was still alive. Toby wrapped it in one of his window-cleaning towels and took it home. He told me it tried to bite him, but thank heavens the creature died before doing any damage.

"Just last week I received a frantic call from Toby. A snake had finagled its way behind some rocks, ate an oversize meal, and couldn't get out. Toby had tried to move the rock, but it wouldn't budge. I told him to forget it, but Toby said the snake's tail was making a funny noise. When I heard that, I didn't linger. I hopped in my car and headed out there."

Mr. Barker shook his head. "I've never fainted in my life, but when I saw Toby sitting six inches from that rattler's head, I almost passed out. Nothing would do but that we get that snake free. Sheer adrenaline gave me the strength. We shifted one of the rocks enough so the snake could slither away. Once it was gone, I gave Toby a lecture on letting Mother Nature see to her own."

Mr. Barker peered at me over his glasses. "You know what Toby said when I was done?"

I shook my head. "I haven't a clue."

"Toby stared me in the eye, and said, 'God made us all—ants and spiders, birds and fishes. Critters can't always help themselves. You helped me, Mr. Barker, and I'd help you if you were caught between two rocks.'"

Mr. Barker shrugged. "I told him I wouldn't sink my fangs into his skin and fill him with poison in return, but Toby wasn't convinced. I don't remember his exact words, but he said something to the effect that no critter should be punished for just being itself. I feel as if Toby has been punished for that same reason—for being himself."

Mr. Barker's voice was hoarse with emotion. "In those last minutes before Toby passed out, he must have felt betrayed by the critters he helped and loved." He cleared his throat. "When the call came about Toby, I'd already gone to bed. I'm on the job by three in the morning, and I don't have the same vigor I had twenty years ago. Martha, my wife, thought she was doing the right thing by not waking me. She meant well, but I should have been at the hospital with the rest of you."

I touched Mr. Barker lightly on the arm. "There was nothing you could have done. Thanks for talking with me," I said. "And for sharing your memories of Toby. I really appreciate it. I won't bother you any longer."

I zigzagged my way between customers, but stopped when Mr. Barker called my name. I turned to see him waving a white sack at me. I met him midway and took the heavy pastry bag he offered.

"Let me pay you," I said, reaching into my purse.

"No. This is on the house. A few extra calories to burn might come in handy if you have a busy day at your flower shop."

"BUSY" WAS AN UNDERSTATEMENT. In addition to the sympathy work for Toby's service, the owner of the Teaching Tots Day Care Center called and needed sixty helium balloons by noon. The children were going to release them in honor of Grandparents' Day.

The supervisor at a River City nursing home telephoned. In a frantic tone, she told us that the woman in charge had forgotten to place an order for a centerpiece and fifteen corsages. A special celebration was taking place at two o'clock. She wanted to know if we could help them out of an embarrassing situation. With a worried eye on the passing time, I reluctantly agreed.

Avery called and confirmed that Toby's casket would be open. I told my crew of two that it would be easier if we all met at the funeral home tonight and went in together. Lew said, "I might not go."

Lois and I both stopped what we were doing. I asked, "Why?" Lois said, "Do you have a hot date?"

"No. Toby didn't like funeral homes. Remember when he said people go in on a little bed and come out in a locked box? That's exactly what's going to happen."

I said, "It's going to be difficult, but attending his visitation is the right thing for us to do. We'll pay our respects, but we'll remember him the way he was the last time we saw him."

Lew mumbled something I didn't catch before heading for the bathroom.

Lois looked after him, shaking her head. "He's either really bummed out, or he's got a bad case of the *trots*. He's been in there off and on since he came to work."

"Being upset has that effect on some people."

Lois shrugged, and we went back to work.

Four babies had been born over the weekend, and, of course, the local sheriff was still in the hospital, recuperating from surgery. If the numerous orders we received for Sid were any indication, he should win his bid for reelection. Knowing Sid, he probably wouldn't appreciate the flowers, but the expressions of get-well wishes ought to make him feel better.

I called the hospital to make sure he was out of the ICU and could receive the floral deliveries. The nurse I spoke with said he was back to his usual self. This observation was passed in a dry tone that made me chuckle. Sid, in a hospital gown, confined to bed, while a high-profile murder investigation was being bandied about in the newspapers wouldn't win any "good patient" award. I had absolutely no plans to visit him. I figured anyone who willingly walked through the doorway to his room had a death wish. I considered sending his nurses a bouquet with a sympathy card attached, but there wasn't time.

When Lew came out of the bathroom for the third time, I said, "I'm sorry you don't feel well, but we have work to do. We also have an obligation to attend Toby's visitation. The three of us will meet at the funeral home tonight, and we'll go in together."

Grimly, Lew nodded.

As I worked, I kept a watchful eye on him. If his illness progressed, I'd have to call in additional help. To my relief, whatever had plagued him seemed to have lessened. He kicked into high gear. It's times like this that I truly appreciate Lew as an employee. He takes phone orders and waits on customers. He wraps plants, pleating the foil paper neatly around the pots and tying perfect satin bows. He delivers. He types cards. He does it all, except he won't learn to design. On slow days, I've offered to give him a lesson, but he always declines, saying he's happy with the status quo.

We made the deadlines for the helium balloons, and the nursing-home centerpiece and corsages. My feet were killing me. I'd worn a pair of shoes that were usually comfortable, but I'd made too many trips to the back flower cooler. While Lois tackled the hospital orders, I did the sympathy work. For most funerals, plants outnumber cut flowers. Since Toby hadn't any family to see to the plants after the service, all the orders were for bouquets. These took more time and thought because I wanted each one to be different and special.

It was midafternoon before the phones were silent and the front doorbell had stopped chiming. Lew had pulled up a stool and sat down. He had his delivery clipboard in front of him, but he wasn't writing. I thumbed the stack of orders and shifted from one sore foot to the other.

Lois said, "Lew, if I can't sit, you can't sit."

"I'm listing my deliveries."

"I don't see your hand moving."

Lew muttered, "That's because you're blinded by that monstrosity in front of you. You're mixing your seasons. Blue iris and yellow sunflowers—spring and fall."

I was accustomed to Lois and Lew's constant bickering. This time Lew's observation seemed more belittling than usual. I looked at Lois's bouquet. She tended to be flamboyant in her designs, but that was her style. She dressed the same way, favoring bright, splashy colors. I sometimes cringed when I saw her bouquets, but if given the choice, customers often picked her designs over my more conservative ones. It was a matter of taste, and I respected that. However, Lew didn't see it that way. He was always nitpicking about Lois's work, which led me to believe that was why he wouldn't try designing. It would be payback time, and Lois wouldn't hesitate in being equally critical.

Uneasily, I watched Lois lay down her florist knife. With eyes narrowed, she said, "I'm not sure I heard you correctly. Would you mind repeating what you said?"

I jumped into the conversation. "We don't have time for this. Lew, you were out of line. Lois, consider the source and drop it."

Lew said nothing, but his hand shook as he picked up a pen. Lois glared at him, willing him to meet her stare. When he continued to ignore her, she grabbed up her knife and whacked off a flower stem with the ferocity of a guillotine.

In a sweet voice, she said, "I wish I were as perfect as you, Lew. How do you stand us lesser beings? It must really try your patience, putting up with our shortcomings. I should apologize for offending your sensibilities with my reprehensible arrangement."

Lew glanced at Lois. "Be careful, or you'll strangle on all those multisyllable words. Your tongue isn't in the habit of using them."

I braced myself for all-out war, but Lois continued in the same subservient tone. "You're so kind. Always thinking of others. We are truly blessed to have you in our lives. I wake up each morning and thank my lucky stars that I have the opportunity to come to work and—"

Lew pounded his fist on the table. "I'm a sniveling coward. A poor excuse for a man." His voice broke. His shoulders slumped in despair.

I was speechless. As long as I'd known Lew, he'd always been in command of his emotions. He might get angry and spout off, trying to psychoanalyze our womanly behavior, but he'd never lowered his guard and shown this kind of personal vulnerability.

The raw anguish in his voice moved me. I went around the table and touched him on the shoulder. "Lew, what's wrong? Are you ill?"

"I'm sick," he said. "Sick of myself."

I shot a quick glance at Lois. She mouthed the words, "I haven't got a clue."

"Lois and I will manage if you need to leave early."

Lew reared back as if I'd smacked him. "Ha! That's what started all my trouble."

Bewildered, I asked, "What trouble? What are you talking about?"

Lew bowed his head. His voice was low. "Remember last Friday, when I got that electrical shock while trying to fix the bad connection on the lighthouse?"

I nodded. "Of course, I remember. You said your hand was burned, and you left early to have it treated."

"That was my excuse. I left early, but it wasn't so I could go to the doctor. I'd devised this fantastic strategy that backfired." Lew lifted his head and met my gaze. His expression was a mixture of guilt and remorse. "I went to Toby's, Bretta. I saw him collapse in the kitchen, and I did nothing."

TWELVE

THE HORROR OF Lew's admission took my breath away. I leaned weakly against my worktable. I wanted to demand a full and detailed explanation, but one glance at Lew told me he wasn't in any condition to take a verbal onslaught from anyone. His expression was that of a condemned man with no hope for a reprieve.

I took a deep breath and let it out slowly. "Tell us what happened, Lew."

His voice was shaky. "When Toby told us about his mother's flowers being stolen, I decided to investigate. I assumed there was a logical explanation. I planned to reach a thought-provoking hypothesis, and then arrive on the scene when you kept your appointment with him on Saturday." Lew hung his head. "In short, Bretta, I wanted to show you up."

I was irritated by Lew's plan to one-up me, but I kept my tone even. "I suppose I can accept that. I know you dislike my sleuthing. Go on."

"I couldn't leave my car in Toby's driveway because this was to be a covert operation. I hunted for a place to park that was out of the way, but not too far. I found an entrance into a pasture. The lane was rutted and narrow. Tree branches raked against the sides of my car, but they also acted as camouflage. The lane suited my purpose, but it meant that I'd have to walk across a field."

Lew wrinkled his nose in distaste. A trace of his old stuffiness broke through his misery. "I don't commune with nature. Uncultivated plants are an abomination. I had a pair of gloves in my car, and I always keep boots and coveralls in the trunk in case of an emergency. By the time I donned my protective covering, and worked my way to Toby's garden, he was parking his bike on the porch. My plan to show you up hinged on surprise. I wasn't sure if Toby would approve of or even keep my visit a secret. I decided to make my assessment of the situation alone, so I hid until he'd gone into the house."

Lew's forehead glistened with perspiration. He pulled a handkerchief from his pocket and mopped his brow. "I—uh—hadn't gone very far into the garden when I heard Toby's first scream. I ran to the porch and tried the door, but it was locked."

Lew's voice dropped to a whisper. "His screams were indescribable. They demanded immediate action. I didn't know what to do. I didn't know what was happening. I was standing at the back door, peering through the curtains when Toby stumbled into the room."

The hairs on my arms stood up as Lew described the scene he'd witnessed.

"Toby was enveloped by a black, undulating cloud. The hornets swirled around him, but hundreds clung to his bare legs, arms, and face." Lew gulped. "It was a nightmare come to life. Toby screamed and swatted at the hornets. I beat on the glass, but he never glanced my way. He shuffled to the phone and poked the pad three times. I assumed he was calling 911. I saw his mouth move, and hoped he was speaking with a dispatcher. From the porch, I cheered him on, willing him to be courageous. Then suddenly he collapsed.

"For a few minutes, Toby's body twitched, as if he was still fighting off the hornets, then he stopped moving. I didn't know if he was unconscious or if he was—uh—dead." Lew bowed his head. "I ran back to my car. I'd just unlocked the door when I heard the sirens."

As Lew recounted events, I struggled with two conflicting emotions. I was furious. Lew had wimped out when Toby needed him. He'd been right there, and hadn't lifted a finger. But I couldn't squelch the compassion that welled up inside me. Lew wasn't a cruel, unfeeling man. If I tallied the hours, I probably spent more time with Lew and Lois than I did with anyone else I knew. I'd invested days, weeks, months, and years in this work-related association. Lew was feeling as guilty as hell. He needed to hear a kind word, but I wasn't sure what to say.

Lois didn't have my problem, though kindness was the farthest thing from her mind. She glared at Lew. "That's the damnedest story I've ever heard. Didn't it occur to you to break the glass, reach in, and unlock the door?"

Lew's tone was stiff. "No. It did not. You weren't there. Everything happened so quickly. There wasn't time to deliberate. Looking back I see that what I did—"

Lois snorted. "That's the trouble. You *did* nothing."

Lew winced. "I know that better than anyone." He turned to me. "What should I do now?"

Taking a deep breath, I let it out slowly. "When you approached Toby's house, did you see anyone?"

"No. Should I tell Sid what happened?"

"I think it might be in your best interests to have a talk with him."

Lew nodded. "A purging of my sin."

Lois rolled her eyes. "There isn't enough water in the Osage River to cleanse this mess. I can't believe you, Lew. And I'm not just talking about Toby. Whatever possessed you to try to solve a mystery on your own? You don't have an interest in sleuthing." She waved her arms in the air. "Good heavens, you've just told us you didn't have the nerve to help Toby. What in the world would you have done if you'd found some ax-welding thief in the garden?"

Lew's chin shot up. "If you had listened, you would've heard me say that I assumed there was a logical explanation for the disappearing plants. I didn't think—"

Under her breath Lois said, "That's been well established."

Lew continued, speaking louder, "—there was any danger. I only planned to inspect the destruction of the plants that had been chopped down."

Lois wouldn't give up. "*Chopped* is the operative word. How do you think they were hacked off? With a butter knife? You were walking into a possibly dangerous situation. At least when Bretta plays private eye, she has some experience. You have nothing."

Lew's mouth drew down. "That isn't true. I have a brain. I have the ability to size up a situation and—" He stopped abruptly. His shoulders drooped. "You're right. I have nothing."

"You have plenty of good qualities," I said. "When you make these deliveries to the hospital, go to Sid's room and talk to him. It won't be easy, but I think it needs to be done."

Lois started to say something, but the front doorbell chimed. We looked up and saw Leona headed our way. She waved to Lois. "Stay where you are. I don't want anything. I've closed the dress shop early. I was on my way to my car when I decided I wanted to have a chat with Bretta."

Leona came around the front sales counter and plunked a sack and her purse on my worktable. "I'm exhausted," she said. "I need a relaxing bath and a nap before I go to the funeral home this evening."

If she was exhausted, it didn't show. Not one blond hair was out of place. Her navy dress was crisp and fresh. I brushed my straggly hair away from my damp forehead and said, "The relaxing bath sounds wonderful, but it's going to be a while before I can indulge in that luxury."

"I know you're busy and I won't stay long. I'd share my gift with you, but I'm too selfish." Leona took a bottle from the sack. "I do alterations on Mrs. Darby's clothes free of charge. In return she gives me little goodies. I found this bag on my front counter." Leona tipped the bottle upside down. The green solution glubbed a weak bubble. "She left me bubble bath and a bag of my favorite cinnamon candies."

"What's the fragrance?" I asked.

Leona squinted at the label. "It says freesia. The liquid seems rather thin. Mrs. Darby shops at Buck-A-Roo." She lowered her voice. "Diana doesn't stock the best quality when it comes to merchandise. It'll probably take the entire bottle to make a froth of bubbles." She put the bubble bath in the sack and pulled out a bag of candy. Holding it up she asked, "Would anyone care for a piece?"

Not waiting for an answer, she tore open the cellophane and passed the candy around. Leaving the sack of sweets within easy reach, Leona said, "Yvonne enjoyed discussing her notes with you yesterday. I wondered what you thought of my theory about Diana and Toby?"

I shifted the disk of candy around in my mouth so I could

speak. "It's an interesting concept, but it's hard to imagine Toby and Diana involved in a romance."

Leona pulled up a stool and sat down. "Toby, no, but Diana, oh my yes. It's rumored that her youngest child belongs to the man who used to do her taxes. He's moved away, but every time I look at that child's brown eyes, I see Raymond's."

She leaned forward. "That's why my theory makes perfect sense. I've witnessed Diana flirting with Toby. She liked to touch him, and she used any excuse to do so. I think Toby was confused by her attentions and rebuffed her advances. She was afraid he would tell her husband, so she put the hornet's nest in Toby's house hoping to divert his attention. I'm not saying she wanted Toby dead." Leona shivered. "I don't think Diana is a cold-blooded killer. She was scared and acted irrationally."

When Leona had finished speaking, Lew snorted. "That's the dumbest thing I've ever heard. I'm going on deliveries."

Leona waited until Lew had left before she said, "Phillip had the same reaction when he heard Yvonne and me hashing out ideas."

I counted out five orange gladioli from the bucket that was near me on the floor. Picking up my florist knife, I stood the first stalk upright and eyed it for height. As I sliced into the stem, I asked, "Does Phillip have a theory?"

"If he does, he's keeping it to himself. He says our law enforcement is paid to do their job, and they shouldn't have to deal with interference from the rest of us. Of course, that's experience talking. He learned the hard way that when you're paid to do a job, that's the job you do. Phillip came back to River City because he was fired from a Canadian company he'd been with for twenty years. Yvonne says her brother bucked the system. He used grant money inappropriately. The money was designated for one project, but Phillip used it for another."

"What kind of project was he working on?"

Leona shook her head. "I don't know. Phillip never talks about it, and Yvonne advised me not to ask. Ten years ago when he came back here, he was out of sorts and restless. He bought a few goats, some chickens, and a couple of cows. He tried farming, planting soybeans, alfalfa, potatoes, and mustard greens."

I looked up from my bouquet. "Mustard greens? I wouldn't think there'd be a big market for that vegetable."

"He never tried to sell any of the crops. Money doesn't seem to be an issue for him, but the same can't be said for Josh."

I added the last orange glad that formed the framework of my arrangement. "Josh? Is he having problems?"

"He's about to lose the video store. By his own admission, he's spending more than he makes. He says he doesn't have time for a second job, but I think he's delivering for some of the fast-food places around here. He leaves work about the same time I do. I go home, but Josh always pulls into the parking lot of a restaurant. I can't figure out his schedule. First he's at one place, and then another. I don't know how he keeps it straight where he's supposed to be and at what time."

Leona heaved a sigh. "At least he's trying to make money in an honest way. I get furious when I think of Abner swindling Toby. And for what? Gambling debts."

I was reaching for some white Fuji mums to mingle with the orange glads when Leona dropped this bomb. "Abner gambles?"

"That's right. He goes to St. Louis to play blackjack on the riverboat. From what I understand, he may have already gambled away his home. His wife is just the sweetest thing. I always call her when I get in a new shipment of denim. She loves those long-waisted jumpers with embroidery on the bodice. I feel sorry for her. She's tried so hard to be supportive, but Abner's arrest has devastated her."

Frowning at Leona, I said, "Apart from the information you told me about Diana, you didn't put any of these particulars in your notes. Why not?"

Leona stared at me. "This is just girl talk."

I didn't agree. Facts were facts, and I wanted more. "Tell me about Harmon," I invited casually. "I know you want to go home and take your bath, but visiting with you makes my work go so much quicker."

This lame excuse seemed to satisfy Leona. She crossed her legs and unwrapped another piece of cinnamon candy. I glanced at Lois. Her hands were idle. She was soaking up this "girl talk" like a piece of floral foam absorbs water. I nodded to the orders that were her responsibility. Silently, I mouthed, "Work." Lois rolled her eyes, but picked up a bolt of red ribbon.

The disk of candy clicked against Leona's teeth as she said, "Harmon is a sad man. He's been married three times. He loved Agnes, but didn't want Toby as part of the marriage bargain. I think he's sorry he didn't try to make things work. He's broody and moody and spends too much time alone. A man needs mental stimulation. I learned that in my own life.

"My husband, Herbert, retired about six years ago from a wonderful job in St. Joseph, Missouri. We came to River City because we loved the feel of the town, and we wanted to be close to the lakes so Herbert could fish. He tried retirement for a year, but he wasn't happy. He needed mental stimulation. I understood Herbert wanting to go back to work, but I didn't want to leave River City. I'd settled into life in this small town, and I loved it. It made me feel like I was part of an extended family. But most of all, it was here that I discovered something about myself."

Leona shook her head. "Talk about a late bloomer. At the age of fifty-eight, I decided that I wanted my own business, serving the women who'd welcomed me when I first arrived in town. St. Joseph was too far north for Herbert to commute each day. We decided our marriage was strong enough for him to live there through the week and come home weekends." Her cheeks reddened. "I call him my weekend lover."

I added three yellow roses to my arrangement. I'd never gotten so much information about so many people without leaving the flower shop. But was everything Leona said fact or fiction? I decided to put her to the test. Giving Leona a smile, I asked, "What about Bretta Solomon? What do you know about her?"

Leona didn't hesitate. "Her husband was the light of her life. When he died she was shattered, but she picked up the pieces and is carrying on very well." Leona shot me a grin. "I understand she has a new man in her life. She loves her work to the point that she's obsessed. She's friendly, but doesn't take the time to make social contacts unless she's on the trail of a criminal. When she does that, she can be relentless in finding out the truth."

It was an accurate assessment, though I might argue the "obsessed" part. I'd rather think of myself as dedicated.

Lois was more impressed. "Wow," she said, eyeing Leona as if she were a soothsayer. "Do me next."

Leona grew thoughtful. "She and her husband, Noah, are still very much in love. Their children are finally gone from home, but she's taken on the care of a niece. This young lady has given Lois trouble, but seems to have settled down, and is loved like one of her own. But that's the way Lois operates. She's outspoken and blustery but kindhearted."

"Thanks," said Lois. "If that's the scuttlebutt floating around town, then I'm pleased."

I'd finished one order and moved on to the next. This one called for red roses, white snapdragons, and a touch of purple wax flower for filler. As I assembled what I'd need to make the bouquet, I asked Leona, "Did you know Agnes very well?"

"Agnes Sutton was the first friend I made in River City. I met her at the pharmacy. She was nice to me, inviting me to attend a garden-club meeting. I agreed to go though I knew nothing about plants and Agnes wasn't much better."

I was reaching for a rose but paused at this piece of information. "Agnes didn't know anything about plants?"

"That's right. She was determined to learn, but I'm afraid I didn't have that same ambition. I don't like dirt under my fingernails." She held out her hands so we could admire her tapered nails that were an inch long. "The deciding factor was when I almost died from an allergic reaction to some poison ivy. Anyway, getting back to Agnes. She wasn't much on flower beds, but she loved shrubs of all kinds. She had heard they were the backbone of any garden. At first she took it slow, planting lilacs and pussy willow along the fence line of her garden. Then she found out she had cancer. She received treatment and the tumors shrank. She went on working at the pharmacy during the day, and gardening in her spare time."

I nodded. "Then the cancer came back."

"That's right. Again Agnes received treatment, and for a time she was fine but then the tumor came back. She quit her job at the pharmacy to spend more time with Toby. I thought she needed her job, but she seemed to do okay financially."

Here Leona paused and sucked thoughtfully on her candy. Musing, she said, "That's always bothered me, how Agnes could quit her job. Yvonne says the railroad gave Agnes a settlement when her husband was killed, but that money had been used up years ago."

Leona gave herself a little shake before continuing, "Anyway, as I was saying, we all thought Agnes was doing well. But now that I know how short the time was before she passed away, I can't help but wonder if the disease might not have progressed so rapidly if she'd taken better care of herself."

I carried the rose arrangement to the back and picked up another container. For this bouquet I chose purple larkspur, red carnations, and yellow daisy pompoms. It was a "Lois" combination. She saw what I was using and flashed me a grin before saying, "Why didn't Agnes take care of herself?"

"She probably thought she was. I blame her early death on the garden. She kept digging and planting shrubs until she exhausted herself. She didn't have any spare energy to fight off the cancer."

I asked, "I've seen the garden and I don't understand why she planted so many shrubs in such a small area."

"She was living in the moment, I guess, never thinking

about how the little bushes would grow. And she had only so much land. She told me she believed that a person who works the soil is closer to God." Leona stood up. "I guess in a way she was right. Agnes worked herself into an early grave and right into the arms of Jesus."

THIRTEEN

IT WAS SIX O'CLOCK before I got home from the flower shop. I needed to eat, and I still had to dress and drive back to town for Toby's visitation. DeeDee had left a salad in the refrigerator. In the microwave was a plate that held a piece of poached salmon nestled on a bed of dilled rice. While I waited for the fish to warm, I watched the seconds tick away.

Leona's visit had started me thinking, and I hadn't been able to stop. Early on in my florist's career, I'd learned that it wasn't my concern if Joe Blow ordered roses for someone other than his wife. It wasn't up to me to pass moral judgment if Cindy Lou had a baby at fourteen and wasn't married. Flowers commemorate an occasion, and when the order is placed with my shop, I'm made aware of the circumstances.

Since flowers aren't normally sent to someone who has a gambling problem or has been fired from his job or whose business is about to go belly-up or who missed the chance to marry the woman he loved, then I'd been left out of this particular informational loop.

I'd always considered myself to be in the know when it came to what was happening around town, and yet I didn't have a clue about the lives of the people I saw every day. Leona called our conversation "girl talk," but was it as innocent as the phrase suggested? Hadn't we actually indulged in some old-fashioned gossip?

I shifted uncomfortably. It wasn't my style to spread rumors, but I willingly listened when people talked. I'd learned that during an investigation, even the smallest piece of information could be a turning point. It was a matter of taking one scenario and following it through to a possible conclusion.

The microwave beeped. I removed the plate of salmon, then juggled it back and forth between my hands because it was hot. I put the dish on the table and sat down. The food was up to DeeDee's high standards, but my appetite was gone. I poked at the salad, eating about half before I pushed back my chair. I covered the leftovers and shoved them in the refrigerator.

At the dining-room doorway, I paused to watch my father and Abigail. The table was piled with papers, books, color charts, and fabric swatches. Clearing my throat, I said, "How's it going?"

They looked up with the same distant expression. My father blinked a couple of times, as if to get me into focus. "Slow," he said, "but it's coming along. Why don't you join us?"

"I have to go back to town for Toby's visitation." Trying to keep my tone light, I asked, "It's surely after working hours. I'm not being billed for this extra time, am I?"

Abigail brushed a weary hand across her eyes. "Of course not. The amount stated in the contract is the amount that is due."

"Do you always spend so much time on a job?"

"I do if it's needed."

"What about your other clients? Don't they feel slighted?"

Abigail licked her lips before replying. "As I told you, I've cleared my schedule so I can concentrate on this job."

"The first third of the contractual amount is due. Shall I write you a check?"

Abigail cast a swift glance at my father. "That can wait until tomorrow," she said. "I understand that you're in a hurry right now."

I was, but something kept me standing in the doorway watching Abigail and my father. She'd answered all my questions, but I had many, many more. I hesitated to put her on the hot seat with my father right there. He eyed me uncertainly, as if he wasn't sure where I would take the conversation next.

I said, "From the paperwork I've seen, you seem to have every detail nailed down. When will the actual painting and papering begin?"

"Soon," said Abigail.

My father frowned. "Are you worried that our work won't be up to your standards?"

I lifted a shoulder casually. "Not at all. I've been impressed so far." I glanced at my watch. "I've got to dress and head back into town." Abigail nodded and turned her attention to the books on the table. My father followed me out into the hall.

"Are you all right, daughter?" he asked, searching my face. "I know this evening will be difficult. Would you like me to ride along with you?"

I was touched by his concern. "I'm fine," I said. "I'm meeting Lew and Lois at the funeral home. We're going in together." I turned to the stairs, but my father put his hand on my arm. When I faced him again, his eyes were sad.

He said, "I don't want you to think I'm fickle, that my interests change on a whim. When we worked that last case together, I felt as if I'd lost five years off my life. It was too much adventure for an old man like me. Working on this house soothes the creative side of me, and it isn't nearly as dangerous. But if you'd like to discuss Toby's death, I'm willing to listen." He winked. "I might even offer a suggestion or two or three."

His last comment had been to lighten the mood, but my throat tightened at the tenderness in his voice. My emotions were fragile due to what I faced in an hour. I mumbled that I'd keep his offer in mind, then headed up to my room. I almost missed the last step as tears blurred my eyes.

FUNERAL HOMES ARE an important part of my business life. In the case of Bernard Delaney, we have a friendship that has nothing to do with my flower shop, but everything to do with trust. When my husband, Carl, passed away, Bernard handled the funeral, easing me through decisions I thought I wouldn't have to make for years and years. Bernard had seen me at my most vulnerable, hanging on to the casket, viewing my beloved husband one last time. Bernard kept confidences. He conducted himself and his business with just the right touch of solemnity, but he kept a sense of humor. I admired his integrity but worried about his failing health. When he passed on, our town would lose more than a funeral director. We would lose a man whose faith and love had eased our journey down life's darkest path.

I was relieved to see that Bernard felt well enough to be at the front door. He was tall and lean, with a high forehead and thinning hair. The circumstances called for a solemn smile, which he delivered professionally, but when he shook my hand, he gave it an extra squeeze. That gesture communicated to me that he was aware of my loss and empathized.

I hesitated, blocking the door, but I wanted to ask Bernard about Toby's appearance. If he didn't look natural, I wanted to be prepared. I gazed into Bernard's blue eyes and whispered, "How does Toby—uh—What I mean is—does he—" I couldn't get the words out.

Bernard bent forward and put his lips near my ear. "I know what you're trying to say, Bretta. Toby looks fine. No swelling. No sting marks. He looks like he's sleeping."

I drew a shaky breath and nodded. A line was forming behind me. It was time to move on. Forcing myself to put one foot in front of the other, I entered the chapel, nodding to people I knew. Yvonne and Phillip were leaving. I was concerned when I saw Yvonne leaning heavily on a walker. In passing, she explained that her knees were worse tonight. She figured a storm was brewing. Melba stopped to give me a hug. I saw no sign of Leona, but in the crush of people it was possible that I'd missed her.

I dislike visitations. The atmosphere often takes on a partylike feel. People are ill at ease. Laughter is often the outlet for pent-up emotions, but the sound grates on my nerves. It doesn't seem appropriate when the individual who's being honored isn't able to participate. On the other hand, this same group of people wouldn't have come together if it hadn't been for the benefit of the person lying in his casket. It was a paradox, a contradiction of sensibilities as to what kind of behavior was expected. At the funeral service, these same people would be appalled if someone were to laugh aloud, and yet tonight the noise level was high.

As I stood in line to pay my respects to Toby, I looked around the room. I was heartened to see that not everyone was in party mode. Apparently, Harmon had already been through the line. He was off to one side, staring into space. The skin around his eyes drooped. His mouth was turned down at the corners. He looked up, caught my gaze, and nodded a greeting.

What was in his thoughts? I wondered as I shuffled forward. Was Harmon thinking about Agnes? Did he wonder what his life might have been like if he'd accepted Toby as part of his marriage to the woman he loved? Had Harmon loved Agnes so completely that a terrible resentment toward Toby had grown over the years? Had he taken those frustrations out on Toby?

As Bailey would say, these were good questions, but where were the answers?

My gaze drifted past Harmon, to Josh. I tried to catch his eye, but Josh worked hard at ignoring me. His restless gaze dropped to his shoes. He lifted his head and smiled and nodded, but never at me. I kept my eyes on him. I had several questions I wanted to ask him, but high on my list was Leona's comment that Josh had a second job delivering fast food.

I continued to stare at Josh. I don't think he would have acknowledged me if it hadn't been for the man standing near him. He touched Josh's arm and pointed to me. Wasting no time, I motioned for Josh to join me. When he hesitated, I took a purposeful step in his direction. When he saw I was determined to have a meeting with him, regardless of my position in line, Josh strolled over.

"Good turnout," he said. "How are you doing?"

Conscious of the people around us, I lowered my voice. "I might like a pizza or a hamburger later this evening, and I thought you could deliver it." I stared at Josh long and hard. "You do that, don't you? Or do you only deliver to *certain* people?"

Color flamed in Josh's cheeks. But he kept his chin high

and met my steady gaze. "I don't know what you're talking about. I'm not a deliveryman. I have my own business—"

"Which is in serious financial trouble," I finished. "Out of respect for Toby, I'm dropping this—for now. But believe me, you and I will talk."

Josh didn't seem to know what to do. He blinked at me wordlessly, then turned and hurried away. Lois elbowed me in the ribs. Leaning closer she said, "I don't know what that was about, but you sure rattled his cage."

I nodded. I felt that Josh was guilty, but was it of only taking advantage of Toby, or had Josh gone way beyond that?

We were about midway in our trek to the front of the chapel. I saw Mr. Barker step away from the casket, wiping his eyes. He walked to a row of chairs and sat down. A woman who I took to be his wife, Martha, sat next to him. They looked like a matched set—short and round, with gray hair and gold-rimmed glasses set on stubby noses. Martha was consoling her husband, murmuring in his ear. He nodded, took a deep breath, and rose slowly to his feet. Seeing me, he crossed the room to get to my side.

"We're not staying," he said. "I have to get up early in the morning." His shoulders drooped. "I haven't been sleeping very well. Toby's death has knocked the stuffing out of me. I keep thinking that if he and Elsie hadn't exchanged words, he might have told me if something had happened to bring about this horrible situation."

"I've been wondering how Agnes went about choosing the people she wanted Toby to work for. I've heard that she was a stickler for healthful foods." I flashed Mr. Barker a smile. "And while your pastries are the best in town, I'm surprised she asked you to let him work at the bakery."

Martha spoke up. "We raised eight healthy, well-adjusted children. We understand kids, and Agnes knew that."

Mr. Barker added, "When Agnes approached me about Toby doing odd jobs, she begged me to keep his diet healthy. I agreed, but I couldn't deny him a cinnamon roll now and again. My kids didn't show any adverse effects, and I knew Toby wouldn't either."

"On the day Toby died, was there anything different about him? Did he say something to you that seemed ordinary at the time, but now might have a different meaning?"

Mr. Barker scratched his head. "Well, one thing is that normally, Toby didn't come into my shop until late afternoon. That day he came into the bakery right after lunch."

"Did he say why he was early?"

"No. He was jabbering about a bowl of white worms until he noticed that the front of Elsie's pants were wet."

I frowned. "A bowl of white worms? Is this another 'critter' story?"

"No story, because I don't know the facts. I wasn't paying any particular attention to what Toby was saying. My mind was on the stock that had just been delivered. I'd ordered a bag of yeast, but the order had been screwed up. I needed that leavening for a batch of dough. When something like that is on my mind, I don't often hear what's going on around me."

Standing a step behind her husband, Martha nodded emphatically.

I gave her an understanding grin, but turned back to Mr. Barker. "Do you know which shop Toby was at before he got to yours?"

Mr. Barker thought for a moment. "Normally it would have been Leona's, but that day it had to have been Melba's because Toby said he was working backward. I didn't question him as to why he was running his route the opposite way. I'm sure that in his mind, he had a good reason."

Lew jiggled my arm. "We have to move forward," he said, nodding to the space that had opened ahead of us.

Mr. and Mrs. Barker murmured good-bye and departed, leaving me with something more to ponder. Was it important that Toby had changed his route? I'd never given much thought to when Toby came into the flower shop. If he showed up, I had something for him to do.

The line inched forward.

But what if Toby reversed his route? What if a store owner was expecting him at a certain time, but he made an unexpected appearance at an inopportune moment? What if he saw something that upset him?

The line was moving more quickly. I shuffled forward.

More important, what if Toby saw something that upset someone else—namely, his killer?

Hear no evil. See no evil. Speak no evil.

Again Lew jiggled my arm, bringing me out of my thoughts. I'd been staring at the carpet. When I looked up, I was at the foot of Toby's casket. My heart dropped, then righted itself, only to pound erratically.

The mahogany finish gleamed richly under the lights. The spray of red and white roses I'd made looked elegant, but neither the casket nor the flowers suited the Toby I'd known. I wished now that I'd used bright, bold sunflowers with assorted greenery, fall leaves with spiral eucalyptus. I wished I'd tucked in miniature orange and yellow roses that were sweet and innocent. I wished I could turn back the clock and visit with Toby more fully about what he'd done with his days.

As I advanced to the front of the casket, Lois, Lew, and I stood shoulder to shoulder, staring down at Toby. Just as Bernard had assured me, Toby appeared to be sleeping. His long eyelashes feathered a pattern on his cheeks. His lips seemed to be tipped up in a smile. Tears welled in my eyes.

Lew reached into his pocket. Through a mist of grief, I watched him slip a key under Toby's folded hands. In a broken whisper, Lew said, "There's no locked box for you. I'm so sorry." Lew's voice cracked as he repeated, "I'm so sorry."

I knew why he was apologizing, but the couple behind Lew seemed startled by the guilt in his voice. Taking Lew's arm, I urged him away from the casket. All Lew needed was for the couple to report to Sid that they'd seen a man at the funeral home standing at Toby's side begging for forgiveness. While Lew pulled himself together, I greeted Avery Wheeler. As Toby's legal guardian, Avery stood in the space usually designated for family members.

Avery's bulbous nose was red with emotion. His eyes were bloodshot and watery. He was a good-size man with a paunch, but tonight he seemed shrunken and fragile. Even though he had his cane in his hand, he was tottery on his feet.

I put my arm around him and said, "Why don't you let me get you a chair?"

He drew away from my embrace. "As Toby's representative, that action could hardly be classed as dignified." He patted my arm. "But I appreciate your thoughtfulness."

"You have to take care of yourself."

"Yes, Bretta, I know. And I will, as soon as the last person goes out Bernard's front door."

I smiled. "You're a proper man, with proper ideas, but you're too stubborn for your own good."

Avery smoothed his prominent salt-and-pepper mustache with his little finger while keeping a watchful eye on me. "In another time and another place, we'll discuss who is the more stubborn, but for now, I'll let your remark pass."

I shook my head at him and moved on. Lois was headed for the door, pulling on her coat. Lew was behind me. I turned to him, thinking I'd ask about his conversation with Sid, but stopped as a sudden hush filled the chapel. Everyone was staring at the entry. I looked in that direction and saw Abner framed in the doorway.

With every eye on him, he stepped into the funeral home. He acknowledged Bernard with a slight nod. Ignoring the line, Abner walked directly to the casket. He stood with his head bowed. His shoulders were squared, as if to ward off the barrage of hostile glares directed his way.

The tension in the room mounted. No one spoke, but there was a restlessness that couldn't be ignored.

After a few moments, Abner faced the crowd. His expression was grim. Without a word, he made the long journey back to the front door. On the threshold, he turned to say, "You've all passed judgment on me. In your eyes I'm guilty, but the law sees things differently. I've been released from custody because they couldn't make a case against me. There's a reason. I'm innocent of any wrongdoing connected with Toby's death."

Someone snorted in disgust.

Abner's lips trembled, and he fought for control. Slowly his gaze traveled the room. "I have an advantage over all of you. I know I'm innocent. But you might want to think about this. If I didn't harm Toby, then who did? Who walking among you is free to kill again?"

FOURTEEN

THE NEXT MORNING I awoke with several thoughts flitting through my weary brain. I'd been up and down most of the night, getting little sleep. Seeing Toby in the casket, hearing the pain in Abner's voice, speaking with others who had loved Toby had kept my mind spinning. Around three o'clock this morning, I'd stared out my bedroom window, across the treetops to Bailey's house. A light had been on, so I figured he'd been working on his book. I needed to talk to someone and would have welcomed Bailey's input, but for what I had in mind, there was really only one person who had the authority to hear my questions.

I threw caution to the wind and went to see Sid at the hospital. I arrived about a quarter till seven. The shifts were changing and the nursing station hummed with activity. From the deliveries yesterday, I knew Sid was in room 621. Since I didn't need directions, I breezed down the corridors as if I had every right to be there before visiting hours.

Sid's door was open. I peeked around the door frame. I wanted to save both him and me the embarrassment if he was perched on a bedpan. Thank goodness he was fully clothed and stood at the window. I rapped on the door.

Sid spoke without turning. "You're up bright and early, Bretta. I saw you get out of your vehicle and race across the parking lot. Even from the sixth floor, I could tell you were hell-bent on some mission. I hoped you had business in some other area of the hospital." He sighed and faced me. "But since you're knocking on my door, I guess I'm the lucky one."

Sid's skin was pasty white, but his eyes were clear and bright. I would have liked a more receptive welcome, but that would've been asking for too much. He'd undergone an appendectomy, not a personality transplant. I took heart from the fact that his tone was mild and he wasn't blustering. I gestured to the empty room. "Where are all your flowers?"

"I had the nurse take them to other patients. I can get out of here faster and with less fuss if I'm traveling light. They say the paperwork should be done by eleven o'clock. I'm ready now. My ride should be here at eight. I have things to do, and waiting for hospital personnel to get their act together isn't one of them." He waved me to a chair. "Sit if you want. I'm standing. My butt is sore from wallowing in bed."

"I'm surprised you're going home so soon."

Sid quickly set me straight. "I'm not going home. I'm going to work, but they don't have to know that. For all the hoopla I've been through, I have a couple of pitiful little laser holes in my belly and some nasty bruises on my arm where some inept witch couldn't find a vein. Hell, I've had worse pain. Grappling with that punk spraying graffiti on county bridges comes to mind. The little snot played dirty, scratching and clawing like a girl."

I ignored that sexist reference. "Last night at the visitation I discovered that Toby reversed his route on the day he died. Mr. Barker said Toby came into the bakery right after lunch instead of his usual time, which was later in the afternoon."

"Does that make a difference?"

"It might if people were used to him coming around at a

certain time, and he dropped by earlier than expected. Perhaps he saw something that got him into serious trouble."

"We checked his route for the day he died, but no one mentioned a change. I'll look into it. Anything else?"

"Mr. Barker said that when Toby came into the bakery, he was talking about a bowl of white worms." I proceeded to tell Sid the other "critter" stories Mr. Barker had related to me.

Sid wasn't impressed. "'Snips and snails and puppy dog tails.' Boys like creepy crawlers."

"I know that, but what if those white worms were maggots?"

Sid's upper lip curled. "That's too damned visual. I had rice for breakfast." He thought a second, then asked, "Where would Toby see such a thing?"

Those questions had kept me awake most of the night. Maggots suggested death and decay. But why a bowl? Were the maggots feeding on something in the bowl? How big was the bowl? Where had Toby been? I hadn't come up with any answers last night, which was why I'd come to Sid. I'd just worked up my courage to put my questions to him when the phone rang.

Sid picked it up. "Sheriff Hancock." He listened to the voice on the other end. "How bad is it?" He muttered under his breath. "Just left her house? Okay. I'll take over from this end. You stay there and go over everything with a magnifying glass. I mean it, Deputy. I don't like coincidences. This ties in. I don't give a rat's ass what anybody says. You stay there. Be on the alert for any corroborating evidence. Got it?"

Sid slammed down the phone. He was already on his way to the door when he enlightened me. "Leona Harper is being transported to the ER."

It took a couple of heartbeats to get me up to speed. By that time Sid was out the door. I hurried after him. He hustled down the corridor, holding his side. I caught up to him at the elevators. He poked the button for the ground floor.

I asked, "What's wrong with her?"

"She's unconscious."

The elevator dinged. The doors slid open, and we got on. Sid leaned weakly against the wall. His skin was the color of oatmeal. His hand shook as he made a quick swipe across his face. "I don't want questions, Bretta, so here's what I've got. Yvonne Pritchard tried to call Leona last night, but she didn't answer. Yvonne assumed Leona was still at the funeral home. Yvonne tried again this morning and still couldn't get an answer. No one picked up the phone at the dress shop, either. Apparently, Melba Cameron, Leona Harper, and Yvonne Pritchard have exchanged house keys. If for any reason one of the three is worried about the welfare of another, she can get inside the house. Yvonne was worried about Leona, so she used her key."

The elevator doors opened. Sid stepped out and headed for the ER. I loped along about a step behind him. I said, "Leona came by the flower shop yesterday afternoon. We visited about the people on Hawthorn Street. I learned from her that Abner has a gambling problem, and that Josh is about to lose his video store."

"Old news."

"You didn't bring any charges against Abner."

"Not at this time. Avery Wheeler is trying to decide if he wants to pursue a case of fraud, but with Toby dead, he's not thinking too hard on it."

"Do you have another suspect in mind?"

"What's in my mind isn't any of your business."

I frowned. "That hardly seems fair. You don't have any reservations when it comes to picking my brain."

Sid slowed and looked over his shoulder at me. "I asked for your help at Toby's house the other day and you stiffed me."

This man could aggravate me faster than anyone I knew. I could have pointed out that *he* had been the one who demanded that before I spoke, I had to be sure of my facts. Now, at his convenience, I was to spout every thought that zipped through my brain.

In a huff, I walked past Sid and pushed open the glass doors that shut the ER away from the rest of the hospital. The noise level was high, the lights brighter. The pace was hectic, and to my inexperienced eyes it seemed disorderly. Several people dressed in green scrubs scurried in and out of curtained enclosures.

Suddenly Sid snorted. "Nurses ought to be in white. Yesterday morning I woke up to a woman standing over me. She was wearing a Mickey Mouse-printed shirt. Hell, for a minute, I thought I was in the children's ward. Professionals should dress accordingly." He touched his blue shirt and sighed. "I miss my khaki." His hand rested briefly on his hip. "I miss my gun."

I rolled my eyes. "I doubt you'll need it."

"Don't matter. I still miss it."

"They're here," said a woman standing near the entrance.

The outer doors swooshed open, and two men rolled in a stretcher. Hospital personnel converged on the patient. My heart hammered as the drama played out not more than twenty feet from me. I heard snatches of conversation. Some of the medical terms I didn't understand, but I got enough to know that Leona's air passages were swollen. She was wheeled into a curtained cubicle and Sid and I moved closer. We kept out of the way, but when the blanket was removed from Leona, I heard a nurse gasp.

"Sweet mother of Jesus," she whispered.

For the blink of an eye, no one moved—except me. I maneuvered myself so that I had a quick glimpse. Leona was naked, her body as red as a rose and covered with oozing blisters. Her eyes were slits in a face that was bloated beyond recognition. Her lips were puffed out, exposing teeth in a macabre smile. The ER staff closed around her, shutting off my view.

A man with a stethoscope dangling around his neck turned, saw Sid, and strode purposefully toward us. I figured he was about to give us the boot, but he said, "I'm Dr. Emery. Are either of you family? This woman is having an allergic reaction to something. It would help to know her medical history."

"I'm Sheriff Hancock."

Dr. Emery turned to me. I shook my head. "I'm not family, but Leona told me that one time she almost died from an allergic reaction to poison ivy."

The doctor frowned. As he moved away, he muttered, "If that's the case, it looks as if she took a bath in it."

Bath? My eyes opened wide. "Sid," I said, "Leona received a gift of bubble bath yesterday. When she stopped at my shop, she was on her way home to bathe."

"Who gave it to her?"

"She thought it was from a customer named Mrs. Darby." I proceeded to tell him about the brown sack, bottle of bubble bath, and the bag of cinnamon disks. "Leona didn't see Mrs. Darby leave the package on the counter. She just assumed that's who it was from because the woman had given her gifts in the past."

Sid said, "I need a phone." He sprinted off.

I hung around the ER, but Sid didn't return. It didn't seem right to go off and leave Leona, so I went to the waiting room and sat down. I picked up a magazine and flipped the pages, but I didn't read a word.

My thoughts refused to leave that bottle of bubble bath. Leona hadn't known for a fact that Mrs. Darby was the one who'd left the bottle on the counter. She'd assumed it was Mrs. Darby, but what if it was someone else? Who knew she was allergic to poison ivy? And why target Leona? What did she know?

I switched gears. How would a person distill the poison? Boil it? Strain it? Mix it with store-bought bubble bath?

I had questions and I wanted answers. I didn't realize how antsy I was until Yvonne and Phillip arrived. I sprang to my feet, anxious to be on my way.

After Phillip had gotten Yvonne settled in a chair, he asked, "How's Leona?"

"There hasn't been any word yet."

He glanced at Yvonne. "I wanted to take her home, but she insisted on coming to the hospital. If she doesn't take care of herself, she'll be in a bed upstairs herself."

"I need to be here for Leona," was Yvonne's wobbly reply.

She was a basket case. Copious tears had reddened her eyes. The heavy folds of skin around her neck and face sagged. I touched her lightly on the shoulder. "I heard you found her."

Tears welled up and dribbled down her cheeks. "I wanted to check on her last night, but Phillip told me I was being neurotic. He said that just because Leona didn't answer her phone didn't mean something was wrong." Yvonne pressed her hands tightly together. "We had a pact, and I broke it."

"By not going over there last night?"

"No. No. Melba, Leona, and I swore that if one or the other of us had to be transported to the hospital, the one who found us had to make sure we were presentable. She was naked, and I couldn't make myself touch her. Her skin was covered with watery blisters the size of teacups."

Yvonne hung her head. "She's my best friend. She takes such pride in her appearance. When she finds out she rode to the hospital without a stitch on, she'll be mortified."

"She'll understand," I said.

Yvonne glared at me. "No she won't. Propriety was important to her. Looking good, dressing well, behaving in a manner suitable for a lady was how she lived her life. She would have made the effort to make me respectable."

Phillip sighed. "Yvonne, honey, it was more important that you called for assistance than whether Leona was dressed in her best bib and tucker."

"I don't agree," she said firmly, "but that's my opinion. And since I knew Leona better than either one of you, that's the end of this conversation."

That was my cue to leave.

FIFTEEN

It was almost nine o'clock when I passed Scent-Sational, Melba's candle shop. The "Closed" sign was still in the window. Worried, I decided to stop in and see if she was okay. Her shop was on the corner, so I turned down the side street off of Hawthorn and parked. I went to the front door and tried the knob. The door was locked. I peered in and saw a light in back. I rapped gently on the glass. No little figure bustled forward. I knocked louder. Still no one.

Concerned, I went around to the back of the building. Melba's alleyway was much narrower than the one that ran behind my flower shop. Her blue Ford was parked close to an old porch. The boards creaked and moaned as I mounted the steps. The door was covered with a piece of sheet metal. Again I knocked and waited. No answer. I tried the knob. The door swung open.

I stuck my head in and called, "Melba? It's Bretta Solomon. Are you okay?"

I listened intently but only heard a radio playing. Uneasily, I stepped inside. I was in her back storage room. The shelves were jam-packed with candles and bags of potpourri. They looked pretty sitting neatly in rows, but the sickeningly sweet odors blended together in an overpowering assault on my nose. Were these intense aromas masking something else entirely? I was thinking about Toby's bowl of white worms.

Had he seen maggots? Where? I felt sick to my stomach and blamed it on the oppressively heavy scent of the candles. Or was it my present situation that made my stomach churn?

"Melba?" I called again, and this time I heard the uncertainty in my voice.

Where was she? Why didn't she answer?

The hairs on my arm tingled. In a rising panic, I thought, *Maybe she can't.*

I got a grip on my imagination. *Think rationally,* I told myself. The music seemed to be coming from the basement. I walked quietly to the head of a staircase and started down.

Now I was reluctant to call out. I wanted to surprise—not be surprised. I descended another couple of steps, hunkering so I could see beneath the floor joists. Off to my left, I caught movement out of the corner of my eye. I turned in that direction and crept down another step. Gripping the rail tightly, I bent my knees so that I was almost sitting on the step behind me.

I had a clear view of an artist's studio. Melba was seated on a stool, her back to me. A portion of the canvas in front of her glistened with wet paint.

I almost laughed aloud with relief. Then I focused on the painting Melba was working on. There was no mistaking the setting. The background was a city with emerald green spires, towering among white, fleecy clouds. The Tin Woodsman, the Scarecrow, the Cowardly Lion, Toto, and Dorothy, were asleep among the red poppies. A young man sauntered down the yellow brick road, headed for the Emerald City. There was no question in my mind. The man was Toby. He was dressed in shorts and a T-shirt, the same as the last time I'd seen him alive.

I looked around the basement and saw stacks of canvases, but only a few were facing so I could view the subject. They were all scenes from *The Wizard of Oz,* but with a unique twist that I decided must be Melba's style.

Melba glanced at me over her shoulder. "I heard you calling my name, but I wasn't sure I wanted company." She turned her back to me. "I should have known you wouldn't go merrily on your way."

Hurt by her tone, I said, "I'll leave, now that I know you're okay." I turned to go, but stopped when she said, "I did this painting years ago, but I had a horse of a different color on the road. I decided last night that before I attended Toby's funeral, I had to paint him on the yellow brick road. It's easier to accept that he's gone if I can picture him like this—headed to the Emerald City. Maybe he'll finally get his wish."

"His wish?"

"To have a mother and a father and brothers and sisters. He wanted a family more than anything else in this world."

"Did Toby know you painted?"

"Of course. He helped me with some of my ideas. His mental capacities were limited in some areas, but in others he excelled." She got up and went across the room. "Take a look at this one. It was his idea to have the good witch, dressed in all her finery, have the face of a crone. While the bad witch in her pointy black hat and gloomy cape would be blond and beautiful."

I smiled. "It is a bit of a jolt seeing that glittery dress on a bent and ugly figure. I wonder how Toby came up with that idea."

"He said it would confuse the witches. If the bad witch looked nice, she might change into a good witch."

"But then the good witch could change into the bad one."

Melba laughed. "Toby didn't reason things out that way or that well. I never told him, but I figured that without his realizing it, he'd made the discovery that just because a person looked nice, it didn't necessarily mean they were kind."

"Interesting. Are there other paintings that he helped you with?"

She shuffled through a stack and pulled out another. "I only finished this painting the day Toby died. I don't care for it, but Toby thought it was wonderful. He wanted it for his room, but I don't let any of my paintings leave this basement. I do them for my own enjoyment. They relax me. I've been captivated by the Oz movie for years, but it was always too much happy ending for my taste. Toby knew what I wanted and seemed comfortable making suggestions."

She turned the picture around so I could see it. I caught my breath at the scene. It was the one where Dorothy and her gang are in the haunted forest and are being hunted by the flying monkeys. Only in this rendition giant spiders had replaced the monkeys.

"Why spiders?" I asked.

Melba shook her head. "I don't have a clue. Toby said that it made more sense for a spider to drop a net. Monkeys don't have nets, but spiders spin webs. He wanted me to paint the picture so that Dorothy and her friends go free, and the spiders team up on the witch, weaving her into a cocoon." Melba sighed. "I told Toby that wasn't the way I worked. It's a rule of mine that I have to stay within the story line. Dorothy has to go to the witch's tower so the hourglass can run out."

"Did Toby understand that?"

"I'm not sure. He said that bad things happen in towers. Spiders need to win. Need to be free." Melba shook her head. "He didn't always make sense, but then neither do the things that happen in life." Her shoulders slumped. "I assume you know about Leona."

I nodded. "I was at the hospital when they brought her in."

She looked up at me with teary eyes. "It's bad, isn't it?"

Again I nodded.

"I thought so. From the way Yvonne described Leona's condition, it didn't sound good. Yvonne was upset because she couldn't make herself dress Leona before the paramedics arrived. We had a pact, you know."

"I spoke with Yvonne, but in this case I think it was best that Yvonne left Leona alone. The skin eruptions covered her entire body. She'd had an allergic reaction to some bubble bath."

"Bubble bath?" repeated Melba, cocking her head. "That's odd. Leona loved using every kind of body lotion, cream, and oil that was on the market. I've never known her to have a reaction to any of them. The only time she had a problem was when she pulled some poison ivy from her garden. She puffed up like a toad."

"I'm wondering about that bottle of bubble bath. Leona thought a customer left it on the counter. What if it wasn't soap? What if someone put something in it that would cause Leona serious problems?"

Melba stared at me in disbelief. Finally, she pulled herself together. "Bretta, do you think this was intentional? Like the hornets in Toby's house?"

"It's possible. If we go on that assumption, then the next obvious question is, why harm Leona? What did she know?"

"I can't imagine she knew anything more than either Yvonne or I. We pooled our information." She stared up at me. "In fact, what we know, you know, too. We put everything in our notes to you."

I wanted to disagree. Leona had strolled into my flower shop with all sorts of information that hadn't been mentioned in the notes. I kept my opinion to myself. Melba was visibly upset. Trying to put her at ease, I said, "Let's not worry about this now. The sheriff is checking on everything and everyone. He'll get to the bottom of whatever is going on." She nodded, but I could see she wasn't comforted.

Melba walked around me and sat back down on her stool. "I couldn't sleep after Yvonne called, so I dressed and came here. I didn't plan to open my shop today because of Toby's funeral this afternoon. I was going to unpack some new merchandise, but I came down here instead."

She turned to stare at the painting she'd been working on. In a quiet tone, she said, "In my mind's eye, I could see Toby on the yellow brick road just as plain as day." She rubbed a hand across her brow. "But now when I look at the canvas, I see Leona at his side." She took a quivering breath. "They're walking hand in hand."

HEAVY OF HEART, I pulled into the alley behind the flower shop. Josh was unlocking the door to his video store. He glanced over his shoulder, saw me, and fumbled faster with the key. Anger replaced my sorrow. I leaped out of my SUV and called to him, "Josh, I want to talk to you."

He didn't acknowledge me. He wrenched open the door and hurried across the threshold. When he reached behind him to pull the door shut, I was there. He jerked back in surprise. "Oh, hi, Bretta," he said nervously. "Can't talk now. I have work to do."

I pushed past him, dodging empty boxes and wads of packing material. "Go ahead and work," I said. "I'll just follow you around, asking my questions, waiting for your answers."

Josh flipped a light switch. A single bulb, dangling from a cord, flashed its low wattage on the room. I'd never seen such squalor. Besides the boxes, there were overflowing trash cans. Four plastic five-gallon buckets were filled with empty soda cans. Flies buzzed in the air. The smell was disgusting. Peering through the gloom, I looked for a bowl that might contain the white worms. If that bowl existed, it didn't stretch my imagination one iota to think that it could be here.

"You don't give up, do you?" said Josh.

"Not usually."

"Fine," he grumbled. "Ask your questions."

"Were you ripping off Toby?"

Josh's chin came up. "That's unfair, Bretta. I would never—"

"Hurt Toby because you owed it to his mother, Agnes, to protect her son." I stared at Josh. "Is that what you were going to say?"

"No. Like I told you the other day, I never met Agnes."

"So how did you and Toby become friends?"

"It was after Agnes died. I was sweeping off the sidewalk and Toby came by on his bike. I told him I'd pay him to wash my windows, but he said I wasn't on his list. I told him he could make more money by enlarging his customer base. After I'd explained my comment, he washed the windows. When he came in to get paid, he was mesmerized by the video I had playing. We had a conversation. I learned he didn't own a television. He didn't know what a video was. He didn't know about VHS players."

"So you enlightened him?"

"Sure. What was the harm? I saw him as a potential customer."

"All right. I assume you set him up with a television and all the equipment he'd need to view the movies he rented from you."

"That's right. He wouldn't go to the electronics store. Said it wasn't on his list. I bought everything and hooked it up in his bedroom. He didn't want it in the living room. I can't say I blamed him." He gave me a quick glance. "You ever been in Toby's house?"

I nodded.

Josh seemed surprised. "Really?" He thought a minute, then said, "But only after Toby died."

"That's right. I saw Toby's bedroom with the *two* televisions. Whose idea was that?"

Josh shrugged. "Here at the store I showed Toby how much clearer and more realistic the pictures are on a DVD. He was ready to update his equipment, but I told him that some of the movies he liked to watch hadn't been released on disc. Toby and I talked it over, and he made the decision to have two televisions. I went shopping again."

"How much over the cost of the items did you pocket?"

Josh bristled. "I told Toby I needed something for my time. He understood that, and he paid up—willingly, I might add."

"Let's talk about the fast food. How did that come about?"

"His mama was a strict woman. Toby had never tasted pizza or drunk a Coke in his life. I couldn't see the harm in treating him to some fat and cholesterol and a few empty calories." Josh grinned. "I'll never forget the look on his face when he took his first bite of pizza. His eyes lit up, and he laughed out loud. He was hooked. From that moment on, he was a junk-food junkie."

My tone was dry. "And you were only too happy to feed his addiction?"

Josh scowled. "You make it sound like I lured him onto drugs. What was the harm? He was happy."

"And you made money?"

Josh shrugged. "Some."

"How much did you charge him for a pizza?"

He hedged his answer. "It varied depending on which kind he wanted."

I persisted. "How much did you charge him, Josh?"

He squirmed, but finally admitted, "Twice the price I paid plus delivery."

I was shocked. "Good heavens. You're as bad as Abner."

Josh's chin came up. "I don't see it that way."

"Of course not. You were lining your own pockets."

"It was business. Don't you have a delivery charge when you take flowers out of town? How much is your markup on the merchandise you sell?"

"That's beside the point."

"No it isn't. Toby knew I was making money, but he didn't care. He wanted out of the protective bubble his mother had put him in. He wanted to experience what other people had. He only rented family movies. He would sit for hours and watch stories that had to do with a mother and a father and kids. He wanted to be part of that scene. I couldn't help him with that, but I could round out his life in other areas. His mother had drilled it into him never to set foot in a fast-food restaurant. She had drilled it into him never to watch television. Before she died, she made out nutritious menus, but it was the same old humdrum stuff he'd been eating all his life."

Josh stopped and wiped a hand across his face. "Look, Bretta, I don't mean to pass judgment on Agnes. She probably meant well, but once she was gone, Toby needed more in his life. She expected him to be content to associate only with the people on her approved list. I wasn't on that list, but I brought something to Toby's life that none of the rest of you did."

On this subject, Josh was more confident. He straightened his shoulders and met my gaze unflinchingly. "What do you think he did the last few years for Thanksgiving and Christmas? He was with me. My family is back East. Toby and I were alone, but together we were a family. He was like a brother to me."

"But you took advantage of him."

Josh's smile was sad. "That's your opinion. I don't see it that way, but more important, neither did Toby."

"Who put the hornets in Toby's bedroom?"

"I don't know."

"If you and Toby were as close as you say, surely he said something that would give you a clue."

Josh shook his head. "I've thought and thought, but nothing comes to mind except those flowers that were chopped off in the garden. He told me you were coming to his house the next day. I was busy and blew him off. I was working the store alone. Two of my employees didn't show up. I told him I had more important worries than a bunch of missing flowers."

"How did Toby take that?"

Josh's shoulders sagged. "He was hurt. He left without

saying good-bye. Maybe if I'd spent time with him, I'd have learned more, but I didn't." Josh breathed in deeply and let it out in a mournful sigh. "He might have confided in me, but I didn't give him the chance."

"If he told you I was coming by his house the next day, then he must have come directly to your store after he left mine."

"I suppose."

"Do you know if that was his usual route?"

"I guess. He came by every day because he rented lots of movies. Do you think his route was important?"

"Mr. Barker says that on the day Toby died, Toby told him he had reversed his route. Do you know why he would do that?"

"Not really, unless he wanted to see someone who's usually last on his route."

"Who would that be?"

Josh didn't hesitate. "That would be Yvonne. He always stopped off there before he went home."

I didn't try to hide my disappointment. I'd hoped for another name—any name that would keep this line of inquiry open. But Josh's answer had stalled me. I already knew Toby had stopped by Yvonne's on the morning of the day he died. While waiting at the hospital for news of Toby's condition, Phillip had told us about the incident with the wet varnish. Yvonne said Phillip had yelled at Toby. I had no doubt that Phillip was capable of reprimanding Toby in a harsh manner. But where did the white worms fit in?

Josh glanced impatiently at his watch. "Look, I have things to do before I open."

I told Josh good-bye and advised him that it would be in his best interests to have a candid chat with the sheriff about his business dealings with Toby. Josh didn't take to the idea. I didn't repeat my suggestion. I walked out of his storage room and crossed over to the flower shop.

When I stepped inside, I looked around. Everything was tidy. The vases were lined up on the shelf. Extra boxes of supplies were stacked within easy reach. Trash had been set out for pickup. This was the way a back room should look.

I stepped into the workroom, where all was quiet. Lois was fussing with a basket and Lew was hanging up the phone. "What's going on?" I asked.

Lew said, "I just took an order for a fall bouquet. They want it delivered later this afternoon."

"Give the order to me," I said. "I'll make it." I glanced at Lois. "Thanks for opening up. I went by the hospital to talk to Sid and got sidetracked. I've got so much to tell you guys, I don't know where to begin."

Lois said, "Before you get started, take a look at this." She gestured to the basket. "I found it outside the back door. We must be doing something right. Some kind and thoughtful soul left us a thank-you gift. It's really neat. All sorts of stuff." She held up a bottle. "This is an aloe lotion for dry, chapped hands. I can't wait to try it. My hands look and feel like sandpaper."

A vision of Leona's abused skin flashed in my mind. I shouted, "Lois, put that bottle down. Drop it now!"

SIXTEEN

STARTLED BY MY HARSH tone, Lois followed my command and dropped the bottle. It hit the edge of the basket, which tipped over, scattering the contents across the table. She frowned at me. "You scared me spitless. Look at what you made me do."

She reached to set everything right, but I said, "Don't touch any of that stuff until Sid gets here."

Lois drew back. "Why? What's going on?"

"I'll tell you in a minute. First wash your hands and use plenty of soap—our soap. You, too, Lew, if you touched that basket."

Lew shook his head. "I looked, but I didn't handle any of it. I wasn't interested. There's shaving lotion among the items, but it isn't my brand."

Lois went to the sink and lathered up. "I'm washing. Now will you tell us what's going on?"

"First I have to get Sid over here. I doubt there will be fingerprints," I said as I moved to the phone. "In fact, I could be blowing this out of proportion, but I'm not taking any chances."

Lew and Lois stared at me as if I was talking gibberish. From their standpoint, I probably wasn't making much sense. I could be wrong, but it was too much of a coincidence. Yesterday, Leona had found a gift on her counter. Today, Lois had found a gift at our back door. Leona was fighting for her life.

The paralleling of events would stop here if I had anything to do with it.

I put through the call to Sid. When he came on the line, all I said was, "Lois found a basket of toiletries at our back door. No card." His response, "I'll be right there," made me breathe easier. It was a pleasant change not to have to beg and plead before Sid took me seriously about one of my assumptions.

I hung up. "He's on his way," I said, turning to find Lew and Lois watching me in wide-eyed wonderment.

Lew asked, "That's all you had to say and the sheriff is on his way over here?"

"He knows this basket could be important."

Lois finished drying her hands and flung the paper towel in the trash. "It's a basket of goodies. Did I miss something?"

"Lots," I said. I filled them in on my morning. After I'd described the condition of Leona's skin, Lois went back to the sink and lathered up again. Over her shoulder she asked, "What do you think was in that bottle of bubble bath?"

I shrugged. "Since Leona said she was highly allergic to poison ivy, I'm leaning in that direction."

Lois looked at me. "How bad is your reaction when you come in contact with the vine?"

"I get a rash, some itching, but nothing like Leona."

Lew snorted. "That's because you've never bathed in it. Imagine a tub full of hot water, and the air is warm and steamy. Your pores are wide open, primed and ready to absorb the emollients from the contents of the bottle you've just dumped into the water. If I remember right, Leona said the fragrance was freesia. So add the fact that the air was also sweetly perfumed. She wanted a relaxing bath, so she lingered"—he paused and gave us a knowing look—"soaking and scrubbing her more sensitive areas as she reclined in the poisoned water."

He'd conjured up a horrible picture. I rubbed my arms. An itch developed between my shoulder blades. I twitched, trying to make it go away. I told myself it was nerves, a case of sympathy prickles. It's like when someone talks about mites or lice or fleas. You immediately feel them crawling across your skin.

To take my mind off my phantom itching, I eyed the bottles on the table. The "gift" had been attractively presented in a wicker basket. The bottles were assorted sizes and had been nestled together with iridescent shredded cellophane. A bow, like the kind sold at discount stores, was stuck to the handle.

"What I don't understand," said Lois, drying her hands once again, "is, how do you get poison ivy into a bottle?"

"We don't know that it was poison ivy," said Lew.

Lois glared at him. "But *if* it was, how do you process it? The plant is very toxic. I've read that you shouldn't even burn it. If the smoke gets in your eyes or nasal passages, you've got some serious medical problems."

Before Lew or I could offer an opinion, Sid blew in the front door. Behind him was one of his female deputies, Donna Meyer. Officer Meyer had been on staff with my husband. I was pleased to see her and offered her a warm greeting before turning to Sid.

He wasn't wasting any time. He came around the front counter to the worktable where he eyed the bottles, changing his positions so he could read labels without making contact.

"Body lotion. Shaving lotion. Hand cream. Bubble bath. These are all different scents from the one that was found in Leona's bathroom. Hers was called freesia. Whatever the hell that is." He leaned closer. "These say they contain aloe." He looked at me. "Isn't that the name of the plant that you slice a leaf off and apply the slimy edge to a sunburn?"

"That's right. It has medicinal properties. Makes your skin feel cool and—" I stopped, thought a second, then said, "What if these aloe products were chosen because they're known for soothing skin irritations?" I shook my head in disbelief. "It's almost as if this person is flaunting what was done to Leona."

Sid made a face. "Forget the psychoanalysis. I have work to do. Deputy, get this stuff tagged and bagged. I want it out to Monroe on the double."

"Monroe?" I said. "As in Bailey Monroe?"

"Yeah. I called him. I need the contents of these bottles and the one found in Leona's bathroom tested. I can transport everything to St. Louis, but I'd go on a waiting list. I don't have that kind of patience."

I was amazed and just a tad proud that Sid had called on Bailey. Deputy Meyer finished with the bottles. She and Sid stepped over to the side of the room and had a quick chat. Deputy Meyer left, and Sid came back to the worktable.

I asked, "So what is Bailey going to do to help?"

"He's taking the evidence to St. Louis, where he has contacts. One of his high-powered friends has agreed to do a rush job."

I grinned. "I'm impressed."

Sid snorted. "Get over it. I want to know, who found this basket?"

Lois raised her hand. "That would be me."

Sid said, "Give me a quick rundown, then I'll ask questions."

Lois said, "Okay," then launched into her story. "I found the basket at the back door this morning when I arrived for work.

I carried it in. There wasn't a card, but I assumed it was a thank-you for some job we'd done. I brought it in here, put it on the table, and went up front to unlock the door. While I was turning on the lights, Lew arrived. I told him about the basket. He glanced at it, and said the shaving lotion wasn't his brand. The phone rang. He answered it. I went back to the basket and picked up the hand lotion. I was reading the label when Bretta came in. I told her what I'd found. She screamed at me to drop the bottle. I did. It hit the rim of the basket and the whole thing fell over. She told me to leave it alone and to wash my hands. I've done so—twice. She called you. That's it."

Sid stared at Lois for a long, drawn-out moment. Finally he said, "Good God, woman. Take a breath."

Lois breathed in and out deeply. "Thanks," she said. "I was feeling kind of light-headed."

"I'm not surprised, rambling on and on like that."

Lois frowned. "I wasn't rambling. I was doing like you asked. I was giving you a quick rundown."

Sid nodded. "That's appreciated, but you did it so damned fast, I've got to stop and review what you said."

"You want me to start over?" asked Lois.

"No," grumbled Sid. "I think I've got it. The main point is that none of you has a clue as to who put that basket by the back door. Do I have that right?"

We nodded.

Sid turned to Lew. "You aren't holding out on me again, are you?"

Lew drew himself up and held his head high. "I know nothing more than what Lois has told you."

"Good," said Sid, and then he scowled. "Hell no. It's not good. It's damned frustrating."

I said, "Before you came in, we were discussing how to get the poison out of the plant. Do you know how it's done?"

"According to Monroe's expert, the sap is extracted by using a cold press, which works just as the name implies. No heat is used in the process. Our perp simply ground away at the raw plant fibers and strained the sap. We're assuming the toxin was added to the bottle of bubble bath. It's a nasty concoction when you add the fact that the recipient was highly susceptible."

Sid's radio squawked to life. He stepped away from us and carried on a short conversation. When he came back to the table, his face was grim. "Forget what I said about that bottle being a nasty concoction. It was a deadly mix. Eight minutes ago, Leona Harper died."

SEVENTEEN

WITH ANOTHER FUNERAL LOOMING on the horizon, I had flowers to order. I took a pad of paper and a pencil and went to the walk-in cooler in back to check on what I had in stock. Flowers are best kept at a holding temperature of thirty-four to thirty-six degrees. It was cold, but I was hot. Hot with anger, flushed with outrage that someone I knew was so devious, so without conscience that they could set Leona up for such a cruel death. She had prided herself on her looks. She'd taken care of her skin, using creams and oils. She'd been a businesswoman, conducting herself with honesty and integrity.

She talked too much, said the voice in my head.

Leona's tendency to chatter was probably the reason she'd become the killer's target. Had she died knowing something that had placed her in jeopardy? Or had she already spilled the beans and none of us recognized the importance of what she'd said?

Since I was gearing up for a woman's service, I made a note to order pink roses, stargazer lilies, blue iris, golden solidago, calla lilies, lavender gladiolus, and hot pink gerbera daisies.

The cold seeped into my bones, but still I lingered, trying to make sense of the information that had come my way. If the bottles of toiletries that had been left at my back door contained something toxic, then the killer must have felt that

Leona had given me some morsel of wisdom that might clue me in. What could it be?

To my growing list of cut flowers, I added baby's breath, caspia, purple waxflower, and some asparagus fern.

I stared off into space, replaying the conversation we'd had. Leona had reduced everyone's life to a neat and concise little package. She'd done it so seamlessly that I had to believe she'd said those same words to others. What word or phrase had provoked a murderous response?

Leona had said she'd witnessed Diana flirting with Toby. Phillip had misused a company's grant money, but he'd been reprimanded by being fired. I'd found out why Josh spent so much time at fast-food restaurants. Leona had said that something had bothered her about Agnes and her job at the pharmacy. I thought hard, but I couldn't remember what she'd said.

My teeth were clenched against the cold. It was time to move on. I stepped out of the cooler and came face-to-face with Lois.

"If you're going to set up camp in there," she said, "you'll need this." She held out a sweater.

I waved it away. "I'm fine, but thanks. At first the cold felt good, but now I'm chilled."

As we walked back to the workroom, Lois said, "Lew and I figured you needed a quiet place to do some heavy-duty thinking. Did you come up with anything?"

I shrugged. "Just that Leona liked to talk. You heard her, Lois. Did she say anything that might give us a clue as to who's behind this?"

"If she did, I didn't pick up on it."

Lew said, "The time element seems like it should be significant."

"In what way?" I asked.

"Who has time to go out in the woods and scout around for a hornet's nest? Or for that matter, collect enough poison-ivy vine to get enough sap from this cold-press method Sid mentioned."

Lois said, "It's not just the time. The act itself is insidious. What kind of person dreams up putting poison-ivy extract in bubble bath? It's so simple, and yet horrifying. When I found the basket by the back door, I figured it was the banker's wife thanking us for the fabulous job we did on the 'lighthouse extravaganza.'"

Lighthouse? I frowned. That word conjured up a feeling of something left undone or unresolved.

Lew interrupted my thoughts. "Bretta, we made a decision while you were 'cooling' your heels."

I made a face at his lame attempt at humor. "And what would that be?"

"Lois and I are going to stay here instead of attending Toby's funeral service. It's raining, but more important, since Leona has passed away, we figure we'll be busy this afternoon."

Rain? I glanced at the front window. Big, fat raindrops splattered against the plate glass. "Great," I muttered. "Just great." I sat down at my workstation. Propping my chin up with an elbow on the table, I sighed. "You're probably right. I'm sure some of the businesses along Hawthorn Street will be closed. I could do that, but life goes on. Since both of you have this place covered, I'm going home. I didn't bring a change of clothes with me, and I don't have an umbrella. I was in too much of a hurry to get to the hospital this morning to talk to Sid."

Lois chuckled. "That's not the way I'd want to start the day."

I would have come to Sid's defense, but to my surprise Lew beat me to it. "He's not so bad." Lew's face reddened. "What I mean is, he could have ripped into me, but he listened, asked some questions, and then thanked me for coming forward."

"Sid thanked *you?*" said Lois in wide-eyed wonder. "He must have been tripping on a morphine drip."

Lew shot her a sharp glare. "He was on pain medication, but he was rational. He understood what I told him and responded like a professional. In a calm, reasonable manner he reprimanded me for not going to him sooner."

Lois snickered. "Sid might have behaved like a professional, but he won't forget. He'll keep digging at you like he did earlier when he asked if you were holding out on him— again."

"You're going to bring up this subject over and over, aren't you?"

A customer came in the front door. Lois went forward to help the woman, but before she rounded the front counter, she looked back over her shoulder. "If it suits my purposes," she said.

Lew grumbled, "That woman is the most—"

The phone rang. I waited for Lew to pick it up. When he grabbed an order form, I knew it was flower shop business. I took advantage of the opportunity and headed out the back door.

By the time I unlocked my SUV, I was soaked. I put the vehicle in motion, switching on the windshield wipers. Rain filled the gutters and dumped in abundance on asphalt. With nowhere to go, the water pooled in low spots, creating miniature lakes and streams. Lightning flashed in the distance. I counted the seconds. The thunder rumbled at seven. According to folklore, that was supposed to mean the main part of the storm was seven miles away. I grimaced. My surround-

ings didn't corroborate that old prophecy. Rain was falling as
if it was being poured out of a bucket.

Passage on Hawthorn moved at a crawl. I figured if I kept
my eyes on the car in front of me, I could safely let my mind
wander. Since today was Toby's funeral service, it seemed
only appropriate that I use this unexpected downtime to think
about him. I didn't want to shuffle among the facts connected
with his murder. I wanted to remember his sweet nature. The
naive way he had of looking at ordinary events and other
things.

On the day of his death, he'd been fit and healthy. Lois had
asked if he'd been working out. I grinned when I recalled
Toby's response. He'd stuck out a tanned leg and said it was
as "strong as a spider's web."

I sped up as the car in front of me made a right-hand turn.
Closing the gap, I pondered Toby's odd remark. It was strange
that he'd use a spider's web as a comparison to something as
strong as a leg muscle. And yet, according to Lew, Toby's
comparison was quite accurate.

The rain was letting up and traffic was moving more
quickly. I concentrated on my driving, squeezing through a
couple of yellow lights and finally making a left-hand turn
onto Chestnut.

Now that I was out of heavy traffic and on the road home,
I resumed my thoughts, but quickly made a face. Forget the
spiders. Think about Toby. But the first thing that came to
mind was Melba's painting of the giant spiders dropping nets
on Dorothy in the haunted forest. The painting had been a
creepy rendition of a scene I'd never liked in the movie.

I turned into my driveway and idled up the lane. I was
weary and glad to be home, even if it was only for a short

time. I wondered how Toby felt when he came home. Did he dread going into the house? Or was he excited to have movies to watch? I wondered what kind of mood he was in when he got home the day he died. Lew had watched Toby park his bike on the porch and enter the house. I hadn't thought to ask Lew if Toby had seemed upset. But I could remedy that with a phone call.

I pulled into my garage with a flourish and hurried into the house. As always, good smells welcomed me. I sniffed as I made my way to the kitchen. DeeDee had her back to me, her gaze on the television set in the corner.

"Hi," I said, going directly to the phone.

DeeDee jumped. "Bretta. You scared me. My mind was on the t-trinity."

I glanced at the TV screen. No surprise there. The set was tuned to a cooking show. Curious, I asked, "What does a trinity have to do with cooking?"

DeeDee grinned. "Everything." She held up a finger. "One is onion. Two is c-celery, and the th-third is g-green pepper." She glanced at the television screen and then back at me. "I'm no e-expert, but I think there should be f-four because nothing says flavor like a h-hunk of garlic s-sautéed in olive oil."

"In my book you *are* an expert, sweetie." I matched her grin with one of my own. Pointing to the hot pan on the stove, I said, "Carry on. I have to make a phone call before I dress for Toby's funeral."

DeeDee nodded soberly. "It's a dreary day for such a s-sad occasion. Don't forget to t-take an umbrella."

I agreed and lifted the receiver from its resting pad. I touched the familiar numbers and after a couple of rings, Lew picked up. In a highly professional voice, he announced, "The Flower Shop. You're speaking with Lew. How can I assist you?"

I rolled my eyes. "Hi," I said. "It's Bretta. You're just the person I need to talk to."

The professionalism disappeared. In a dull, flat tone, Lew muttered, "Oh. What's wrong now?"

"Nothing is wrong," I stressed impatiently. "I want to know how Toby acted when he arrived home the other evening."

"We're kind of busy here. Is this important?"

My tone sharpened. "Lew, the faster you answer, the quicker you can get back to whatever it is you need to do."

"I don't know. He shuffled along, parked his bike on the porch, then went inside his house."

"Shuffled along? Like he was sad? Upset? What?"

Lew sighed. "If I had to guess, which I do, I'd say he was lost in thought. He didn't act as if he was aware of his surroundings. He parked his bike and went into the house. He didn't look around. He didn't display any passionate emotion. He didn't make any wild declaration. He simply unlocked the door and went inside. Is that it? The other line is ringing, and Lois is up front waiting on a customer."

"Fine. 'Bye." I hung up. That phone call had netted me nothing unless I counted the aggravation. One of these days, Lew was going to push too hard and I'd fire him on the spot. I didn't want to look for a new employee, but he was—

"—worried about Bailey."

I turned to DeeDee. "I'm sorry," I said. "My mind was on something else. What did you say?"

Her face was flushed. I assumed it was from the heat of the stove, but her first words let me know that wasn't the case.

"Your m-mind is always on everything except B-Bailey. I'm w-worried about him. I was outside a while ago, and I saw h-him leave the cottage. He h-had a s-suitcase."

I smiled reassuringly. "Bailey is fine. Sid has asked him to help with the investigation by taking some evidence to an agent friend in St. Louis."

"W-What about his b-book?"

"He's still working on it, but he's taking a breather. I think deep down he misses being a federal agent. I haven't talked to him since Sid asked for his help, but I imagine Bailey jumped at the chance to zip off to St. Louis for some male bonding with his buddies." DeeDee still looked unconvinced. So I tried harder, putting a positive note in my voice. "He needs a break. He's been working very hard on his book."

I smiled to myself as I remembered him reenacting the search-and-seizure scenario so he could get into the "moment." Patting DeeDee on the shoulder, I said, "Bailey is fine. Our relationship is progressing. We don't have to spend every minute together. We each need our space. Don't worry so much."

DeeDee still didn't look convinced, but enough had been said on the subject. I left the kitchen headed for the main staircase and my bedroom.

As I crossed the foyer, my father stuck his head out the library doorway. "I thought I heard you, daughter," he said. "Come in here for a moment, if you have time."

I glanced at my watch. "Okay, but I have to dress and drive back to town for Toby's funeral."

"I know, but this will only take a few minutes."

When I entered the library, Abigail looked up from a spiral-bound book of paint samples. When I saw what was in her hands, I shook my head. "I'm not in the mood to make color choices."

"That's not why I asked you to join us," said my father. "Abby has been doing some research on the blends Phillip used in that fabric we glimpsed last Sunday at his workshop. We think we've got a likely candidate."

I relaxed. No decisions to make. No wondering if I'd blurt out something that would cause another rift between Abigail and myself. I smiled at her. "So you've narrowed it down. Good job. It seems we have more in common than I thought."

Her happy smile shriveled to a tentative twist of her lips. "What does that mean?" she asked.

Again I'd said the wrong thing, and again, I didn't know what it was. "I just meant that we both like a mystery. We're curious. We like to unearth the truth."

My father's laughter sounded forced, and he seemed nervous. "Yes, well, we—uh—why don't you tell Bretta what you think Phillip used to make that fabulous fabric."

Abigail cleared her throat. Her face was flushed with color, but her tone was positive. "Since I had my fingers on the material so briefly, I've had to rely on what Albert saw, too."

My father said, "It was exceptional, but then I'm not the authority Abby is. She's shown me different fabric swatches but, while several had similarities to Phillip's, none was what I'd consider a match." He winked at me. "That is, until a friend sent her some new blends that are being explored."

Abigail took up the tale. "Deanna has been an interior decorator for many years. She's older and more experienced. When I described what we'd seen, she said it sounded like a kenaf blend."

Kenaf? I'd never heard of it, and I wasn't sure that it

mattered. But to keep everyone happy, I said, "Really?," in a tone I hoped conveyed the correct mixture of curiosity and interest.

Abigail nodded. "It's exciting that modern technology is giving a second life to old tradition. I've been doing some research on the textile industry and the information is amazing. In the 1580s, Spanish galleons took pineapple plants to the Philippines. The variety had larger leaves than the ones grown today. The natives stripped the leaves down to the fibers and spun the threads into a soft fabric that had more texture than silk and was much cheaper to produce."

Confused, I asked, "So Phillip's cloth is made from pineapple leaves?"

Abigail shook her head. "No, I'm just giving you some background. Piña cloth comes from pineapple leaves. Abaca is a fabric made from the fibers of a plant that's related to the banana. Henequen is derived from the agave and is used to make rope and binder twine. Coir is the prepared fiber from the husk of the coconut." She sighed. "Isn't it fascinating? Wouldn't you love to see these textiles manufactured?"

I shrugged. "Since it takes a tropical climate to grow the plants you've mentioned, then yes, I'd like to go to some warm, stress-free island and have nothing better to do than watch plants become fabric." I tapped the face of my wristwatch. "But right now the seconds are ticking away."

Abigail frowned. "Fine. Kenaf is native to Africa and yields beautiful fibers that are strong and resist mildew and rotting. Because it can be mass-produced here in the United States, it is economically competitive with cotton. The kenaf fibers by themselves yield a naturally strong fiber that is popular for making rope, but once it's blended with another plant tissue, its commercial viability is endless. The plant is a relative of the okra plant."

"Okra?" I said. "Well, that's fairly common and easy to grow."

Abigail nodded. "Exactly. Okra is part of the mallow family."

I'd been inching toward the door, but stopped. That piece of information struck a chord. "Mallow?" I said. My heart was beating faster. I knew enough botany to recognize that classification. "You said your friend sent you a swatch of this kenaf material. I'd like to see it."

Abigail turned and picked up a square of fabric that was about a foot across. "This isn't exactly like Phillip's work because I'm sure he used a different blend of fibers to achieve the shimmering quality we saw in his cloth. I won't be able to isolate those blends until I see the material again." Abigail chuckled softly. "Now that I have the background and can talk intelligently on the subject, I'm hoping to initiate a conversation and charm the information from him."

I ran my hand over the nubby fabric and tried to corral my excitement. Keeping my tone steady, I said, "The plants in the mallow family typically have large, showy blooms. If I remember right, the genus *Malva* includes the hollyhock, the rose mallow, the marsh mallow, cotton, and, as you mentioned, okra. But there's one more plant that is fairly common and is a member of this same genus."

Abigail opened her mouth to supply the answer, but I wanted to be the first to say the word.

"Hibiscus," I blurted out. Then in a shaky voice I proceeded to piece the information together. "Kenaf is grown for its fiber. We don't have kenaf plants in this area, but our climate will allow hibiscus, which is a cousin of the kenaf plant, to grow. It stands to reason that the hibiscus could produce fibers that, when processed, might be woven into a piece of cloth like the one we saw at Phillip's workshop."

Abigail nodded. "I can't be absolutely positive, but I'm sure beyond a reasonable doubt. I'm hoping that over the next few weeks, I can gain his trust. I'll have to see him quite often as I pick up and drop off the pieces of furniture we want him to refinish. If I can convince him, I want to showcase his fabrics in several of the bedrooms upstairs." Her eyes sparkled with excitement. "Wouldn't that be fabulous?"

Fabulous wasn't the word I was thinking of. *Murderous* was more the case. But where was the motive for Toby's murder? Why steal the hibiscus plants? Toby was more than willing to trade his time or his groceries for money. If Phillip wanted the hibiscus, why hadn't he offered to buy them? The only thing I could figure out was that he didn't want anyone, even Toby, to know that he was interested in the plants. But why? What was so important about Toby's hibiscus plants?

All these questions were driving me crazy. I needed answers. Toby's funeral service was a formality—the final good-bye to a very special man. I needed to be there. I wanted to be there, but my final gift to Toby's memory *could* be the apprehension of his killer.

In the blink of an eye, my mind was made up. While all the suspects were attending Toby's service, I had some serious investigating to do. Toby's garden and the hibiscus topped my list.

EIGHTEEN

"THIS WASN'T MY IDEA," said Abigail from the passenger seat of my SUV. "But I'm looking forward to seeing the hibiscus."

My tone was cool. "I know whose idea it was, and it's not necessary. Regardless of what my father thinks, I don't need a companion."

Abigail chuckled. "Back home he's known as the Missouri mule."

"Back home?"

Abigail grew still. "Where Albert used to live. He's told me stories about having to—uh—draw on his Missouri heritage when it came to getting his way, especially in business dealings."

"This really doesn't concern him, or you, for that matter." I glanced at Abigail. She was hardly dressed for a trek through Toby's garden. Her thin cotton shirt and lightweight slacks would offer little protection against the cold rain and the wilderness of plants. I'd seen this even if she and my father had refused to face facts. With wasted minutes ticking by, I'd given in. I'd grabbed an old denim jacket from the closet and handed it to Abigail. My father had seen my gesture as more than capitulation. He'd acted as if I'd bestowed a priceless gift on Abigail. He'd patted my shoulder, telling me what a generous person I was. How kind and thoughtful I could be.

My mouth drew down in a frown. I was feeling anything

but kind and thoughtful. I said, "I'm surprised you have the time to make this trip. Don't you have other clients?"

Abigail's hands had been busy plaiting her long hair into a loose braid. She stopped and looked at me, then quickly away. "As I've said before, I've cleared my schedule to do the work on your house."

"But you do have other clients here in town?"

It took her a moment to answer. "My business is just getting started."

"I'm guessing that means I'm your one and only customer."

Reluctantly, Abigail admitted, "At present, but I'm working on a couple of ideas."

I shifted uneasily in my seat. "I never asked you for references concerning other jobs you'd done. You have done other jobs?" I glanced at Abigail, but she was staring out the window. When she didn't answer, I said, "I should have had this conversation with you on Saturday when you gave your presentation, but I was distracted by other events going on in my life."

She perked up and turned to me. "I'd like to hear more about Toby's murder. Your father told me someone put a hornet's nest in his bedroom."

Her need to change the subject was too obvious. "Abigail, you do have references, don't you?"

She licked her lips. "Not really, but I can call my friend Deanna if I run into a problem. She's been a decorator for years."

"How did you meet my father? How did you convince him that you had the right qualifications for this project?"

Abigail gave her finished braid a final pat. "Let me ask you this. Aren't you pleased with my ideas so far?"

Slowly I nodded. "Your ideas are very good, but they're

all on paper. Do you have the expertise to execute them? Can you carry through to the end?"

"Yes. I know I can, especially with Albert helping me."

"But you hardly know him. Why all the confidence in him?"

Her voice trembled. "He's a nice man, and he was willing to give me this opportunity." She squared her shoulders. "I know I can do it."

"How did you meet him?"

She ducked her head. "I don't really remember."

I kept pressing. "You don't remember? That seems odd when he's giving you the chance of a lifetime to show your talent."

Abigail twisted around on the seat so that she was facing me. "Do you think we could forget Albert, the decorating of the house, and just get to know each other? I think we have plenty in common to make for an interesting conversation."

I said nothing as I put on my left-turn signal.

Abigail tapped a fingernail on her knee. "The majority of Albert's concerns for you stem from your interest in solving mysteries. Back at the house, when he said he'd seen 'that look in your eye,' I'm assuming you had a flash of insight concerning Toby's death. It must have been important for you to give up going to his funeral."

I navigated the left turn and stepped on the accelerator. Tight-lipped, I answered, "I'm hoping that will be the case." For a few minutes we traveled in silence, then I said quietly, "I don't know what's going on between you and my father, but at some point I'm going to get answers."

I pulled into Toby's driveway and shut off the engine. I zipped up my coat and opened the door. After I'd climbed out, I looked at Abigail. "It isn't raining, but the garden will be wet and drippy. If you want to wait here—"

She didn't let me finish. She got out. After giving the door a solid slam, she stared at me over the SUV's hood. "I'm not waiting here. Let's go."

She stalked ahead of me as if she knew where she was headed, but paused at the corner of the house for me to lead the way. I thought she was about to say something, but she pressed her lips together. As I passed her, she stubbornly tilted her chin and fell into step behind me. I shook my head. This was ridiculous. We were bickering like siblings.

I wanted my mind free of outside aggravations as I inspected the hibiscus plants. To do that I had to break the strain that existed between Abigail and myself. She hadn't answered questions about her relationship with my father, but now wasn't the time to press. So I broke the silence by talking about the reason for our jaunt to this garden.

"Toby Sutton was a unique young man," I said. "With some people, you have to make an effort to like them, but with Toby, it was easy to care about him." I continued into the garden, spilling my thoughts if Abigail wanted to listen.

"On the day Toby died, he came to my flower shop to wash the windows. Sometimes he carried out the trash. Other times he unpacked freight or swept the sidewalk. He was easy to be around. He didn't make demands or ask personal questions. By the same token, my employees and I didn't probe into his life. If Toby initiated a topic, that's what we discussed."

I led the way into the tangle of bushes. "From the looks of the shrubs and the size of the weeds, Toby hasn't worked in this area of the garden since his mother died. And yet, when we get to the hibiscus, you'll see a marked difference in the upkeep."

Abigail asked, "Why only the hibiscus?"

"I'm not sure. Toby said his mother taught him how to start seeds on the kitchen windowsill. He promised her he would plant six new rows each year."

"So the hibiscus were an ongoing project?"

"I'm sure of it, but I don't know why."

"Maybe Toby was growing the plants to please Phillip."

"But why didn't Phillip grow them on his own land? Why would he cut the stalks on the sly? Why not tell Toby he was taking them?"

Abigail didn't have an answer, and neither did I.

We followed the path around a curve of sunburned azaleas to be confronted by the wall of burgundy-colored leaves. I said, "Beyond this barrier of red barberry are the hibiscus."

Before I could stop her, Abigail reached out as if to brush the barberry branches aside. She yelped in pain and pulled her hand back. "Thorns," she muttered, rubbing her pricked skin.

"Sorry. I should have warned you. Barberry makes a perfect privacy fence. The dense foliage combined with the thorny branches is impenetrable."

I turned in a circle, waving an arm at our surroundings. "In fact, this entire garden is a deterrent. There's no attraction, no design. Every shrub that grows well in Missouri can be found right here. Lilacs are planted next to pussy willow, which has wild, unruly, upright stems. I love the burning bush, but its vase-shaped growing habit is lost because it's planted too close to the arching limbs of that forsythia, which in turn is being smothered by the Hall's honeysuckle. I'm accustomed to seeing mugo pines sheared and well kept. These specimens are four-foot haystack-size monsters. Powdery mildew has all but covered the lilacs. The potentilla has spider mites. Aphids are living and reproducing like mad on the crepe myrtle."

Abigail pointed to a particularly thick tangle of leaves. "What is that horrible vine that's covering everything?"

"Bindweed. Its vigorous growth takes over an area, smothering everything in its path. The roots grow under the surface of the soil, and they're next to impossible to destroy. If you leave a fragment of root behind when you pull up the vine, the cycle is reestablished, and you have to wage another war or use a strong herbicide. Not everyone wants to handle chemicals. This entire area is a gardener's worst nightmare. Every negative thing I've learned, planning my garden at home, has been put into play here."

"Maybe it was intentional," said Abigail.

Slowly I nodded. "Maybe so. Leona told me Agnes joined a garden club to learn about plants because she knew nothing. Looking around us, it's as if she ignored all the dos and concentrated on the don'ts. *Don't* plant shrubs close together. *Don't* prune at the appropriate time. *Don't* water, fertilize, or spray for pests."

"Why would she do that?"

I shrugged. "I didn't know Agnes well when she was alive, but since Toby's death, I've learned several things about her. And the one fact that stands out is that she never did anything without a purpose." I looked around and sighed. "She programed everything about Toby's life, so I have to assume this garden has taken on the look she had planned. Leona said Agnes liked the idea of shrubs. Maybe she set up this part of the garden to be something special."

Abigail snorted. "Well, I'm not seeing it. There's nothing aesthetic about this plot of land. It's a hodgepodge of sun-burned, pest-infested, overgrown vegetation with nothing going for it except perhaps the reason we came. Bretta, my curiosity is running as rampant as these shrubs. How do we get beyond this thorny barricade so we can see the hibiscus?"

"Follow me," I said. "There's a gap down this way."

We walked about twenty feet and came to the break in the enclosure. Using the sleeve of my jacket, I pushed a branch aside. Abigail slipped through. I ducked my head and followed her into the enclosure.

"I haven't walked the perimeter, but Sid told me a narrow path lies between the barberry hedge and the hibiscus. Over there are the stubs where the hibiscus was chopped down. Their growth habit is for a single plant to develop into a clump. With each passing season, that one plant can yield up to as many as eight stalks."

Abigail looked around her in disbelief. "There isn't a weed anywhere."

"I didn't see a water source in the other area of the garden, but there's one right over there." I pointed to a sloppily coiled hose. "Toby watered these plants when we had a long, dry spell this summer. He took his mother at her word—on this subject, at least."

Abigail looked at me. "That last comment makes me think that he didn't follow her instructions on other matters."

I nodded. "He didn't. Another time I'll explain, but right now I want to examine these plants. The last time I was here, Sid hurried me away."

"Are we looking for something specific?"

"I don't have a clue. I hoped with the information you gave me about the kenaf, I'd have a new perspective."

Stepping carefully, I worked my way among the towering plants. My passing shook raindrops from the leaves. The water trickled into my hair and rolled down my cheek. I wiped my face as if I was wiping away tears.

"Are you all right?" asked Abigail.

Blinking away the moisture, I said, "Yes. I'm not crying, if that's what you're thinking. I'm not that desperate—yet." Speaking quietly, I explained, "This is what I love about becoming involved in a mystery. The brain power. The collecting of facts and connecting them with my personal observations. It's like that bindweed you pointed out earlier. Everything ties together: this garden to Agnes. Agnes to her son, Toby. Toby to his association with the people on Hawthorn Street."

Abigail added, "These hibiscus to Phillip."

I shook my head. "Sid would call that supposition. It hasn't been proven."

Stubbornly, Abigail said, "It isn't supposition in my mind. I'm *sure* that cloth was kenaf."

I tried to keep the amusement out of my voice. She was a persistent woman. And I liked that. It reminded me of myself. "I can appreciate your gut feeling. I've had it many times, but absolute certainty doesn't cut it unless you can back it with hard evidence."

"We'll find it," she said. "I don't know what I'm looking for, but we can cover more ground if we split up."

I wasn't sure if that was a good idea, but she'd disappeared among the plants. "Abigail," I called. "Don't wander far."

"I'm not a child," she said.

I shook my head and moved out of the plants and back to the barberry hedge. Using caution against the thorns, I sidled along the path. I counted thirty-six rows of plants in all stages of growth. The ones closest to the entrance were older, with more stalks to a clump. By concentrating on one row at a time, I saw there was a slight difference in the coloration of the foliage. The first twelve rows were a healthy shade of green, but row thirteen showed a marked difference that carried through the next twelve rows. Here the plants were darker, thicker of stem, and the leaves had developed a slight crinkling pattern. At a glance, the difference wasn't discernible, but I wasn't glancing. I was examining each row, and finally each plant segment by segment.

I stepped back on the path and counted rows. Toby had said his mother wanted him to plant six new rows of hibiscus a year. Thirty-six rows and Agnes had been gone six years, so it looked like Toby had followed her instructions. The plants that had been chopped down started at row twenty-five and ended at row thirty. All six rows were gone, with just the green stubs of the stalks left to show that the plants had existed. The next six rows were intact. I assumed they were last year's seedlings. The plants were small, but showing healthy, vigorous growth. This year's plants were shriveled up on the windowsill in Toby's house.

I studied the six rows of whacked-off plants. Something wasn't adding up. I went back to the path and surveyed the area. The plants right before the ones that had been cut down had a supple difference in color and a crinkle in the leaves. But those plants hadn't been touched. Or had they?

I went back to rows nineteen through twenty-four. At random, I picked a row. Shuffling along, with my gaze on the base of the plant, I spotted something brown. Stooping, I scraped away the muddy soil and found a dried-up stub. When I pushed on the stub, it keeled over. I searched for more and found them. It looked to me as if several stalks had been cut, but they'd been taken here and there among the plants.

But why cut the entire hibiscus in the next section? What had made them more special than any of the others? Since they were gone, I didn't have a clue, but I knew the hibiscus in rows twenty-five through thirty were important—to someone.

I went to the path and called, "Abigail, where are you?"

"Over here," she answered. Her voice had come from the far corner of the plot.

I said, "I'll meet you by the opening in the barberry hedge."

"I'll be right there."

While I waited for her, I pondered the situation. I'd been thinking about kenaf and hibiscus plants, but I hadn't allowed my thoughts to put those pieces of the puzzle into the framework that surrounded Toby's death. Was there a connection? The hibiscus was on Toby's land. If he'd kept quiet about the plants being cut, would he still be alive? Or were the hibiscus just the tip of a larger, more devious scheme?

If the hibiscus were valuable, why weren't they under lock and key? Why were they being grown in the open? I looked around me. They weren't in the open. No one would suspect that in this weed-infested jungle there was an immaculate piece of ground covered with well-tended plants. But what had Agnes told Toby to make him keep these plants flourishing? Why would he devote time to this area and not the rest of the garden?

"I'm a muddy mess," said Abigail, coming up to me.

I turned and grinned. Mud was smeared across her cheek. A cluster of leaves and twigs was caught in her hair. "Are you okay?" I asked. "What happened?"

She made a face. "I'm annoyed, but fine. Back at the farthest corner, I saw something caught on the barberry hedge.

It was a piece of yellow fuzz." She pulled it out of her pocket and mashed it between her fingers. "Feels like wool, probably from a sweater or a scarf."

This time I laughed out loud. "You got mud on your face and leaves in your hair from finding a piece of fuzz?"

Her eyebrows drew down. "No. I did more than that. I found a place where the barberry hedge isn't as dense. By using my—your—jacket for protection against the thorns, I eased my way through to the other side. I was busy fighting the groping branches and didn't notice that the ground sloped."

"So you fell?"

Her eyes flashed. "I caught myself, and I found a lovely place to have a picnic."

Disappointed, I turned away and headed for the break in the hedge. "Swell," I muttered under my breath. "That's just what we were looking for."

Abigail said, "You don't think the fuzz is important?"

"I don't see how. We don't know when it was caught on the hedge. For that matter, we don't even know for sure what it is. It could have been dropped by a bird who was trying to feather its nest with something soft."

"Or it could have come from the sweater Phillip was wearing when he trespassed to steal the hibiscus."

I didn't verbally comment, but I rolled my eyes. Was this how Sid felt when I handed him my theories on a case? I didn't like the flash of guilt that weaseled its way into my consciousness.

Abigail was still talking. "—a willow tree by the stream. I had to look beyond hoofprints and piles of poop, but it was picturesque."

I was ready for a change of subject. "I found evidence that some of the hibiscus was cut last season or even the season before. This was in the middle of the patch, so Toby might not have noticed. Something has been bugging me. I need to know how long it would take to turn a stalk of hibiscus into a piece of cloth."

Abigail stopped and stared at me. "Gosh, Bretta," she said, "I don't have any idea."

I motioned for her to keep walking. "What about the technique?"

She was silent until we got back to the SUV. As we climbed in, she finally spoke. "Turning fibers, whether they're plant or protein, into fabric is a process. My thimbleful of knowledge says that the stalks are cut and the fibers separated. Generally speaking, the fibers have to be softened so they'll blend with one another. Wire teeth, like you'd find on a wool card, might work. It's like combing the tangles out of your hair. It brushes, and cleans, and separates the fibers so they're ready for spinning into yarn. Depending on the quality of the fibers, the yarn could be woven on a regular loom. But since our interest is kenaf, I'm not sure if a regular loom would work."

I started up the SUV and put the lever into reverse. Craning my neck so I could see out my back window, I said, "It's just as I thought. There are numerous steps, which takes time."

"That's right, but I don't know how much."

"Longer than from Friday, when Toby noticed the plants had been chopped down, until Sunday, when we saw the cloth at Phillip's workshop?"

"Oh, yes, I'm sure it would take longer than a couple of days." Her jaw dropped as realization struck. Shaking her head, Abigail said, "I see what you're getting at. There's no way the cloth we saw came from these missing hibiscus stalks." She slumped back against the seat. "All of this has been for nothing. What a waste."

I put the lever into drive and smiled. "Don't give up so quickly, Watson. Last year's stalks could have produced the cloth, and this year's harvest could be hidden away ready for spinning and weaving."

I stepped on the accelerator. As my SUV gathered speed, my heartbeat picked up its rhythm, too. I couldn't suppress my excitement. "I'm basing our next action on conjecture, but what the hell. Sid isn't here. Who's it going to hurt to do a little snooping?"

NINETEEN

"WHY ARE WE PARKING HERE?" asked Abigail. "Surely you aren't hungry?"

I'd pulled the SUV into a slot in front of a Mexican restaurant a block or so down the street from Yvonne's antiques store. "I'm always ready to eat," I said, turning off the SUV's engine. "But not right now." I darted a quick look at her. "I couldn't very well leave my vehicle parked in Phillip's driveway."

Abigail's eyes widened. "That's what you meant when you said 'snooping'?"

"Are you interested?" I asked.

Abigail stared at me. "This is crazy, but you don't have to ask me twice. I'm in." She slipped off her seat belt.

So our hands would be free, I suggested we hide our purses under the seat. "If you have your cell phone, you might want to slip it into your pocket."

Abigail grimaced. "I left it on your dining-room table to recharge."

Wasn't that just the luck? The one point at which Abigail might prove helpful. Oh well. "Okay, let's go."

"And let the chips fall where they may," she muttered as we headed down the sidewalk.

I wasn't sure what that was supposed to mean. "Act naturally," I said under my breath. "Don't pay any attention to the street traffic. We don't want anyone to notice us. We're just two women out for a stroll."

Abigail's approach to "act naturally" was just like my father's. She flapped her jaws, telling some story about a purple carpet in a peach bedroom. I pretended an interest, but hardly heard a word. Was this asinine? Phillip had told me he kept everything locked. What was I hoping to find? Even if he had woven a piece of cloth from the stolen hibiscus, what did that prove? How did it tie into Toby's death?

Free-word association has been a trick I've used in the past when nothing I've learned seems to connect. It's like gathering an assortment of flowers from the cooler and assembling them into a bouquet. I might have a general idea of where each flower might fit into the arrangement, but until everything is laid out on my worktable, I don't know which ones will take center stage.

I shut out Abigail's voice and let my mind wander. The first thing that popped into my mind was the comment she'd made as she got out of my SUV: "And let the chips fall where they may." I pursed my lips and tried to relax.

The word *bindweed* was next. It all ties together.

Chips. Chips.

Was I hungry? I frowned. Buffalo chips. Hoofprints and piles of poop. Road apples.

Frustrated, I scowled. A mind is a terrible thing to waste.

We were almost to Yvonne's shop. Abruptly, I took Abigail's arm and pulled her to a stop at the display window of a hardware store. Pointing to a Coleman lantern, I said, "When the traffic light changes, we'll duck around the corner. Drivers should be watching the car in front of them, so maybe they won't notice what we're doing."

Out of the corner of my eye, I checked the light. "It's green," I said. "Let's go, but keep your rhythm slow and easy. A quick movement will draw attention."

Nonchalantly, we walked around the corner of the building and down the alley. Abigail wanted to hurry ahead, but I kept a tight rein on her.

Rein? Why not "hold" or "grip"? Why rein? Something was bugging me, but I couldn't tap into it.

Walking slowly, we crossed a patch of grass and slipped behind a couple of Dumpsters. Now that we were out of sight from the street, we picked up our pace. Skirting the antiques store, we moved around it to the woven-wire fence that enclosed the barnyard.

Quickly I sized up the situation. The coast was clear. No car was parked at the house. My body opted for the gate, which would have been an easier climb, but it was in full view of the street traffic. My brain said it would be prudent to use the store to shield our stealthy scaling of the fence.

"Up and over," I said. Drawing on my country background, I looked for a sturdy post. I grabbed it for leverage and put the toe of my sneaker into woven wire. With a grunt, I heaved myself up. The wire wobbled, but I clung like a leech to the post while I swung my leg over the top of the fence.

Straddling the wire, I looked around for Abigail. To my amazement and chagrin, she was already on the barnyard side, waiting for me. Gritting my teeth, I lifted my leg over the top wire and made a scrambling descent.

Once I was safely on the ground, I stepped away from the fence. I gave my jeans a sharp tug to settle them back in place. "That wasn't so bad," I said. But Abigail wasn't paying any attention to me. She'd spied Sugar Cube, standing near the side of the barn.

"Hey, guy," she called. The horse turned toward the sound of Abigail's voice. She pointed her index finger. With a happy nicker, the hulking brute ambled forward like a trained robot. "Aren't you a sweetie?" she said, rubbing the horse's ears.

The horse answered by lifting his tail and depositing a good-size pile.

"Yuk!" I said.

Abigail chuckled. "What goes in must come out." She hugged the horse's neck. In a soft voice, she crooned, "I miss Rex and the roundups, and the bran—" She stopped abruptly.

Instantly, I was alert. Had she almost said "branding"? As in "branding cattle." As in my father had gotten rich by inventing a gizmo that "branded cattle." I swallowed and stared at her. "Who's Rex?" I asked.

"My horse," she said hurriedly. "What do we do next?"

I narrowed my eyes. "What roundups?"

Abigail shook her head. "We're wasting time. Phillip and Yvonne should be back from the funeral before long."

I barely glanced at my watch. "We've got maybe half an hour. They probably went with the cortege to the cemetery." I waited a second, then said, "What aren't you telling me, Abigail?"

Her head jerked around, but she didn't meet my gaze. Her voice was shaky. "I'm not sure why we're here, Bretta. What exactly do you have in mind? What are we looking for?"

I stared at her until she turned away. The first time I'd met her, in the library, I'd been struck by how well she got along with my father. They'd seemed to be on the same wavelength, each anticipating the other's thoughts without any verbal communication. But it was more than that. It had bothered me from the get-go that my father was adamant that I hire Abigail. I'd let several things slide—like how uncomfortable she became when I discussed my relationship with my father. Or how worried he'd been when she hadn't answered her cell phone. Everything about their association seemed to be a long time in the making. I'd never witnessed any of the awkwardness that comes from a newly established friendship.

My gaze intensified as I studied her profile. No resemblance that I could see, but my gut was telling me things I wasn't ready to acknowledge. I walked past Abigail and Sugar Cube, skirting the horse poop.

Suddenly I stopped. "When you went beyond the barberry hedge in Toby's garden, you said you found hoofprints and piles of poop." I couldn't keep the sarcastic tone from my voice. "With your background of *roundups,* and I assume you were about to say *branding,* as in cattle, I'd like your most expert opinion. Did you see horse or cow poop under that tree?"

She gulped. "Without a doubt, it was from a horse. In fact, if I were to hazard a guess, I'd say a horse had been tied to the tree. There was a bunch of hoofprints in the dirt that the rain hadn't washed away."

I started walking toward the barn. It seemed feasible to me that Phillip might have ridden Sugar Cube over to Toby's, bypassing roads and sticking to the pastures. He would have tied the horse to the tree, cut the hibiscus, and ridden back home with his bundle of stalks. He could have wrapped them up in a blanket or secured them with twine to his saddle and no one would have paid the least bit of attention to horse and rider.

I circled around the silo and stared across the open pasture to the boundary fence. Down by a line of trees was a gate. I reasoned that if I were to cut across the pasture in a diagonal line, I might not be far off the route Phillip could have taken if he'd brought the hibiscus back to the barn.

If, might, and could were wishy-washy, but I had nothing. Maybe Phillip had dropped a leaf or a branch. I needed some hard evidence to prove I was on the right track.

To get my bearings, I glanced back at the barn and moved to my left another fifteen feet so I was in a more direct line with the gate. Abigail hadn't followed me. She hadn't asked any more questions. At the moment, she and the horse were nosing around a junk heap. All farms had them. Trash collectors didn't take certain items, so the discarded pieces were piled in an out-of-the-way spot. From my vantage point, I could see an old cookstove tipped over on its side. There was part of a hay baler, and some other farming equipment, mixed in with weeds and brush. I figured there might even be a snake or two, but I'd let Abigail find those on her own. I glanced down the line of trees to the gate and started off in the direction I hoped might prove informative.

Suddenly Abigail called, "Bretta, I don't know what I've found. It's vegetation, only it looks as if it's been put through a grinder."

At the word "vegetation," I reversed my route, lengthening my stride so that I was at her side in a flash. "See?" she said, pointing. "It's a bunch of mashed stems."

I looked where she'd indicated. My stomach leaped with excitement. Using a two-foot length of pipe, I probed the squashed stems, and unearthed a piece of vine with a shredded leaf attached. With the tip of the pipe, I smoothed the leaf as best I could. There was no doubt in my mind.

I tossed the pipe aside. "That's poison ivy," I said. "Did you touch it?"

Abigail shook her head. "Nowhere close. Why was the vine ground up that way?"

"Actually, it's a method called cold pressing. The juice was put in a bottle of bubble bath."

Abigail's eyes widened. "You've got to be kidding. Was it used?"

"Yes. She died from an allergic reaction to it."

The color drained from Abigail's face. She leaned weakly against the silo. "How horrible."

"We've gotten a portion of what we came for. Let's go."

Abigail didn't move. In a musing tone, she said, "Phillip would never extract the juice from a poison-ivy vine in his house or at the antiques store. He gives his customers free run of the barn, letting them snoop around, looking at the furniture he's working on, but I've never seen inside the silo."

Slowly she turned and touched the brick wall. "As you've said, we've gotten a portion of what we need, but we don't know everything." She tapped a brick with a fingernail. "It's here, Bretta. I know it is. All the answers are on the other side of this wall."

My gaze traveled up the thirty-foot tower. As I studied the brick exterior, I remembered Toby's aversion to the brick lighthouse that had been at the flower shop. I remembered Melba saying that Toby had said that "bad things happen in towers."

I sighed. "I want answers, too, but they might as well be on the moon for all the good it will do us."

Abigail moved around the structure. "There are steel rungs cemented into the bricks."

I followed her. "I know, but the first one is ten feet off the

ground. How do you propose we close the gap? I don't see a
ladder lying conveniently around here, do you?"

Abigail grinned. "We don't need a ladder. We have Sugar
Cube's broad back."

When it dawned on me what she was suggesting, I shook
my head. "Oh, no. I'm not getting up on that horse."

"You don't have to. I'll make the climb. Once I'm inside
I'll unlock a door and you can walk in."

It was tempting, but I didn't like the idea of Abigail going
inside on her own. We'd found the cold-pressed poison-ivy
vine. Surely Sid could use that as a toehold for getting a
search warrant. I shook my head. "Let's go find a phone. I'll
call Sid. He can deal with it."

Abigail put her hands on her hips. "I can't believe you're
this close to finding out the truth and you're going to turn your
back and walk away."

"I'm showing sense," I said, but Abigail wasn't listening
to me. She stomped away. I thought she was headed back the
way we'd come, but she only went as far as the old cookstove.
She hopped up, whistled to Sugar Cube, and pointed her
finger. Obediently, the horse went to her.

"Abigail," I said. "Don't do it. You don't know what's
inside the silo."

"That's the whole point," she said, swinging her leg over
the horse's back. Sugar Cube didn't move. "Come on," she
said. "If you don't want me to go alone, then come with me."

"That's not a choice. I don't like horses or heights."

Abigail stroked Sugar Cube's mane. "What's not to like?
He's a sweetheart. As for heights, just don't look down."

"That's easier said than done," I muttered, but I walked to
the stove. How could I back away now? I wanted answers. I

had liked Leona, but I cared deeply about Toby. If Phillip was behind Toby's murder, then I wanted to know why. I wanted to be the one who gathered the evidence that would put him behind bars.

I got up on the stove. On this level Abigail and I were eye to eye. Staring at her, I said softly, "Your mother is divorced from *our* father."

She licked her lips and finally said, "That's right."

I didn't change expression. "What if we get to the top and the silo is empty?"

She blinked a couple of times. "Then we climb down and beat it out of here. But you and I both know that won't be the case."

Resigned, I put a hand on Sugar Cube's back. It was warm and bristly. Abigail took hold of my arm and pulled. With a few grunts and groans, I found myself on the horse's back, seated behind Abigail. I closed my eyes, wrapped my arms around her waist, and hung on for dear life. We swayed our way slowly around the silo.

Abigail said, "Whoa, boy." She twisted so she could touch my arm. "Open your eyes, Bretta. You have to watch what I do so you can follow suit."

I did as she directed. "Sure. Right. Let's do it." My intention was to speak in a calm, rational manner. Instead, I delivered a squeaky, squawky rendition of a woman scared witless.

"If you stretch your arms up, you can grab the bottom rung." Abigail demonstrated. "See? That's easy. Once you have a tight hold, then you can pull yourself upright." She came nimbly to her feet, balancing herself on the horse's back. "Now that you're up this high, you can reach for the third rung and from there on it'll be a snap."

Without Abigail to hold on to, I felt as vulnerable as a bug at a square dance. For reassurance, I put a hand on her leg. I needed personal contact. I needed to know that I wasn't alone. That's when it occurred to me that once she was up the ladder, I'd be left with only the horse for company. What if I couldn't make Sugar Cube obey? What if he galloped off across the pasture with me on his back? I shuddered as the image played out in my mind.

Tentatively, I said, "Maybe I should go first."

Abigail looked down at me. "If you can do it, that might be best. That way I can keep Sugar Cube steady until you get on the ladder."

She squatted and swung her leg over the horse's neck. Once she was settled in front of me again, she maneuvered Sugar Cube so I was closer to the silo. I wasn't as nimble as Abigail, but I amazed myself. I grabbed the rung with both hands and slowly stood up. There was no time to think. I stretched to another rung and swung myself off the horse. With Abigail's help, my sneaker found a toehold. Reaching over my head, I found the next rung and pulled myself up.

Below me, Abigail called encouragement. "Go up a couple more, and then I'll be right below you."

I didn't speak. I needed all my concentration for the job at hand. And so I climbed. I never looked down, but I did look up, though the sight was far from reassuring. Dark storm clouds raced across the sky and collided like bumper cars. The wind was cooler and the threat of rain was imminent.

I tried not to think about what I was doing. Letting go of one rung to reach for the next was agonizing. At this height the wind tore at my clothes and whipped my hair into my eyes. My legs trembled with fear and fatigue. My hands were like perfectly formed claws that fit around each iron rung. I wasn't physically fit enough for this kind of exercise. Maybe I needed to join Lois at that health club. My heart was hammering by the time I got to the top.

The top!

I closed my eyes and took a shaky breath. What a fool I was! How could I have been so stupid not to have looked this far ahead? Now that I was at my destination, I had to climb over the rim.

Below me, Abigail called, "Bretta, don't stop now."

"I don't think I can—"

"Sure you can. Dad says you have more courage than anyone he knows."

That wasn't the best argument she could have used. I was hurt and angry that my father hadn't been honest with me. Why couldn't he tell me that I have a half-sister? He'd told Abigail all about me. Why hadn't he given me that same courtesy?

My tone was waspish as I replied, "And what does *our father* say about you?" I waited, but there wasn't a reply.

My spark of anger prompted me to ease myself up the final rung. Leaning over the brick rim, I peered down into the silo. What I saw made me blink in amazement. Below the silo rim was a glass roof with open vents. Hot air, mingled with a foul odor, rose like a vapor to greet me. I leaned over farther so I could see the inner wall.

I called to Abigail. "There's another set of metal rungs on the inside that are identical to the ones here. I'm going down."

Her voice was calm. "I'm right behind you."

Taking a deep breath, I swung my leg over the rim and grabbed the first rung. Carefully I squeezed through the open vent, and I descended into the silo's interior.

TWENTY

I KEPT MY EYES ON the brick wall. It represented stability, which I needed to keep my anxiety in its proper place. What was proper? I had every right to be apprehensive. I was trespassing, and this wasn't your average garden-variety climbing-over-a-fence-onto-forbidden-land intrusion. I'd scaled a thirty-foot silo. That by itself was a stunning feat. Add the fact that I suspected the owner of having murdered twice and my anxiety level should have been off the charts.

My heart pitty-patted at an accelerated rate, but I wasn't distressed beyond what the situation demanded. All my senses were on alert to any new development, and one was wafting up from below. The stench was horrible. So were the flies that buzzed around my face. I tossed my head like an old cow, trying to shoo the insects away.

I paused to look up at the glass roof. Abigail was at the top, with one leg over the rim. I waited for her to descend, but she didn't move. She stared off into the distance.

"What's wrong?" I asked.

Her voice was just above a whisper. "Sugar Cube trotted over to the gate. I can't see anything, but my guess is that Phillip and Yvonne are home from the funeral. What do we do now?"

I gulped. So much for calm and rational. "Climb like mad," was my reply.

She put action to my words and scrambled down the rungs

"Probably to keep the spiders happy, but I don't have a clue as to why. As you said, Phillip went to considerable expense to have this glass roof installed. It allows light and ventilation into this upper part of the silo. Maybe it's some sort of scientific experiment."

Abigail's eyes widened. "Like an invasion of the super-size spiders?"

I shook my head. "I doubt that, though I do suspect the spiders are important or Phillip wouldn't have established this entire area for their well-being. We're at the top of a thirty-foot silo. I'm assuming the rest of the building will yield more answers, but we may not have time before Phillip—"

Below us a door slammed. The floor shimmied as heavy footsteps thudded upward. I tried to keep the panic out of my voice. "We have to hide."

As one, we turned to the table. The black plastic fell in folds to the floor. If we crawled under it, we would be concealed from immediate view. The maggots were a mighty stumbling block, but so was the idea of confronting a possible killer.

Gingerly I held up a piece of the plastic cover, and we scurried under the table just as the door opened. We heard a click and the room was flooded with light. Peeking under the edge of the black plastic, we watched a pair of spit-and-polished black oxfords cross in front of us. When Phillip spoke, my stomach lurched.

"How are my ladies?" he said quietly.

Next to me, Abigail jerked. I squeezed her arm, cautioning her to be silent.

"Such pretty little ladies," he crooned. "This buffet is all for you, my dears. Maggie Mae, you're looking a bit sluggish. Did you get too hot? How about you, Beatrice? You've been busy. Eight flies wrapped in silken shrouds. Planning a midnight snack?" He chuckled softly. "Heloise, you and Jeannette are much too timid. Be aggressive, ladies. Eat up. Now is not the time to watch your figures."

The man was talking to the spiders! He'd given them names. Maggie Mae. Beatrice. Heloise and Jeannette. How creepy!

Abigail and I held our collective breaths as he walked across the room. We heard the sound of the crank being turned. "Not a tight fit," he murmured. "The rubber seal must be warped."

Abruptly, he crossed the room, snapped off the light, and closed the door. The floor vibrated as he clomped down the stairs. We waited. Below a door banged shut.

We took it as a signal that the coast was clear. I scrambled out from under the table, swiping at my face. "I need a shower," I said. "I feel so filthy I may have to take two or three showers before I feel clean again."

Abigail brushed at my hair. One look at the disgusted expression on her face and I knew better than to ask. The thought of maggots crawling on me sent spasms of revulsion down my spine. "Let's get out of here," I said. "I can't take much more."

I went to the door and eased it open. Light filtered up from below and showed a small staircase hugging the silo's circular walls. The treads were only two feet long and about a foot in width. The handrail was a piece of rope attached every ten feet to an upright post that wiggled when I gave it a test shake. Ordinarily, I would have balked at taking this precarious route, but since my alternative was the iron rungs on the outside of the silo, I didn't hesitate.

Slowly we went down. I ignored the rope and plastered myself to the bricks. We hadn't gone far when I noticed we'd traded the sickly stench of rotting fruit for another odor. Behind me, Abigail sniffed the air like a bloodhound hot on the trail.

Whispering, she said, "I'm getting a whiff of something that smells like my grandmother's attic—all musty and unused."

I paused on the staircase to ponder this bit of information. "You have a grandmother?"

"My mother's mother."

I sighed. "I never knew my grandparents."

"We can share Nana. She's a hoot. Not at all like my mother."

Her sharp tone told me problems lurked in that area. I dropped the subject and moved on down the staircase. As my eyes grew more accustomed to the dim light, I could make out objects in the room. I shivered as I caught sight of the cages. Stepping off the staircase, I said, "We've been smelling mice."

But it wasn't just mice. Cages of hamsters also lined one wall. Above each cage was a name and a date. Each compartment had fresh bedding, clean water, and plenty of food. At first glance the rodents looked healthy, but on closer inspection I saw several had strange lumps protruding from their sides. Flossie seemed to be the most affected. She tried to scamper into a corner when I peered into her cage, but the lump severely restricted her movements.

"What's going on here?" I said out loud.

"I don't have a clue," said Abigail. "But there's a desk over there with a slew of papers on it. Maybe we can find some answers."

Abigail moved to the desk. I circled the room, skirting a stainless-steel table that held two strange contraptions hooked up to an electric outlet on the floor. I counted twelve syringes in several different sizes. Delicate pale hairs were scattered across the tabletop. There was a microscope with an open box of slides nearby. A peek into a refrigerator revealed stacks of petri dishes. On the far wall was our source of light.

A string of fluorescent tubes, which I assumed were meant to simulate sunlight, shone down on some plants. There were three species. I recognized two. One was alfalfa. A high-protein crop used for grazing and baling into hay. The other looked like a weird reproduction of a potato plant. The leaves were crinkled and the stems thick and gnarled. Leaning closer, I saw a label on the third plant. The tag identified it as tobacco. I didn't know anything about the habits of this plant, but the leaves were a strange shade of lime green with heavy black varicoselike veins crisscrossing the surface.

"Does this look like a tobacco plant to you?" I asked Abigail.

She didn't glance around. "I don't know anything about tobacco, but listen to this." Mumbling to herself, she ran a finger down a piece of paper, flipped it over, and finally said, "Here it is. '—consisting of stiff sheets of crystallized protein floating in an elastic rubbery matrix.'" She looked at me. "What's that mean?"

"It sounds like you've taken a sentence out of context. What does the rest of the paper say?"

Abigail eyes zipped back and forth as they traveled down the page. "This is a letter addressed to Phillip from a molecular biology professor, and it's talking about genetic engineering. I'm quoting the letter—'Prospects include a possible gene insertion into fungi and soy plants. In Germany the genes have been spliced into potato plants after accomplishing the task in a mustard plant.'"

"'Mustard plant'?" I repeated. "I remember Leona talking about Phillip being at loose ends when he came back from Canada, so he raised mustard plants."

Abigail swiveled around. "Phillip was in Canada?"

"He used to work there."

"Here's a notebook imprinted by a company called Bio-Rite Technologies. Under the logo it says Canada."

I took the notebook and laid it on a corner of the table. I tried to read through the pages, but words like *synthesize, genome, amino acids, alanine, repetitive sequences,* and *synchrotron* kept me from absorbing any information.

I pushed the notebook aside. "I can't understand any of this without a dictionary. It's out of my league. I don't have a clue."

She handed a paper to me. "Read this."

I read the typed words aloud. "'As spider silk is a protein, its chemical composition is encoded in the genes of the organisms that make it. The best approach is using that silk-producing gene and splicing it into another living organism. Plants could serve as hosts. If a robust plant expressed a silk gene, the fiber could be harvested in vast quantities.'"

I stared off into space, taking what I'd read and adding it to the information I already had. Toby's death was tied to the missing hibiscus. The missing hibiscus was tied to Phillip. I had to assume the "robust plant" mentioned in the notes was the hibiscus. Had Phillip taken the silk-producing gene from a spider and spliced it into the hibiscus that was in Toby's garden? Had Phillip then harvested the hibiscus and woven it into a length of cloth?

If this scenario was anywhere close to accurate, then what was the reason? Why commit murder for a piece of genetically engineered fabric?

TWENTY-ONE

MY SHOULDERS SLUMPED WEARILY. "Let's get out of here, Abigail. We've pushed our luck long enough."

"But we still don't know what's going on."

"We know more than we did. We know that Phillip is trying to use spider genes to change the genetic makeup of the hibiscus in Toby's garden. I don't know why he's been working on this. I can't believe the procedure is against the law, but something has made it necessary that he keep it highly secret. I say we take what we have to the sheriff and let him decide what should be done."

Abigail nodded reluctantly. "This info is fascinating. I just wish I could understand more." She took the notebook I handed her and slid it in a drawer. After fussing with the papers on top of the desk, she said, "I think I've put everything back the way I found it."

I left that detail up to her. I'd been too busy looking at the plants and the table to notice how the papers had been arranged. I crossed the room to the door that would take us to the bottom floor. I opened the wooden panel a crack and peered out.

The area in front of me was as black as pitch. I pushed the door wide open so the light behind me could shine out. My heart sank. This staircase was narrower than the one that had brought us to the second floor and it didn't have any rope as a handrail.

"Be careful," I whispered. "Stay as close to the wall as possible. Try to get your bearings, then you'll have to close this door or Phillip will know someone was here."

Abigail looked past me. "I don't like this, Bretta. I could take all the other things because we could see what we were getting into, but this is frightening. We don't know what's below."

"I agree, but what choice do we have? I don't want to go back up to the maggots or climb down the outside where anyone could see us. This is it. Let's go."

Abigail took a shaky breath and eased the door shut. It was worse than I'd thought. The darkness closed around us. "One step at a time," I whispered around the lump of fear in my throat. I pressed my hands to the brick wall and started down. There had been fifteen steps from the third floor to the second. I hadn't been able to see how many steps we faced going from the second floor to the first, but I was betting on the same number.

So I counted. One step. Two steps. Three steps. "Pretend you have your eyes closed," I said.

Abigail gave a nervous giggle. "Open. Closed. Who can tell? I feel as if I'm walking to my death."

"Don't be so melodramatic. We're fine."

"You might be, but I'm not. What if there are more spiders? What if there are rats running loose? What if—"

"Stop it! That kind of talk doesn't accomplish a damned thing."

Abigail's useless chatter had made me lose count. Had I been on the eighth step or the sixth? Annoyed, I decided I'd better assume it was the sixth. Seven. Eight. Nine. Ten. It helped keep my mind off what I was doing if I counted to myself. Thirteen. Fourteen. Fifteen.

I eased my foot forward and couldn't find the step's edge. Hunkering down, I pushed my foot out farther and sighed. "I'm at the bottom." I turned and groped in the dark for Abigail. My fingers brushed her leg. "Here I am," I said. "Give me your hand. Let's stay close together until we have a better idea of what we're up against."

Abigail's hand was cold and clammy. A perfect match for mine.

"How will we ever find the door?" she whispered.

I pulled her forward until we were standing side by side facing the brick wall. "We'll feel our way around the room, starting right here at the end of the staircase."

The bricks were rough, the mortar lines smooth and slightly indented. It's odd how little details escape you when you depend only on sight. With my vision obscured, my fingertips picked out minute deformities I might never have noticed. Besides touch, other senses slowly came into play. The smell was earthy and moist, mixed with the scent of plant juices. This aroma was agreeable. It was familiar, with pleasant memories attached. Newly mown grass. Freshly cut stems. I knew without seeing that I was in the area where Phillip had processed the hibiscus.

As I led the way around the wall, I became more optimistic. Our adventure would soon be over. We'd find the door. It would open, and we'd be in the little alleyway that connected the silo to the barn. That door would open, and we'd make our way out of the barn and across the pasture to the fence. From there it was only a hop, skip, and jump back to my SUV. Freedom was so close I could practically taste it.

Abigail's hand was slippery. It was getting harder to hold. Pulling away, I said, "We're fine now. Just stay close to me and near this wall."

Irritation and fear threaded her voice. "You keep saying we're fine, but I don't believe that for a second."

A hand clamped down on the nape of my neck. I tried to shrug it away, but the pressure increased. Annoyed, I said, "That hurts, Abigail. If you have to hang on to me, take my arm."

"What are you talking about? I'm not touching you."

I twisted suddenly to the right, but the hand on my neck stayed where it was. My optimism took a nosedive. I nearly jumped out of my skin when I reached up and touched a thick, muscular wrist.

With a cry of surprise, I kicked back and connected with a solid thud. There was a sharp groan of pain, and the grip on my neck loosened. I didn't wait to see what would happen next. I lowered my head and launched myself into the area behind me. I was amazed when I made contact. From the sound of it, I'd rammed my head into a stomach. Air swooshed out in a rush.

Surprise was all I had on my side. Using both fists, I slammed and punched the air in front of me. Several times I connected. I couldn't see if I was doing any damage, but with each moan, I took strength from the fact that I'd found my mark and was making progress.

A sudden clout to the side of my head brought a bright burst of light. It wasn't the kind that unveiled hidden secrets. I was still in the dark, but my eagerness to fight my way out of a harrowing situation had lessened.

Staggering back against the wall, I fought the wave of

nausea that rose in my throat. My ears rang, and Abigail's screeching didn't help matters.

"Bretta! Bretta! What's going on?"

Her voice was like a knife to my befuddled brain, slicing and dicing the abused gray matter. I wanted to tell her to be quiet, but I didn't have the strength.

Out of the gloom, Phillip's voice overrode hers. "Shut up," he said, slowly but distinctly.

Abigail gasped. "Bretta?" she whispered.

Gritting my teeth, I forced myself back into the thick of things. I had to swallow a couple of times before I could speak. "We have company, Abigail. Phillip has joined our party." Thinking fast, I added, "Now would be an excellent time to scream." I took a breath and shouted, *"Scream!"*

Abigail cut loose with a mind-boggling shriek that echoed around our tiny chamber. I used the sound to mask my getaway. I scrambled farther down the wall, but kept my eyes pinned on the spot where I'd last heard Phillip's voice.

Groping in the dark for anything I could use as a weapon, I fumbled around and found a bucket. It was empty, but if I put enough oomph behind it, I could clobber him a good one. I just had to get within arm's reach, and make sure I had Phillip in my line of fire and not Abigail.

I didn't know where she was. She'd stopped screaming. All was eerily quiet. If I spoke, I'd give away my new position, but if I didn't locate her soon, I might slug her instead of my intended victim. What to do? What to do?

Straining my ears, I listened. A whisper of movement. A mere breath of sound. It was just in front of me. I took a firm grip on the bucket's handle and swung with all my might. Nothing. I swung again and again while advancing across the floor. Nothing. I turned and swung in that direction. Again nothing.

I was making too much noise. My sneakers scuffed the grit on the floor. The bucket swooshed as it cut through the air. I kept moving, dodging and darting, but taking very small steps. I was afraid of Phillip, but I was also apprehensive of my surroundings. What kind of equipment did he use to prep the hibiscus for spinning and weaving? Somewhere in Phillip's possession was the knife he'd used to chop down the hibiscus stalks. Was it the size of a machete? Was the cutting edge honed razor sharp?

If I let it, my fear would consume me. Fighting kept the adrenaline pumping. I continued to work my way around the silo. Suddenly I had a horrendous thought. Why hadn't Abigail called out again? Why wasn't she saying anything?

Lowering my arm, I set down the bucket. Resigned, I said, "You have Abigail, don't you?"

There was a faint click, and the lights came on. I had to blink several times before my eyes adjusted. My heart plummeted. Over by the staircase, Phillip held Abigail captive. Her back was pressed tightly against him. His hand was clamped over her mouth. Her eyes were filled with terror.

"Let her go," I said.

Phillip's voice trembled. "I can't take any more screaming."

"She won't scream," I said. "Keep quiet, Abigail."

She tried to nod, but Phillip's grip was tight. Tears welled up and dribbled down her face. When he felt the moisture, he dropped his hand and pushed Abigail away. She stumbled and would have fallen but I grabbed her arm. I gathered her close, patting her back, murmuring words of encouragement.

Once she'd regained a measure of composure, we faced Phillip. I refused to cower. I forced my shoulders back and lifted my chin. Abigail took one look at my stoic expression and arranged her face in a similar fashion.

I said, "What now? We know you killed Toby. We know just about everything."

Phillip shook his head. "You know nothing."

I cocked my head. "So enlighten us."

Phillip nodded to the door that led from the alleyway into the barn. "You were close, but the door has to have a key to be unlocked. The only key is always in my possession."

I waved a hand. "Fine. You've made your point. We're trapped. As I said before, now what? Are you going to kill us?"

Phillip hung his head. "Killing isn't in my nature."

I snorted. "Tell that to Toby and Leona." My tone was sarcastic. "Oh yeah. They're dead. You can't tell them anything."

Phillip looked like an old, old man. His movements were slow as he sat down on the staircase. "I haven't got a gun or a knife. I'm weaponless, and that's to your advantage. But I wouldn't try to make a break for it. As I said, the door is locked, and I have the key." He patted his pants pocket. "You could try to overpower me, but I'd put up a good fight."

I rubbed the side of my head. "I already know you're capable of slugging a woman."

Phillip's smile was sad. "I'm sorry I had to do that, but you were hurting me." He gestured to the floor. "Have a seat. There isn't much you can do in your present situation, so you might as well relax. Your fates are sealed. The decision has been made, but it'll keep for a while."

I crossed my arms over my chest. "I'd just as soon stand."

Phillip leaned forward and bellowed, "This is my show. I said sit down, and I mean it."

There was no ignoring the ferociousness of his tone. Abigail and I dropped to the floor. Once we were settled, Phillip leaned back against the brick wall.

"Have you ever had a dream?" he asked quietly. Not waiting for an answer, he continued, "I'm not talking about building your fantasy home or winning the lottery. I mean that you could use your knowledge and abilities to save a life or better mankind.

"For years I worked for a biotech company in Canada. Our objective was to produce artificial spider silk with the same strength and elasticity as the real thing."

I asked, "What would the artificial spider silk be used for?"

"A diverse range of things. Because of its strength and elasticity, it's a good candidate for both the medical and industrial fields. I'm talking ropes, nets, seat belts, parachute cords, even the cables that stop planes as they land on aircraft carriers, bulletproof vests, biodegradable bottles, bandages, surgical thread, artificial tendons or ligaments. The list is endless."

I nodded. "Tapping into either of those fields would make the money endless, as well."

"That's correct. Within the research community, there's a race to bio-mimic Mother Nature's creation—the spider's web. Billions of dollars are up for grabs."

Abigail said, "So why don't you just gather up a bunch of spiders and let them do their thing, like the silkworms do theirs?"

"I wish it were that simple. It takes four hundred spiders to make one square yard of cloth. However, spiders are territorial, as well as cannibalistic. In close quarters, they'll eat each other."

"But what about your spiders upstairs?"

"There are four, not four hundred, and I keep my ladies' appetites well sated. They have no need to go hunting for more nourishment."

I rubbed my head where Phillip had hit me. "I'm not sure I understand. Where does Toby's hibiscus fit into all of this?"

Phillip sighed. "For you to understand fully, I need to go back to the artificial spider silk. Orb-weaving spiders generally produce seven different types of silk. The strongest is the dragline silk. It's what the spider spins to construct the outermost circle of a web and all the radiating spokes. Decades have been spent on decoding the protein gene that makes up dragline silk. Once the sequence was cracked, the race was on to mass-produce it. The gene has been introduced into the cells of hamsters and mice. The results yielded a goodly amount of protein, which was placed in a syringe. Once the protein was squeezed though the syringe, we got a silk fiber that was thinner than a human hair, but it didn't have the strength of spider silk.

"While we were working with the hamsters and mice, another division of our company discovered that the silk gland of the spider and the milk gland of a goat are almost identical. By inserting the orb-weaver's gene into the mammary glands of the goat, we were able to produce a complex protein that contained the spider silk. The next step was to spin the protein into a fiber, but more funding was needed. Our CEO took the news of our discovery to a substantial medical corporation. The result was a grant to our company to pursue the goat/milk research. But no matter what we did or how we approached the problem, spinning that protein into a viable fiber eluded us."

Phillip stopped to stare at us. "When you were upstairs, I heard you reading a letter from my coworker, a molecular biology professor. He tries to keep me updated on the most recent research breakthroughs because he feels as I do that my position with Bio-Rite was wrongfully terminated."

Abigail asked, "What did you do?"

"As I said, the grant money was designated for learning more about the goat/milk protein. I used a portion of the money to pursue a line of research into plants as carriers of the spider-silk gene."

"Plants like Toby's hibiscus," I said.

Phillip nodded. "It seems so obvious and feasible to me. Natural fibers are used for the spinning and weaving of fabric. I firmly believe that once the silk gene is spliced into the cell of a high-fiber plant, that gene will evolve. Given time, it'll take over the host plant, and the molecular wall structure of that plant will undergo a metamorphosis. But new plants have to be started from the older one, either by tissue culture or by mature seeds that have been collected from last year's plants."

I said, "That's why Toby was taught by his mother to plant six new rows each year."

"Correct. With each passing year, the silk gene has become more dominant." Phillip lifted a shoulder. "I'm getting closer. I admit I was wrong to switch around funding to aid my own concept, but time was being lost while I tried to convince a board of directors to listen to my theory. Before I was fired, I managed to make copies of my notes and smuggle them out of my lab. My friend thinks I've given up my research. Any information he passes on to me is a courtesy. He thinks it will make me feel better about events if he can substantiate the fact that I was on the right track years ago."

I grimaced. "How did you put it? 'Save a life or better mankind.' You killed Toby. You killed Leona. How do you explain or justify their deaths?"

Phillip's eyes narrowed. "I will explain, but not justify. I did kill them. I have no excuse. They were in my way."

Abigail sucked in a breath. A shiver swept over me. Phillip was so cool, so detached. It took me a moment to find my voice. "But why?" I asked. "How were they in your way? What did they know?"

"On the night before Toby died, I worked for twelve hours straight testing the hibiscus. I never had to worry about Yvonne coming out to check on me. The pain in her knees keeps her pretty close to the house or her antiques store. When she does make a trip to the barn, it's for an extended period of time. She always says she has to make the journey worthwhile. If she needs me, all she has to do is poke a button and a bell rings out here or in my workshop in the barn."

He waved a hand. "Anyway, as I was saying, I'd worked for twelve hours straight and I was exhausted. I needed a quick shower and a cup of coffee, so I left the doors unlocked. In the space of twenty minutes, while I was gone to the house, Toby wandered in. He found the silo door unlocked and climbed the stairs. When I found him, he was standing in front of the caged animals. He was upset. He didn't like the bowls of maggots on the third floor, but he most assuredly didn't like to see the mice and hamsters behind the wire mesh."

I said, "So Toby didn't touch any wet varnish? That was just a cover story?"

"The wet varnish was a lie. But my losing control and yelling at Toby was all too true. With years of research at risk, I lost my temper. I screamed at him. I threatened to dispose of the animals if he didn't keep quiet. He was shocked by my threat, but he was terrified by my screaming."

Phillip shook his head. "In all the years I've known him, I've never raised my voice to him in any situation. I knew better than to holler at Toby. He was sensitive. I calmed down and tried talking to him, reasoning with him, but nothing I said made an impression. I backpedaled and searched my brain for something that would grab his attention. Something he could relate to. Something his mother might have told him. Agnes was a great one for proverbs, little platitudes that sized up life in a few words. I seized on the three monkeys: See no evil. Hear no evil. Speak no evil. That seemed to work. I told him the animals would still be here, but he had to keep them a secret from everyone he knew. He quieted down, but after he left I couldn't be sure he would keep the contents of the silo to himself. I'd done all this remodeling when Yvonne was in the hospital having her knee-replacement surgery. No one had seen the inside of this silo until Toby found the door unlocked."

"But you cut down his mother's hibiscus? Surely you knew he'd be upset, that he'd tell someone."

"Yes, but they are simply perceived as flowers. Who would pay any attention? It could have been vandals. I figured the topic of the missing stalks would be discussed for a few days, then the subject would be dismissed."

"And Leona?" I asked. "Why kill her?"

"Yvonne kept saying that Leona was trying to piece together Agnes's financial background. My sister had known that Agnes received money when her husband was killed in a railway accident. She speculated that the money was gone years ago, which it was. Agnes had only her paycheck from the pharmacy to live on when I met her."

Phillip shrugged. "There's never been time in my life for a relationship. My work has been my life. I came back to River City to lick my wounds and mend my pride after being fired from a job where I knew I could make a difference. I had a feasible concept, but I had to find a suitable host plant. When I read about kenaf, I decided to do some extensive tests.

"I met Agnes though my sister. Agnes was a quiet woman who analyzed every step she took. Most of the time her major concern was for Toby, but as we got to know each other, I realized that she possessed the same qualities that have carried me through years of research. We both contemplated every situation, predicting how events would develop. Neither of us was afraid to manipulate anything or anyone to achieve our goal."

I asked, "So you and Agnes fell in love?"

"I cared for Agnes. I think she might have loved me, or maybe she only saw me as a way to keep her son safe."

My hoot of derision made Phillip wince. He said, "My action in placing the hornet's nest in Toby's room was at odds with all I've done for him since Agnes died. My research is based on records I stole from my old company. They could claim ownership. I've always felt there was a chance that someone from Bio-Rite might look me up. Repairing and refinishing furniture was far removed from the studies I'd conducted, but there was always a concern on my part that my ongoing work would be discovered. I had to find a place away from this farm where the hibiscus could grow. That meant that I had to bring someone into my confidence.

"I chose Agnes. She was dying. She needed money. Her only relative was a son with less than average mental comprehension. Her home was within easy reach. I could take a rambling route over connecting pastures and be at the back of her property in less than ten minutes."

Abigail said, "We figured that out. You rode Sugar Cube over to the garden, tied him to a tree, and went through the hedge to chop down the hibiscus."

"That's right."

I said, "Did you give Agnes a lump sum of money? Is that why Leona was suspicious?"

"No. I supplied the money for Agnes to buy stock in my old company. Regardless of how I was treated at the end of my employment, there are brilliant scientists working there. Agnes received a nice dividend check each month. That stock was moved into Toby's name at Agnes's death. I convinced her she had to hold on to that stock. Once I'd perfected my theory and had substantial proof to present to the board of directors, I was sure the stock would skyrocket."

"But what does this have to do with Leona's horrible death?"

"Once Toby's will was read, and the name of the stock disclosed, Leona would know immediately that I was guilty. She knew I'd left a company in Canada."

I nodded. "That's right. She told me you'd been fired."

Phillip's lips turned down in a frown. "You mean she'd already told you before she died?"

"That's right. You were too late. No need to give her that bubble bath concoction." Slyly, I interjected, "Nor was it necessary to leave the basket of toiletries outside my flower shop's back door."

Phillip lifted one shoulder. "I needed some extra insurance against your prying."

Abigail said, "Wouldn't Yvonne recognize the name of the company where you used to work?"

"Yes, but she would never betray me."

My mind was in a whirl from the information Phillip had given us. There had to be more questions that needed answers. Given our predicament, I asked the only one that had immediate relevancy. "What are you going to do with Abigail and me?"

Instead of answering, Phillip pulled a piece of paper from his shirt pocket. "I have here the name and phone number of the CEO of Bio-Rite. I'd like you to contact him. Tell him everything. Describe what you've seen upstairs. Convince him that it would be in his best interests to get here as quickly as possible."

Phillip put the paper on the step next to him. He stood up. "You'll have to do some fast talking, but I'm positive that you can do the—"

Heavy pounding sounded on the door. "Bretta!" shouted Sid. "Are you in there?"

Abigail and I sprang to our feet. We rushed to the door. "Help us," yelled Abigail. "The door is locked, and Phillip has the only key."

I whipped around to the stairs. I was afraid Phillip might be at our heels, ready to throttle us, but the staircase was empty. The door to the second floor was open. A prickle of uneasiness crossed my skin. Why had Phillip gone upstairs? There was no escape that way.

Or was there?

A feeling of dread washed over me.

In the alleyway outside the silo, I heard Sid say, "Get a crowbar or a hammer." In a louder voice, he said, "Keep calm. We'll get you out as fast as we can."

Abigail looked around at me. "Where's Phillip?" she asked.

I hesitated, then finally pointed up.

She breathed deeply. "We're safe for the moment." Her

eyes widened. "Unless he's gone to get something to use as a weapon."

There was only one reason Phillip would ask me to contact his former employer. Slowly I shook my head. "We're the last thing on Phillip's mind."

Out in the corridor, a man yelled, "Sheriff, someone has climbed out the top of the silo. Deputy Meyer says you need to come—"

A high-pitched scream ripped the air, followed by the words, "No. Phillip. *No!*"

I recognized Yvonne's voice. Tears filled my throat and worked their way up to blur my vision. Closing my eyes, I waited. I envisioned the wind tugging at Phillip's clothing, the stench of the rotting fruit wafting up through the open air vents. Would he venture a quick look down?

My heart pounded. I opened my eyes when Abigail took my arm. In a ragged whisper, she said, "Surely Phillip won't jump."

But I knew he would. His research had been an obsession that had taken a disastrous turn. He'd lost sight of what was truly important, putting his work before everything and everyone. Even his present choice of how to bring this investigation to a close hadn't caused him to lose sight of his goal. He'd placed his trust in my hands to see that his research was directed to someone who would make the most of his discovery.

Outside, the voices rose in volume, and then suddenly subsided. Yvonne made another heartfelt appeal. "Please, Phillip," she sobbed. "You're all I have."

In the breathless silence that followed, the sound of impact was minute.

For some of us, the reverberations would last a lifetime.

EPILOGUE

On this October night, a week before Halloween, Hawthorn Street was filled with costumed customers. A store owner, one who wasn't of Agnes's "select few," had come up with the idea that we needed to outdo the Westgate Mall shops. Every year on Halloween, these shops hold marathon sales with free goodies for the children. It was a huge draw for the outer-loop shopping district, but it took attention away from our street.

At the first planning session of the Hawthorn Street store owners, it had been unanimously agreed upon that while we'd been River City's focus during the murder investigation, it was time to replace those tabloid impressions. Coming under scrutiny for a festive occasion seemed the best way to put the ghosts of Toby, Leona, and Phillip to rest.

I hadn't been against the plan, but I hadn't been gung ho, either. Once Sid had declared the investigation closed, I'd done as Phillip had asked. I'd contacted the CEO of Bio-Rite. The Canadian company hadn't wasted any time sending a crew of scientists to River City. Sid said that once they were done, nothing had been left in the silo but the framework.

Yvonne had been paid an undisclosed amount for her brother's research. She'd put her antiques store and the surrounding land in the hands of a realtor. In a matter of days, she'd jetted off to California where she'd checked into a health spa. Before she left town, she'd given Sugar Cube to Abigail. Since Abigail lived in an apartment, I'd had an area fenced off on my property. A small barn was being built so Sugar Cube would have a warm home this winter.

I leaned against my workstation table and surveyed the crowded flower shop. I'd let Lois and Lew do the planning. When asked, I'd offered suggestions, but this was their show, and they reveled in the merriment.

Lois was dressed as a harem girl. The puffy lime green pants were gathered at the waist and the ankles. A hot pink camisole topped her outfit, along with an assortment of purple and orange scarves. When she walked, she jangled. Every piece of gold jewelry she owned was either hanging from her neck or her arms.

Lew had amazed everyone with his costume. Always the epitome of the well-dressed man, he'd arrived at the shop as a hobo, complete with magic tricks. He was a hit with the kids, especially when he pulled a quarter from behind their ears. I didn't have a clue how many coins he'd given away, but he seemed unconcerned, laughing and teasing everyone, young and old.

At home I'd mentioned that Lew and Lois wanted to serve simple refreshments. To my surprise, DeeDee had volunteered for the job. She'd baked a ton of cookies, decorating each with a Halloween theme. She'd concocted a fizzy apple punch that was fantastic. For me, the highlight of the evening was the way she reacted to the people who entered my shop. Posing as a gypsy, she smiled readily and ventured into conversation with strangers.

My father and Abigail had offered to keep watch over the crowd so none of my merchandise was trampled in the melee.

They'd opted for costumes that brought smiles to the faces of my evening customers. My father was dressed as a sheep with snowy white fleece and a big pink bow tied around his neck. Abigail was Bo Peep. She wore an elaborate blue-flounced dress, a broad-brimmed straw hat, and carried a crooknecked staff. Twice I'd seen her use the oversize hook to grab my father's arm and pull him to her side, where they'd shared a laugh with those who'd witnessed the corralling of her "wayward" sheep.

"You're being a wallflower," said Lois, coming to stand near me. "Why don't you spread some of your sunny charm over by the door?"

The emphasis on the word *sunny* referred to my costume. I was a sunflower, dressed from foot to neck in a green jumpsuit. My arms were encased in material that had been sewn to resemble huge leaves. A giant sunflower blossom surrounded my head, with my face exposed as the center. When I'd seen the outfit in the rental store, I'd snatched it up, feeling it was apropos for a florist. What I hadn't counted on was the awkwardness. The yellow petals were stiffened with wire and stuck out from my head a good twelve inches. If I didn't keep my neck muscles taut, I lost my balance, wilting like a flower left too long without water.

Turning my head carefully, I smiled at her. "I'd better stay back here, out of trouble. I'd hate to assault a customer by falling on him."

"But you're okay?" persisted Lois, eyeing me sharply. "You're not wallowing in sorrow, are you?"

"I'm wallow-free, just watching everyone have a good time. I don't know about the other shop owners, but I'd say this evening has been a success."

Lois grimaced. "Not so much for the old cash register. We've had a few sales but nothing spectacular. Everyone wants the freebie stuff."

"We didn't do this for immediate sales. Our main objective was to give Hawthorn Street a new image."

Lois looked around. "By the way, where's Bailey?"

"He said he'd be late. He's winding up another chapter in his book."

"What's he coming as?" Lois's wink was lascivious. "He's such a handsome hunk. I hope he's displaying plenty of skin."

I made a face. "Just because you look like a floozy doesn't mean you have to act like one. As for Bailey, I wouldn't pin any high hopes on him arriving in costume—brief or otherwise. He isn't the type to don a—" I stopped because Lois wasn't listening to me. She was looking over my shoulder, with eyes wide and mouth open.

"Wow!" she breathed. "Forget showing skin. He's incredible."

I moved too quickly and almost toppled over. Once I'd recovered my balance, I thought I'd end up on the floor anyway when I saw who had caught Lois's attention. Bailey was making his way toward me. He was dressed in a black tuxedo. The jacket lapels were satin, as were the wide stripes down the outside of each pants leg. His shirt was white, the vest a shimmering silver. He wore dark glasses, which he slowly slid up over his forehead to rest on top of his head.

"My sweet flower," he said, taking my hand in his. Staring deep into my eyes, he whispered, "I'm sure there's a better place and time for this, but I can't think where or when. The people who are important in your life are here."

Suddenly he went down on one knee. I tilted my head

to follow his action and nearly fell on top of him. Lois grabbed my arm and held me upright. "Steady, girl," she whispered in my ear.

Bailey looked up at me and smiled. His coppery eyes were full of warmth and love. "I had a fancy speech all prepared about life's journey, and how I don't want to go through it alone. I thought about all the reasons I could give you for us becoming a couple, but I don't want to *persuade* you to marry me."

"Marry?" I squeaked.

Bailey nodded. He pulled something from his pocket that glittered in the light. Holding it between his thumb and two fingers, he held up a ring so I couldn't mistake his intentions. When I didn't comment, he slid the ring on my finger.

Holding my gaze with his own, he said, "I want to play a larger part in your life, Bretta Solomon. I want to be your husband, your confidant, and your lover. I'm asking you to be my wife. Bretta, will you marry me?"

I wanted to close my eyes and savor the moment, but instead I found myself gazing at the faces around me. DeeDee's expression was watchful. I could tell she was afraid to hope that I'd say yes. Lew's smile was gentle, almost benevolent. He wanted whatever was best for me. My father nodded encouragement. I couldn't read Abigail's expression, but then I barely knew this woman who was my half-sister. But time could remedy that.

Finally there was Lois. She was squeezing my arm until it felt as if she was cutting off the circulation.

Slowly I smiled and nodded. "Yes," I said, "I'll marry you, Bailey Monroe."

Lois let out a whoop of joy and loosened her hold on my arm. I would have pitched forward, but Bailey was there. He gathered me close, folding me into his loving embrace.

In my ear he whispered, "For richer or poorer, in sickness or in health, and even during one of your sleuthing missions, I'll be here."

I closed my eyes and sighed. How could I ask for more?